THE
CURSING
STONE

ADRIAN HARVEY

D1369000

URBANE
Publications

urbanepublications.com

First published in Great Britain in 2016
by Urbane Publications Ltd
Suite 3, Brown Europe House, 33/34 Gleaming Wood Drive,
Chatham, Kent ME5 8RZ
Copyright ©Adrian Harvey, 2016

A CIP catalogue record for this book is available
from the British Library.

ISBN 978-1-911129-18-9
EPUB 978-1-911129-19-6
MOBI 978-1-911129-20-2

Design and Typeset by Michelle Morgan

Cover by Julie Martin

Printed and bound by CPI Group (UK) Ltd, Croydon, CR0 4YY

urbanepublications.com

THE
CURSING
STONE

TO LONDON

"The moment you doubt whether you can fly, you cease for ever to be able to do it."

J.M. Barrie, Peter Pan

part one

The Kingdom of Hinba

one

You cannot see her face. No matter how hard you look, you cannot make it out. It is not even that it is a blur; rather, an absence, a loss. Her precise shape, her features, slide from view as soon as you try to focus upon them. You are aware that you know the face, you have seen it a thousand times, yet still you cannot bring her image to mind. Neither can you remember her name, even though you are certain that this too you know. Just as you know that she is beautiful, if only you could see her. This face should be familiar to you; it is important, although you cannot recall precisely why.

All else is clear, crisply defined: each purple flower on the clumps of heather, the curve of the beach stretching off to the west, the white caps on the distant waves. It is only when you turn to look at the woman that your eyes cloud and the memory of precisely who she is becomes lost, just out of your reaching. What magic is this, you wonder?

It is now that you realise that you are not standing on the low cliff beside this woman, known but unknown. Rather you are hovering, about a metre above the ground. The air feels solid enough, and you feel no danger of injury, of falling. Only the elusive face gives you cause for anxiety.

An insistent wind presses into you. It seeks out every crease and fold, every weakness and softness, relentless. It is cold, but not bitterly so; it is almost as if the air lacks a temperature. It is simply the solid cold of raw meat; as cold as death and just as implacable.

Yet despite its force, the breeze cannot budge you. It tugs and prods and nudges, but you remain stationary, hovering a little above the ground on the solid air. Somehow you are anchored to this place, tethered but not connected. Above you, the sky is bright in the blue and clear way that skies above the island are. And the ground below your feet is dressed in vivid green, the heather and grass tugging against the force of air.

Tethered but disconnected. The sensation of flying – better, of levitating – is not unusual. In fact it feels commonplace, as though you have always been floating just beyond the surface. Never quite touching the land on which you were raised. The heather and gorse and grass of the hillside still ruffle in the breeze. The green is overpowering, encompassing. You drink in its vibrancy and fecundity, made urgent in the sunlight, and breathe in the solidity of the island, of your heart's love. The world is yours and it is safe and solid, knowable. Then you start to move.

Slowly at first. A gentle gliding, barely noticeable in the rushing wind. But soon you become aware of slipping across the island's surface, away from your sweetheart. You try to resist the motion, but neither your limbs nor your mind can control your trajectory. You are gaining speed. Over your shoulder, you see her, and then the island itself, slip into the distance. And you are alone, gliding over the sparkling sea, pushing ever faster towards the west and the open ocean, away from the dry land and out into the featureless deep blue. Faster that the fastest sail boat.

The Arctic terns are your only company, their tiny bodies and rigid wings arcing above the rising waves as they slide seemingly powerless on the wind, unable to rise or to drop into the water. They are closer than they should be and you can clearly read the curiosity in their eyes as they pause alongside you before slipping away to a safer distance. The smoothness and whiteness of their feathers, the crisp demarcation of their black caps, is impeccable.

You begin to imagine yourself as a tern, half remembering the thousands of miles of ocean over which you have travelled, the months without sight of land, until you are no longer sure if you had only imagined yourself in human form in a brief moment beside the woman on the hill above the bay. You feel the ghost of a forked tail, its long tines trailing in the air behind you. You try to turn your head to see your own shape but cannot twist sufficiently to look down along your body: you are invisible to yourself. Only the shape of the resistance of the wind and the dim throb of a misplaced memory tells you that you are real, solid, human.

The terns have abandoned you now, wanting the closeness of their nesting grounds on the land that you have left behind. Over open ocean, with no land visible, you cannot imagine how this journey will end, cannot recall how it began. There is only the sea. You cannot conceive of any moment in your entire existence, up to this point and forever more, that was not, is not, will not be spent gliding six feet above the rushing waves of an empty ocean. You are taken suddenly by a dumb despair.

In that instant, you start to climb. You are no longer skimming over the waves but rushing upwards, like a rocket, straight into the sky. It takes several moments for your body to adjust to the force of acceleration, to the drag and to gravity pulling at your limbs.

You hurtle upwards and the surface of the ocean becomes indistinct beneath you. Soon it is just a single polished surface, with no waves or creases visible. There is only the sheen of blue and the curve of the world. There is no more. You have become accustomed to the speed and the growing altitude, to your separation from every substantive thing in the universe. There are no scents, no sights; the only sensations come from the rush of air and the tug of gravity.

Then you stop. You are hanging in blue space, and everything is still. Your organs turn anxiously inside you and the giddiness of weightlessness provokes a little nausea, disorientation. You can no longer recall how long you have been like this, stationary in space and time. Perhaps this is where you will spend eternity, suspended just below the sky, with only blueness for company. Your disappointment becomes dismay as you realise that you are not suspended at all, but beginning to fall.

Your body tumbles and cart-wheels through the sparse air. Fingers clutch at it, vainly seeking to catch hold of something that could slow the descent. But nothing tempers the acceleration until the body reaches terminal velocity. A body could not survive: it would die, smashed against the surface of the ocean that is now racing upwards through the unreliable air. As the body plummets towards the hard shining surface of the sea, you imagine the pain that will flow through it with the inevitable impact.

You remember that the falling body is yours, that you inhabit it. You have once more caught up with the tumbling form and re-occupied the speeding mass in time to be overwhelmed by the terror that resides within it. You want to depart once more, to trail the falling man, to witness the crushing of this body, from beyond its confines: to sense its agony vicariously. But it is moving too fast, and with too little control.

Despite the speed at which your proto-corpse is falling, the sea moves only slowly up towards you. So great a distance is left to fall. The descent itself seems to last an eternity and you cannot remember how long it has taken to attain the altitude from which you are falling, let alone the means of achieving it. In the slow rush of your impending death, you half-remember some monstrous bird, climbing to the edge of the sky, its talons pressed tightly into your chest before, weary or bored, it released you to this cascade, to your death.

Or maybe you had been an angel once, an angel that had fallen from the heavens. But you have no wings. Do angels always have wings? The thought that you might be an angel makes you question the certainty of your death. If you were not a mortal, then the impact could not kill you. You would survive. But you would be stranded in the midst of an endless sea with no way to return to the heavens, nor even to find a shore and the company of men. And it would hurt. The impact. Even if it did not kill you, it would hurt beyond all pain that you can imagine. You struggle to find your wings so that you might evade that pain.

The first of the white caps on the waves appear and you know that it will not be long now. In an instant, the tiny specks of spume become individual waves, clearly discernible one from the other. There are small birds, soon much larger, gliding above the surface. You struggle against the racing air to stand upright, so as to limit the impact, to limit the pain.

Then you are under the water, intact, sinking deeper and deeper in to the darkening haze. Down and down through the slow stickiness, the momentum of the fall carrying you farther into the cold wetness. For the first time that you can remember, you are cold. And it is dark: already, before you think to pull against the water, to kick out with your legs, it is dark. You can see nothing, yet can sense the creatures circling you in the gloom. The rushing hush of salt and sand whisper in your ears, threatening in a language you cannot understand. A panic seeps in and you thrash upwards towards the light and air, away from the hidden serpents and sea-daemons.

It takes an eternity to swim back to the surface. Weed and fatigue bind your limbs. Your wet clothes slow you still more. But the grey light grows around you until you can see the fractal surface above. With all your remaining strength you kick and pull upwards and, breaking the shifting tension, you find your face in the air, your skin suddenly chilled. You gulp in heavy breaths and struggle to clear the water from your eyes.

two

Fergus woke slowly. He slipped loose of sleep with a smooth comfort, even though the sweat still crackled through his hair, clung to his body, pulled the sheets tight to his skin. Sunshine reached in through the curtain's crack to search through his belongings, scattered about the room. The pile of yesterday's clothes left in a heap on the carpet. Beside it, a stack of books teetered, topped with his old school atlas, still opened at the page covering Eastern Europe. On his desk-cum-dressing table, the index of British post codes was propped open; a hairbrush, tangled with lengths of strawberry blonde hair; a deodorant spray; a half-eaten tube of Polo mints, its flayed skin curling in the light.

As these relics came into focus, he rolled across the damp bed to the night stand. He drank deeply from the glass of water left there since the night before, then pulled open the draw to hunt out first his note book, then the fat pen his mother and father had given to him on his 18th birthday. The world was forming again into a crisp clarity, as lucid and as solid as his dreams. His eyes traced the curling lines doodled onto the notebook's cover before pulling the pages apart where his fingertips found the folded corner. Halfway through.

He had dreamed again, of course. He dreamt every night: precise, tangible dreams, dreams that left their savour in his nose, on his tongue. He could recollect them perfectly, more so than the events of the previous day, but still he recorded them, in exact detail, each and every morning, before his mother called him to breakfast.

This was his eighth notebook. Like all the others it was a slim pale yellow exercise book, taken from the little shop downstairs, offset against his wages. Each book was filled with tight, dense handwriting, detailing in tidy but inelegant longhand his nocturnal adventures these past six years. They were varied, these adventures, but all shared a consistent feature: in his dreams, Fergus could fly. More accurately: levitate. Simply float at will, rising above whatever place he found himself. Gliding smoothly into and through the air, sedately and calmly.

It was early still. Only his grandfather would be up and dressed. Sitting at the long kitchen table with a mug of tea and a pipe of tobacco, staring out into the bay. The boy fancied that he could hear the old man's laboured breathing rising through the floorboards, could smell the sweetness of the smoke. The fantasy brought a smile, a calmness. But the moment passed soon enough and he returned his attention to the task at hand.

Leaning against the headboard, Fergus wrote carefully but swiftly, capturing the dream before it began to lose its shape, became indistinct and opaque; just a feeling, a sense of wonder and dread that would hang unnoticed over the day. This was why he recorded them, the dreams. By writing them down, in the fullest of detail, he could hope to retain a calm mastery of his subconscious. Others carried through their days an elusive idea that something, somehow, was not quite right: on some days, people seemed to feel simply apprehensive, fearful, out of sorts for no good reason that they could place. Fergus was sure that by capturing and containing his dreams, by searching through every twist and turn of the night, he would rob them of their power to creep up on him, unannounced and unnoticed, and spoil his mood.

Of course, he also wondered if they might mean something. Premonitions or windows into deeper truths. Sometimes he would read back through the carefully dated entries, especially after significant or unexpected events, to see if he had predicted their occurrence in some literal or obscure way. Before making big decisions, he would interrogate the records of his dreams from the previous month or so, trying to detect guidance from a higher power. God maybe. Or simply his true and lucid self. His writing recalled the sensation of not being able to see the face of the woman – it was Shona, of course – and it gave him a momentary flicker of doubt about his plans. But, to date, the notebooks had held neither warnings nor answers. He put his doubt aside and moved on to note the colour of the gorse flowers and the dead chill of the wind.

As he wrote, he could hear the muffled voices and movements of his parents in the next room, then the creak of the bathroom door, and the sound of the sudden deluge as his father fully opened the taps to fill the bath. He had maybe twenty minutes before the bathroom was free for him, then another ten before breakfast would be on the table, an hour before he needed to be at the harbour side to collect the mail from Mr McCredie's boat. It was plenty of time to finish his notes and then pick out some clothes for Shona's birthday party, before shaving and starting his rounds in good time. But Fergus knew not to dawdle, to mistake a lack of urgency for a surfeit of time. Better to use its excess than to fritter it away, his grandfather would say.

It had been many years since Fingal Buchanan had actually performed any of the duties associated with the role of post master of Hinba. He had never actually forsaken the title, but simply allowed his son, Davey Buchanan, to carry the burden, hoping that Fergus would come of age in time to inherit the sinecure directly. In the meanwhile, Fingal chose to spend his time explaining his son's many inadequacies from his high-backed chair at the kitchen table. The old man held court there for most of the day, except to take long walks along the beach as far as the headland or, on the frequent inclement days, until The Harbour Bell opened.

In many places, post master might be an insignificant title, but on Hinba it was the birth right of the most respected family on the island. The Buchanans had been post masters since the Royal Mail had come to Hinba, some two hundred years before. It had been the most natural thing in the world for Fingal Buchanan to be given the seals of office by the gentleman from the mainland, since the Buchanan's had long been the leading family. Only the MacLeods could rival their claim to dominance and, while they had the Bell, it was the Buchanans who maintained an iron grip on the island's only shop and the duty to uphold the security of the post.

So Fergus's father did not begrudge the indignity of his treatment by his own father, since he was the *de facto* headman of the island. Hinba itself was small, the western-most of the Small Isles, if you discounted the fragments of guano-streaked rock that littered the sea before the Western Isles marked the edge of the ocean. It was a small and distant kingdom and he was only regent, but Davey had only ever known Hinba and to him it was as much as the entire world.

He had visited other places of course. He had been to Eigg, for example, where his wife, Morag, had been raised. He had met her at the funeral of Cal Coltrane, the skipper of the Small Isles ferry for 30 years. And he had been to the mainland too, numerous times, to the Highlands for a holiday and even to Glasgow to escort his daughter to the university. But like his father, and like his son, Davey Buchanan had never really seen the point of leaving Hinba for very long.

Fergus heard the water draining from the bath, listened to its throaty gurgling, waited for the key to turn in the lock and his father's feet to pad across the hall carpet and back into his bedroom. He took one last quizzical, uncertain look at the suit of clothes he had hung from a coat hanger on the wardrobe door, then he made his way into the bathroom. His mother would postpone her own bath until the men were at work; she was already down stairs, making arrangements for breakfast, exchanging pleasantries with her father-in-law. Since coming to Hinba some 22 years before, she had had to share her breakfast times with the cantankerous old man. Even then, when he still actually did something useful with his days, he was bitter and proud and unforgiving. Every day of her married life had required enormous effort to maintain her courteousness, to ask after the quality of his sleep, the pains in his legs, or the likelihood of rain.

That she had managed it, had never once exchanged truly angry words with him, astounded her. She had, early on, shaped as if to defend her new husband from one of the old man's tirades, but Davey had caught her eye with a look of warning and reproach, and she had known that she should not intervene. She had said nothing even on the day when Fingal had raised his hand, left it hanging for a moment above Davey's head, weighted with violence, when her husband had simply flinched with practiced acquiescence. Despite herself, she had never broken into the strange dance of contempt and surrender that played out each day between father and son; she had never questioned Davey about it, even in the privacy of their room or when Fingal was out on one of his walks, nor when Fergus and Mary were too small to understand, or away in Mallaig at the school, or in any of the many other quiet shared times they had had during their long marriage.

She had however insisted that he did not treat his own son in that way. Fergus was to be treated fairly, with respect. And Davey had been true to his word, even if the task had been made easier by the high regard Fingal himself had for Fergus. The old man adored his first and only grandson, and often compared Davey unfavourably to him. In the eyes of the patriarch, it was Fergus that kept the shop running efficiently, aided by his tidy mother; Davey was simply an encumbrance, and Fingal knew that he could not contemplate dying yet, not until Fergus had reached his majority and could himself take on the duties officially. Morag toyed with this idea with ever greater frequency the nearer came her son's twenty-first birthday: it was now the spring of that year and Morag found it easier to smile at the old man as he complained about his hip and the pains in his chest that had kept him awake all night.

If she had drawn level in the battle with her father-in-law, by bringing her universally-cherished son into the world, she had lately scored a significant victory in her own right. When Mary, just a year or so before, had declared a desire to go to university, Davey had looked to his father. Naturally, Fingal objected. It was not the business of a Buchanan to be leaving Hinba to go to the university; her husband had naturally agreed. But Morag had given neither man a choice: if Mary, her youngest, wanted to study, then Mary would study. If that took her from these windswept islands, so much the better.

That both men, father and son, had backed down so easily provoked mixed emotions in Morag. She felt a renewed confidence in her own strength of character and, after so many years feeling impotent under Fingal's tyranny, this pleased her enormously. Suddenly, she no longer felt the silent subject in her own house. But the reaction also prompted questions about what might have been, had she taken a stand sooner. If she had not been cowed to silence by her husband's look all those years ago, what might her life, the life of her husband, have been? Would Davey have been his own man, unlimited by his brow-beating father? And would Fingal have retired graciously at the allotted time, foregoing the years of carping obstinacy? And would she have felt the mistress of her home, able to speak her mind when she had things to say, rather than pushing down her discontents, drowning them in soapy dishwater?

She would never know of course, so she simply revelled in the sudden light and space that her daughter's determination had allowed her. Fingal and Davey still danced their dance, but they treated her with greater respect than she had ever thought possible; on occasions, Fingal even held his tongue when Morag was present, saving his indictments against his son for those times when his daughter-in-law visited one of the wives of the island or popped out into the kitchen garden to poke around between the lettuces. From out in the garden, she could still hear the rhythm of Fingal's bitterness, if not the specific complaints, but she would smile and think about how soon it was until her son's twenty first birthday.

Fergus slid into the kitchen that morning just as his mother returned from the garden. It was a quarter to seven and the spring sun was now clear of the mainland. It was the vernal equinox, the day the sun came back to Hinba. From now on, the days would only get longer, the nights shorter. That in itself was reason to celebrate, but it was a day of much greater significance: the eighteenth birthday of his Shona. The birthday itself was of course important, and Fergus had spent most of his savings on a pendant sent over from the mainland, and most of his spare time working on a more personal gift. It was this that he was most excited about: the pendant was merely insurance in case Shona did not appreciate his handiwork as much as she might. But the day also meant that she was a woman. There was nothing now to stop Fergus from making official his long betrothal to Shona MacLeod.

As he poured tea into his cup, Fergus thought about the his three gifts for Shona: the shop-bought pendant; the hand-carved wooden likeness; and his grandmother's engagement ring, which Mr McCredie had taken over to Mallaig to have stretched so that it might fit more comfortably on Shona's hand. He had already made his plans for when and how he would present these gifts, having decided that if he left his proposal until tomorrow, Shona's joy, and his own anticipation, would be extended.

'Did you sleep well, boy?'

Fingal smiled at his grandson, tall and lean. He offered no commentary on his own uncomfortable night, instead waiting for Fergus to reply.

'Aye, not so bad. More dreams, of course, but they didn't interrupt my sleeping. You?'

Fergus pulled out a chair and sat opposite his grandfather, taking a swallow of tea and reaching across the table for a piece of the bread freshly cut by his mother.

'The same. Too little of course, but can a man ever sleep too much?'

The old man stared off out through the kitchen window, across the bay and over the sea towards Rum. Fergus was already lost in his guide to UK postcodes, feeling that he had already done his duty by way of passing the time with his grandfather. He chewed on the bread and jam and studied the maps marked with letters and numbers. Fergus had taken as a duty the learning of the UK's postcode system, its principles and its geography. Especially its geography. While he would explain his interest in postcodes as the necessary training of a future post master, he also took pleasure in the fact that the country beyond Hinba was codified, contained and made intelligible through a rational system of classifications, just as his notebooks made sense of his fathomless nights. Every town and village and house was located in a unique but comprehensible series of six – or seven – digits. Wherever he might roam, he would be able to find himself precisely.

Of course, he did not intend to roam, preferring instead to see the world from the safety and certainty of maps. He travelled vicariously, through the movements of packages and letters. This was his destiny, his birth right. While the other islanders were either here or away on the mainland, one or the other, he and the other Buchanan men were able to be both here and abroad simultaneously.

The bread and jam was done, the tea drained, and on the wind Fergus could hear the pulse of the mail-boat out in the bay. Moving to the window, he watched it make its steady way in towards the harbour. It was time to set off, to collect the post and to start his round of deliveries, a daily ritual he had begun as much from boredom as obligation. He shouted through to his father, who was at his books in the shop, then turned smiling to his grandfather, his tone breezy and familiar:

'OK, that's me. I'm off to work. It's a big day today, granddad, a big day. Even the sun's come out to see it.'

Fingal smiled broadly, his face creasing deeply beneath his long whiskers. They were now lank and thin, the colour of soured milk, where once they had been thick and tawny as marmalade, wilful and unkempt: his daughter-in-law had refused throughout her marriage to trim them for him and, on account of the weakness of his eyesight and the strength of his pride, he too had refused to tend to them. With neglect, they had grown wantonly; with Fergus's exit, lemon green light rushed into the kitchen to burnish the memories of gold and copper that lurked within its cascade.

three

Mr Galbraith was already away. There was no answer when Fergus rang the doorbell, and through the open curtains he could see that the house was peculiarly lifeless, inert. The living room was quiet and somehow chill in its temporary abandonment. He would be away to the mainland no doubt, taking advantage of the empty week of half term to run some errands and stock up on whatever it was Mr Galbraith brought back from Mallaig on his excursions. Fergus dropped the letter and magazine through the door and turned back to the road, where he had propped his bicycle against the wall to Mrs Robertson's tidy garden. Hers was his last call and once across the road, he crunched his way over the gravel towards the red door, flicking through the post destined for the widow.

The window was open a little, as always. Mrs Robertson was at the sink, filling the kettle, lost in her thoughts, humming an old tune. She was dressed in her habitual house coat, her grey hair curled tightly to her head. It was three years now since Mr Robertson had passed: yet the condition of the paintwork and of the flower beds by the path was testament to the continued health and vitality of his wife.

Fergus knocked sharply but respectfully on the window pane to attract her attention. She looked up without surprise and he smiled, held up the bundle of letters for Mrs Robertson to see; then he waited. He always liked to exchange a few words with the widow on his rounds, to make sure she was fit and well, keeping herself occupied. While he waited for her to shuffle to the door, Fergus looked along the path, which was fringed with delicate pink and blue flowers clinging low to the soil. He did not know their names, and wondered why they would choose to bloom here so early in the year, when the risk of late winter storms was not yet passed. But in the spring sunlight they were a welcome sight, breaking the monotony of green and grey that had been the island's palette for so many months. Their cheeriness presaged the long days of sunshine that the summer would bring and Fergus flushed at the thought.

Behind him he heard the stiff door scrape open. As usual he would offer to take a look at it for her, maybe take a plane to it, even put a coat of paint on it, later in the summer. As usual Mrs. Robertson would mutter that it was no matter, that he shouldn't trouble himself with it, that she wasn't so old yet that she couldn't manage a little gloss paint. Then he would ask after her health, her mood, her news, before introducing the post to her.

'Just three letters for you this morning. One's a bill I'm afraid, Scottish Power. But there's also a handwritten one, from Glasgow no less, and there's a little lilac note for you from your sister in Fort William, so that should take the edge of the electric shock.'

Mrs Robertson laughed at this well-worn joke, as she did every quarter, even as she took her glasses from the pocket of her house coat to study the mysterious missive from the distant city. Fergus looked down at her, unsure whether it was he who grew taller, or she shorter. When he had first known her, she had been a tall, straight-backed woman in her fifties, the wife of his grandfather's best friend. Fergus had trailed after the two men as they walked along the low cliffs above the rolling sea, smoking their pipes and exchanging memories. Always a few steps behind, on account of respect and the length of their stride, Fergus had felt himself privileged to be allowed into their world, to walk with them, to hear their stories, to be among grown-ups.

After each of these walks, Fergus would return to the cottage to be fed scones and fizzy pop by Mrs Robertson, whose own grandchildren lived far away on the mainland. For more reasons than he could begin to count, Fergus felt a debt to the old woman, a duty he performed each morning even when there was no post for her. That her cottage was the last door on his round was a deliberate choice: he wanted to be able to take the time to chat without worrying that others would be waiting on their letters and parcels. He would tell her about the comings and goings down at the harbour, about books he'd read, television programmes she might enjoy, even about Shona and his plans and hopes and anxieties. She in turn would tell him about her health, the different flowers and vegetables growing in the garden, on the moor, about the comings and goings on the road. And she would talk about the past, both that which they shared and that which was beyond his reach, about the island when she was a girl, about the stories her grandfather had told her about his own boyhood, about the storms and feuds, the island myths, the Buchanans and the MacLeods.

On other days, he would suck in these stories as if they were fizzy pop through a yellow straw. But today, he was eager to be about his business. It was already eleven, and he had things to do. Mrs Robertson was in any case distracted by the letter and didn't notice the sly glance at his wrist watch; reassured, Fergus took the opportunity afforded by her quiet concentration on the unexpected envelope to take his leave.

Waving from the gate, the door scraping shut behind him, Fergus walked his bicycle further up the hill, then pushed off to ride the last half mile to Mr Duncannon's yard, which lurked on the outskirts of the village. Duncannon was an odd man, one who kept himself to himself, despite the difficulties of doing so on an island with fewer than 50 inhabitants and only one pub. He lived alone. His spent his days taking in the base detritus of the islanders and of the oceans, somehow turning it into money. In all honesty, no one quite knew how Duncannon made a living from all the junk that he took into his barn and, aside from the repairs and odd-jobs he would do for the islanders, he had no obvious customers. But the junk disappeared into the barn never to be seen again, and Duncannon survived.

True, he had no wife, no children to care for, but even so the mystery of his business intrigued his neighbours; some suspected supernatural goings on, others simply criminal. None of them would ever dream of asking. It was not that Duncannon was unfriendly. If you made the first move and passed the time of day, he would smile and nod the greeting in return. He would even pass comment on the changing of the season, about the likelihood of a storm or of fair weather, but he offered nothing of himself. It was clear that his reticence was a curtain behind which he preferred to stay and this was something his neighbours were happy to accept.

Although Duncannon was a private man, he was not a selfish one. He often let Fergus use his shed and his tools for his wood-working. Not joinery: Fergus got no pleasure from making practicalities like cabinets or boxes, even though he was more than capable of doing so, of cutting dovetails so neatly that they required no glue to keep them tight. Since he had been in the school at Mallaig, where he had first learned to bend timber to his will, he had found comfort and solidity not in forcing wood into unnatural angles, but in collaborating with it to release the shapes that it held within itself, to uncover its true essence.

In the school workshop, he had become accomplished with saws and clamps and planes, but it was with the tools of carving – with chisels and gouges – that he had sharpened his skills to the point of artistry, and it was to these that he felt connected. In the years since, he had developed a close affinity with the warm fluidity of timber, and he had learned to coax from it the unique personality of each piece. For Fergus, the most important thing was first to select the right lump of drift wood or unwanted timber lying around Duncannon's yard; after that, carving was easy, as the grain and density and spirit of the timber would tell him what to do with it. Perhaps it was this perceptiveness that warmed Duncannon to Fergus, a recognition of something shared, something held in common.

Leaving his bike by the wall, Fergus headed straight to the shed: Duncannon would in any case be out along the coast, seeing what the sea had brought to the island. Fergus had come here to work at his carving, not to make awkward conversation with an unwilling interlocutor. He had a couple of hours before McCredie's boat was due once more and in that time he had to bring the finishing touches to the piece he had been crafting to mark Shona's 18th birthday.

The air inside the shed was dusty and slow. It was as if the place had been undisturbed for years, yet Fergus himself had spent an hour here only the day before: the chisel he had been using still lay on the bench, alongside the fine rasp and curved file. Fergus drew deeply on the scent of wood and mildew before reaching up to the high shelf, his heels barely rising from the beaten earth of the floor. He pulled down a sizeable parcel wrapped in a heavy, supple canvas, the stiffness twisted and bent out of it through years of use and reuse, its original white made dirty grey by the hands of many men over many decades.

Fergus placed the package on the workbench and unwrapped it reverently. He pealed back each petal until the canvas was flat on the bench and the carving was revealed. It was a likeness of Shona, made from memory, a perfect rendering of her face. The work was still rough in parts, unfinished, but it was unmistakably her, unmistakably beautiful. The head was maybe five inches high, with the wood stopping abruptly at her throat on the right hand side, but continuing just beyond the curve of her shoulder on the left. He had found the knotted tree branch, from which he had fashioned the sculpture over the course of months, on the beach at the western end of the island and he had known, simply known, immediately that this timber contained the likeness of his heart's love. He had carved from memory, half-consciously, and had produced a semblance so exact that had he worked from photographs he could not have been more faithful to the real Shona.

Now he had only to file and sand the features and contours to match the softness of her porcelain skin, the lustre of her hair. He pulled the stool closer to the bench and perched on its edge. Delicately, he turned the carving in his hands, inspecting it closely, then began to smooth away at the coarseness of the surface with steadily finer sandpapers. For maybe forty five minutes, Fergus worked at the wood until every trace of imperfection was removed. Satisfied, he chased away every particle of dust with a paint brush before applying a blend of beeswax and linseed oil until the whole took on a warm sheen. For some time, Fergus stared at the face looking out from his cupped hands, lost.

The cry of a tern wheeling in the sky outside brought him back to himself. Looking at his watch, Fergus repackaged the gift, this time in a piece of clean muslin, and stowed it carefully in his empty shoulder bag. He bustled into the bright daylight, but instead of going immediately to his bicycle and the lane back down to the village, he set off across the coarse field, up the incline to where the land fell suddenly away.

There was no fence here at the cliff's edge. Only the sheep and Duncannon, and sometimes Fergus, came here. None needed restraint to keep them from falling. At the brink Fergus paused. The wide sea stretched far and calm beneath the startling blue arc of the cloudless sky. It was a fine and peaceful day. Sometimes summer brought such days to the island, but it was auspicious weather for March. Fergus stared out across the shimmering blue, his hand shielding his eyes against the late-morning glare. The purple bulk of Rum and, in the distance, the grey stroke of Skye obscured the mainland from view. Under the mountains of Rum, Fergus could make out the wake line of the *Tern* cutting across the placid sea on its return from Mallaig, maybe half an hour out. He had a little time yet before McCredie reached the harbour.

The only sounds were the sounds of the birds above him and the perpetual rush of the sea below. In all his years, he had never strayed too far from that sound. Even during the five years he had spent at school in Mallaig, sleeping on the mainland during the week, he had been able to hear the same sea nudging into the shoreline, or tearing through the night in the frequent storms of winter. He loved the sound, the lullaby and the scream, and could not imagine its absence.

On the mainland, the storms were less urgent than here. Only five miles long and a mile across, Hinba lay in the open sea, beyond the shelter of Rum and Eigg, facing the full force of the south westerly winds, the relentless roar of the Atlantic gales. Even back from the shore, the sea could be deafening for days, an unavoidable reminder that you stood on the very edge of things: precarious and resilient. The sea's rage could not displace the men and women of the island, and Fergus felt his pride swell with each winter spent there.

On days like this, the sea's soft shushing was a reassurance, a keepsake, a promise that everything was right in the world. Down by the harbour, or along the rock pools that cratered the north shore, the water would be gulping and gurgling to itself as the waves arrived and departed. It was a more intimate sound, the sweet nothings of deep connection, the small change of mutual love and respect; the ocean sharing its whimsy with the islanders, all of whom delighted in this quiet communion.

It was maybe odd then that neither Fergus nor his fellows on Hinba had ever, in their five thousand years on the island, been keen seafarers. The earliest inhabitants had built their settlements in the middle of the island, farming the land rather than harvesting the sea. When the Norse men came, with their ships and sagas of faraway lands, the island had turned itself out towards the world: the main settlement was refounded by the landing place on the shore and the interior was left to the sheep and the ruins of churches and hill forts. But even to this day, the boat belonged to the mainland; McCredie himself was not of the island, born and raised in that other world, returning to it each night. The few vessels that remained on Hinba were like lifeboats, an insurance against disaster.

But today, there was no threat from the ocean or sky. The warmth of the air and the sun's brightness fed his contentment. In this light, Fergus knew that Hinba was the most beautiful place in the world: that he had seen so little of anywhere else did not diminish this conviction. An important, beautiful day. Fergus allowed himself to daydream about what Shona would be doing right then, and to think of her mouth, of the bow of her lips. He stroked his shoulder bag and through its nylon wall, and the muslin taken from his mother's sewing box, he stroked the carving as if it were Shona's own cheek.

Slowly, he felt eyes upon him. Duncannon was on the beach, motionless, staring. Over his right shoulder, he had a tyre and knot of orange rope; his left hand was raised to shield his eyes against the sunlight. Fergus waved to his absent host and, sure enough, Duncannon returned the gesture, raising his left arm in a broad sweep. He was maybe 500 yards away, and Fergus could not make out his features, could not tell if he was smiling or scowling.

— ◎ —

The sun prickled the skin under his hair. It was almost too warm, as it had been throughout the summer holidays. With his exertions, Fergus's hands were slick on the basalt. He could feel the tearing of his trainers against the rocks below and he felt his courage flow out through the ragged apertures rent in their fibres. He no longer knew why he was here.

The day had seemed obvious; another in a line of new adventures. Soon he would be old enough for big school and be sent across the sea to study, but for these few, endless weeks his world was only Hinba and he was free to revel in its possibilities. Morag and Davey, Fingal even, had known that this was his last weightless time and so Fergus had been excused of his chores, such as they were, and set loose upon the island.

His companion in these adventures was Jamie McCulloch, a classmate. His father had the farm at Tarbet. The relative seclusion of the farm, some two miles out of the village, and the absence of a mother had left in Jamie a coarseness that Morag Buchanan felt inappropriate for a friend of Fergus. Father and grandfather had waved away such concerns. Today, however, Fergus felt that his mother may have been proven right.

At first, they confined themselves to the gentle bow of the cliff's upper reaches, where the slope provided tufts of grass for hand holds, and old nest platforms gave stable footings. But there were only puffins here and their eggs were not so well prized. Jamie had urged them on, to descend further, beyond the point where the exponential curve became irrevocable, to where the guillemots made their nests.

Some fifteen feet below the lip of the cliff, Fergus had all but lost his nerve. Below him, white tailed eagles patrolled the shoreline, sliding effortlessly through the thick air, building the courage to set off in search of silver-backed fish. The boy longed to be able to glide above the surface, to be free of this insistent gravity. He felt tears burn behind his eyes, but smothered them through force of will. He would not, could not, cry if there were witnesses, especially if that witness was the fearless Jamie McCulloch.

'Hey Fergus! Down here! There's a whole clutch. Enough to take a few, for sure. Fetch that knapsack down, will you?'

Jamie was perhaps two body lengths below him, precarious on a ledge and surrounded by shrieking seabirds. For all his irreverent bluster, he was a farmer's son and knew not to take more than nature would allow. But whatever respect this evoked in Fergus was lost in the prospect of a further descent. The breath juddered out of him as he ran through the options available to him. The least acceptable, staying where he was and clinging to the rocks around him, was the most appealing; down or up, both held their own terrors, but up would be surrender, even if it took him back to the soft, firm grassland above. Fergus opened his eyes, looked down to Jamie to smile and nod, and to seek out some foothold that would make his task possible.

It was then that Jamie lost his own footing. His grin melted into wide-eyed stupefaction as his body slid from the ledge and accelerated downwards. His flailing arms did not prevent his descent and this puzzled Jamie, who's body had until that moment been a reliable anchor in the world. Above him Fergus was surprised to see that the cliff was not in fact perpendicular to the sea, but fell away in a long slope. Jamie's drop released a cloud of loose earth and gravel, but there was friction enough to prevent it becoming freefall. When he struck the outcrop, his leg crumpled and there was a small bounce, but at least he did not continue to fall.

Time restarted with Jamie's wail. From the top of the narrow basalt column, the boy clutched his leg and screamed primal sounds to compete with the cries of the startled guillemots and kittiwakes that span and circled his plinth. His eyes were balled tight shut but Fergus could only see the top of his head and the outstretched good leg, the hands clasped to the bad.

'Jamie, hold on, yeah? I'm coming down. I'll fetch you, don't worry!'

All his own fear had fallen with Jamie. It had clattered onto the rocks that backed the beach and lay there impotent, spent.

Instead, Fergus was gripped by purpose and no more able to resist the impulse to climb down the cliff than he had been to cling to it moments earlier. He was swiftly down to the ledge where the eggs lay yet, undisturbed; ignoring the direct path carved by Jamie's falling form, he picked out a more stable route that led via a series of broad ledges down to his friend's perch.

'It's my ankle. I think I've turned it. Can't put any weight on it. God, it hurts. I'm sorry Fergus, I shouldn't have made you.'

Jamie's eyes were open now but red-rimmed; mucus bubbled from his nose with each heavy, halting breath. His back was jammed against the cliff wall and still he clasped his ankle, his knuckles whitening. He blinked his fear at Fergus.

'It's OK. I can help you. It's easy: look, there's quite a path if you follow these ledges. We've got all day, we can take it slow as you like. From there, we can get up to that crag without much bother, and then it's easy street. See?'

Fergus led the line they would take with his outstretched arm, up towards a rocky point just below the grassy slope. And he took Jamie's hand and led him off the column that had saved him. They picked their way slowly up the cliff, inching over suspect rock and unreliable grit. All the while, Fergus supported as much of Jamie's weight as he could within the confines of the slender space they had. Later, on account of Jamie's fear of what might occur should his father find out that he had disobeyed a direct and strict instruction not to venture onto the cliffs, Fergus would tell his parents that they had been out to the ruins, where they had played on the low stones, leaping one to the other, and where Jamie had mistimed a leap and landed awkwardly, twisting his ankle. Later still he would repeat this version of events with Mr McCulloch and in school in front of Mr Galbraith and all the children, including Shona MacLeod. Neither he, nor Jamie McCulloch would ever say where they had really been, nor what had really happened. Fergus's courage and Jamie's gratitude remained a secret between themselves, even after they had drifted apart in the school at Mallaig.

As the pair crested the outcrop just below the safety of the turf, Fergus looked back down to where they had been and to where they might have ended. There, below on the beach, a figure stood watching them. It had to be the strange man his grandfather warned him against, the man that lived alone out on the cliff top, collecting the rubbish rejected by the sea. He was maybe 500 yards away, and Fergus could not make out his features, could not tell that he was smiling, did not know that he had watched the fall and the rescue transfixed in his own private terror.

four

An eagle wheeled above Fergus and its shriek startled him. He watched it arc out to sea, out to where the little boat was tugging gently at the current around the headland: McCredie would soon be at the pier and Fergus was anxious to greet him when he arrived. He waved once more towards the figure on the beach and turned back towards his bicycle, leant against the gatepost to Duncannon's yard. He gave two or three heavy steps on the pedals, then let the hill carry him down. The lane raced back down to the village, squeezing between Galbraith's and Mrs Robertson's, then past the little school house where the five newest islanders were taught to read and to count, to paint bright houses and smiling families, to name animals and towns from far away; then through the glut of white-washed houses gathered on the rise above the little harbour, where the Harbour Bell and the Post Office faced each other across the curve of the old quay. Finally Fergus flew past the church, built to house the hopes of the herring curers who briefly made their homes here before the wandering fish moved on.

The lane ended at the little hut that served as warehouse and waiting room for McCredie's cargo, human or otherwise. Fergus rolled slowly to the end of the new concrete jetty just as the *Tern* was nudging into the tyres strung along its edge. Most days, McCredie came twice, once early and once in the afternoon, but he could be persuaded to make additional trips as needed and to make the crossing to Rum and Eigg, or even to Skye. The flat bare deck between the bow and wheel house was most often filled with barrels of beer for the Bell and the other bulky requisites for island life. Once a week, more often in the summer, the larger ferry that served Rum and Eigg would continue onto Hinba, but otherwise, McCredie was the only regular connection the island had with the mainland.

When Fergus waved, McCredie's face folded into a smile, his nose almost disappearing into his grey beard. He liked the young man: he was honest and decent, had respect for his elders. When he came to pick up the mail, he was always polite, always had time to talk, to ask after Mrs McCredie and the news from the mainland. And he was diligent, industrious. Punctual. He had grown into a fine young man. Tall and broad, but lean as well: not an ounce of wasted flesh. Too young for a beard yet, but that would come in time.

'And how was the crossing? Did you see any dolphins this time?'

Without waiting for the gangplank, Fergus hopped across the gap and onto the *Tern*, as McCredie shook his head. They had speculated about dolphins that morning when Fergus had collected the mail and now he picked up the conversation from where it had been left.

'No, I think the calm has given them the courage to go further out, into deeper water, chasing the fish. Like a mill pond still.' McCredie clasped the outstretched hand and shook it firmly. Fergus looked at him expectantly.

'Do you have it?' His excitement drove him from pleasantries faster than would ordinarily be the case, and he felt a twinge of guilt. He hoped McCredie would understand his impatience.

'Steady on, lad, no need to fret. I've got it. I stepped over to MacBride's between runs and fished him out of his workshop. He's done a grand job, I'd say. Looks perfect, like it'd never been any different.'

McCredie took a wrap of paper, decorated with pink and grey flowers, from his jacket pocket and held it out towards Fergus. The tiny package was sealed with a swipe of Sellotape and held with gentle firmness between the old seafarer's calloused thumb and forefinger. Gingerly, Fergus accepted the offering, squeezing it between his own thumb and forefinger. He could feel the ring's smooth, cold hardness through the paper, and knew without looking that everything was in order. He hid the precious parcel in his jeans and took a roll of bank notes from the same pocket. Sliding out four twenty pound notes, he took McCredie's wrist in his spare hand and pushed the crisp paper into the waiting palm. McCredie's fingers folded tightly over the money; he held the notes up to his face and seemed for an instant to smell them, before burying them in the inside pocket of his jacket. A smile broke between his whiskers.

— ◎ —

Later now, and the sun had slipped low in the still cloudless sky. Soon it would bleed its colours across the island's horizon and paint the mountains and the moorland black before their time. To the east, a whisper of darkness foretold was beginning to gather over Eigg. Fergus looked at Shona, and she back at him, and they smiled a secret smile each to the other. The little waves, barely ripples, dropped lethargically onto the very lip of the beach, their flat murmur wrapped tight around the lovers.

The picnic was over. His mother's best blanket, which he had taken to use as a rug, was strewn with the debris. The remains of the loaf Morag had made that morning; one and a half tomatoes; the nub of cheddar that was yellowing and hardening in the dying sun light; the shattered shells of boiled eggs and the dusting of the salt that had accompanied them; the crumbs and wrapper of a packet of chocolate biscuits. Only the meat pie had entirely disappeared, without trace or residue: Morag was a renowned baker of pies. The bottle of sparkling wine had been drained an hour before and now lay empty in the sand, beside the paper cups that had played the part of crystal. His mother had frowned at first, unsure that alcohol was appropriate, until Fergus had pointed out that Shona was now 18 years of age. He had told Shona this as he had poured out the first beaker, and she had laughed as he had laughed at the thought of all the times that the two of them had stayed behind in the bar after her parents had shut up the pub, talking, drinking whisky, wine, anything that might not be noticed in the morning. They had been 14 years old when they had first been left downstairs, and Fergus had suggested trying the sweet pink wine that was dispensed from the glass cabinet behind the bar.

Fergus touched the silver pendant that hung around Shona's neck and she allowed it, even though it meant he was also touching her breast with his fingertips. He had bought it for her from a catalogue, in case his handiwork had let him down. McCredie had brought it over with the mail weeks before. It was shaped as a love heart, across which Shona's name was engraved as a ribbon; in the top right ventricle, a diamond had been embedded. It had been wrapped in a neat package onto which his mother had glued a little bow; Shona's eyes had gleamed as she tore of the paper and opened the little hinged box, and they had continued to shimmer as she let out a little squeal and threw her arms about him. For a long time after he had fastened the clasp under her hair, all the while watching the fall of her neck and the wisps of downy hair, she had felt for it as a talisman and looked down at it, smiling, inhaling sharply.

Even after she had opened the larger gift, the carving of her, she kept returning to the pendant. It was not that she had not liked the bust, but there had been something that looked like disappointment as she tore off the paper only recently arranged over its awkward shape. As Fergus had washed and changed, hiding his grandmother's engagement ring in his room, Morag had taken paper and tape from the shop to wrap the carving. His father, nervous under Fingal's gaze, had pretended to begrudge this infringement, unable to read whether the old man would view it as fecklessness or as a laudable indulgence of his favourite grandchild.

They, at least, had all admired the craftsmanship and the refinement of the wooden bust. The old man had held it close to his failing eyes to inspect its lines, while Davey looked on in deep and silent pride at his son; his mother had put her hand to her chest and sighed through half-formed tears, saying it was without doubt a thing of beauty. Yet there had been no squeal of delight from Shona herself, when presented with her own likeness. She had smiled, of course, thanked him, marvelled at the time it must have taken him, the skill employed. But she had been able to contain herself. Maybe she was embarrassed, but the doubt he had feared had crept into him and he was pleased that he had thought to buy the pendant as well.

He touched its cold gloss again, this time moving his hand a little too far across the wool of her sweater. To his surprise she did not try to fend him off. Instead she pulled closer to him, locking her lips onto his, wriggling into an embrace, pulling her body against his. They kissed for several delicious minutes; only when his hand slid too far down her back, beyond the sweater, beyond even the pocket on the back of her jeans, did she stiffen and wrestle away from him.

'No Fergus! I've told you a million times!' She was smiling, a little flushed. Her lips were pinker than usual, more indistinct, and her eyes twinkled with mischief and feigned indignation. Fergus raised his palms in surrender.

'What time is it, anyway? It must be getting on, the sun's almost behind that hill.' Shona nodded towards the squat drum of Carn A'Ghail, a grey-black hat box atop the shelves stacked above the shore. Squinting in the golden light, Fergus checked his watch.

'Christ! It's five thirty. We should be heading back. You'll want to be getting dolled up before the party.'

Shona giggled then sprang to her feet, brushing crumbs and sand from her clothes. Fergus was on his knees, packing the debris into the hamper, watching her run her palms over her body. While she arranged her hair more firmly into the comb and checked her face in her compact mirror, Fergus stood downwind to shake what was left from his mother's blanket. He returned, blanket folded neatly, to find that instead of her mirror she was holding the carving tenderly before her, contemplating deeply its shapes. A little smile played around his lips.

'Fergus, this is really beautiful, you know? I am amazed. And flattered, really flattered.' She paused, then looked up. *'You really love me, don't you?'*

They embraced briefly on the sand, Shona pulling him to her with a sudden sob. Then they were trudging up the beach to the track that let back to the village. In the Bell, Mrs MacLeod would already be setting out the buffet and hanging the decorations. Her husband would be bringing up the case of Spanish 'champagne' from the cellar. Later, with the whole island gathered, they would toast their only daughter's majority, and lavish on her clothes and jewellery and electronic devices they did not understand, all in plain sight of their neighbours. Then they would open the bar and, for this night only, no money would change hands, all would be in their munificence.

five

Wednesday morning came slowly to him, carried on the insistent whine of his alarm clock. He fumbled with the large, round button that silenced the thing, prodding it with uncommon malice, before sinking back into his pillow. His eyes, his throat, were sticky and a little raw. Like treacle, the night before came back to him. Eventually, when it had all arrived, had reconvened in his mind, he was able to place himself in space and time. Davey could hear his wife breathing next to him: shallow, hurried breaths. She needed no alarm clock, simply rising when he made his way to the bathroom, as she had every day, barring Sundays, for the past two decades. She had learned quickly the rhythms of the island and had accommodated herself to them and to the ways of the Buchanan men. He was immensely grateful to her for that.

He turned softly towards her and watched her pale profile, mouth slightly open, chin rising and falling with her chest. She was still a good looking woman, even now, in her early forties. Back when he had first seen her at the sea captain's wake, she had been startlingly beautiful: tall and slender in her black dress, her fresh face framed by strawberry blond hair. She had been seventeen years old, just a touch younger than him, and he had known in an instant that he would woo her. Morag's father, a farmer on Eigg, had been wary of the match at first, since he did not want his daughter to leave the island. But he had recognised that Davey Buchanan's prospects were good, as heir to the Post Office on Hinba.

At that time, farming was a precarious professional. Furthermore, Eigg was still subject to an absent landlord, while Hinba had been its own island for centuries, since the Clanranalds had granted a thousand year lease to the inhabitants. The reasons for this generosity were lost in time, but it was widely believed among the remaining sixteen families that the Buchanans and the MacLeods – rivals even then – had joined forces to convince, bribe or blackmail the old laird somehow. Some believed that there had been a curse involved, some old magic, a rare weapon that the Buchanans and MacLeods had buried out on the moor to preserve a precarious truce once the island was free. But whatever the truth, these legends alone made the two families' continued dominance over island affairs inevitable. The prospect of a union with such a prominent family stilled the sentiment of Morag's father, and ultimately he had acquiesced with grace. Morag and Davey had been married and their life together on Hinba had begun.

Davey began breathing in time with his wife, a secret ritual he had maintained since the first morning he had woken beside her, synchronising his body with hers at the start of each day so that they might remain in step throughout the waking hours, even when apart.

Too soon, it was time to rise. His father would be sitting at the kitchen table, smoking his pipe and drinking from a mug of tea. Davey dared not appear, washed and dressed, later than seven thirty each morning, for fear of the old man's scorn. Even when there was nothing to do in the shop or the office, when the storms meant there'd be no boat and no mail, he would go down, exchange a few words with him over the breakfast Morag would prepare, still dressed in her housecoat. On those empty, pointless mornings, he would simply disappear into the office and work through his book of crosswords, listening to the wind howl.

But today was another fine March morning, and there were things to do. Only his head and his stomach did not want to do them. He was 44 years old, and while he could still drink whisky as he had the night before, he found it ever more difficult to live with the consequences on the following day. The bathroom mirror showed him another man to the one he had expected to greet him: a pale and sagging face with insipid eyes that fluttered against the sudden light. He looked shocking, and he felt as bad.

The party had been loud and long. The free bar had brought the whole island to the Bell to celebrate. Everyone bar Duncannon of course, who would sooner die than spend an evening of gaiety with his neighbours. And Mr Galbraith, the master at the island's little school. He was away on the mainland, apparently, and Davey had wondered what nature of business would have kept him from such a grand event. Unlike the retiring Duncannon, Galbraith was always immersed in the life of Hinba. He was originally from the mainland, somewhere near Loch Laggan, and yet he was as committed to the island as any native; maybe more so.

He had arrived 15 years before, full of talk about St Columba, earnest and enthusiastic. Undoubtedly he had felt himself to be underused professionally in his tutoring of the handful of docile children that the island produced, but the lack of demands made upon him meant that he had been able to throw himself into his research, traipsing over the fields and moors between the two old ruined churches, and up to the old Dun at the western end of the island. Always his nose in a book, looking for the traces of the saint's time on Hinba, relics of the man or the monastery he founded there, destroyed by Pictish raiders even before the Norsemen arrived.

Galbraith had taught Shona from her first day at the school until her last, when, with all the others, she had set off to Mallaig and the high school. That he should miss her day, when he had attended every other eighteenth birthday since he arrived, was inexplicable. His absence had been noted, frequently, before the whisky and beer took hold of the conversation in the bar. When Mr McCulloch had unlatched his squeeze-box and the dancing and singing and carousing had begun in earnest, Galbraith's absence melted into nothingness and the people of Hinba simply celebrated the coming of age of one of their own, their own sweet Shona.

Just eighteen, she had looked every inch the woman. It would soon be time, he was sure. Now that the girl had reached adulthood, and with Fergus on the cusp of attaining his majority, he felt sure that it would not be long before they would be making wedding preparations. There had been talk of that late on, with the older ones cooing over the couple as they danced together, smiling knowing smiles, as if recalling fondly their own youth and fecundity. Old Mrs Robertson had shed several tears as she gazed on Fergus and Shona, his arm around her bare shoulders, his fingers pressing slightly into the plump firmness of her skin, his eyes searching for hers as they stood beside the improvised dance floor in the centre of the bar. While Fingal Buchanan had whirled Mrs Robertson to the floor and danced her round the room as if it were still 1958 and her marriage and his had never happened, Davey's eye had settled once more upon his son and his girl, as they stood in a slow, liquid embrace, oblivious to the clatter that surrounded them.

He had had doubts about Fergus marrying a MacLeod and yet it had been inevitable: the two had been practically betrothed since primary school. Inseparable, already reconciled to an eternity together by the age of eight. That she had turned out so bonny and caring made the pill easier to swallow and Davey, encouraged by his wife, had long since warmed to the match. He suspected that his father still rankled at the idea, but even Fingal did not voice any objections.

At the thought of his father, Davey looked at the clock above the bath and reluctantly pulled up the plug. He came to his feet, still dizzy with the residue of whisky, and fumbled for his towel. The wash had helped and he no longer felt sick, although the heat of the water had done nothing to make his head more stable. He stood there, naked and dripping, too busy steadying himself against the wall to dry himself with the towel. He did not feel sufficiently confident of his footing to move just yet and it was only once the wetness of his skin and hair began to chill him that he cautiously clambered from the bath tub. He looked again at the heavy hanging folds beneath his eyes, pulling them taught either in hope or remembrance. He had not always been in such a state of disrepair: while he had never been as handsomely made as his son, he had been lean and evenly formed. His time was almost past, he knew: his son would take up the reins of the house and the business directly from his grandfather and he, Davey Buchanan, would inherit neither the title nor the acclaim.

This indignity did not ignite rancour either for the father or for the son, but rather for Cameron MacLeod. The two of them had known each other since they were children, had even once been friends; but their eventual feud had been written before they were born, forged in the heat of centuries of hatred between the two families. No-one knew of any incident that had ignited the slow tension that the island had contained for as long as anyone could remember. There were no stories, no legends, to explain the spark of the enmity: it was in fact simply that both families craved dominance. And while

Cameron MacLeod had inherited the Bell from his own father in the natural order of things, Fingal clung stubbornly to the title of post master, undermining Davey's rightful superiority.

Davey shook the thoughts from his head, and padded softly back to the empty bedroom, where he dressed. No sound from Fergus's room, only the murmur of voices from the kitchen, the clanking of plates, cups and saucers. Let the boy sleep, he thought.

'Well, Davey my boy – how's the head?'

That Fingal was smiling as he entered the kitchen was surprise enough; that he had greeted him with an enquiry after his health astounded Davey. He felt unnerved, expected some imminent rebuke. Morag pulled out a chair for him, guiding him into it before placing a cup of tea beside him and stroking his still-damp hair. She too was smiling.

'If I'm honest, I feel like shit. Pardon my French.' He lowered his eyes apologetically in the direction of his wife, but she was already laughing a girlish laugh. She fetched over some aspirin before slipping out into the garden.

'I think we all overdid the drink. I'll say one thing for that MacLeod, he stocks a fine cellar. Nicer when it's free, of course.'

Davey could not remember a morning when his father had been as open and genial, nor as interested in the world beyond himself. He could not decide whether it was better to wait and watch or to mirror Fingal's uncommon fluency.

'I wish he'd had a pay bar after all, mind you. I might not have drunk so much of his whisky if he'd been charging. Fergus seemed to be OK,

mind you. He spent most of the night gazing into Shona's eyes rather than the bottom of glass. I should shout him, I suppose.'

'Fergus? Oh, he left an hour ago, before I'd filled my first pipe. Got things to sort out, I shouldn't wonder.'

Fingal ended this with a smiling wink, something Davey had never seen. He wondered if he was still drunk. Drawing deeply on the cooling tea to wash down the aspirin, he leant over the table towards his father and placed his hand in the old man's bare forearm, without thinking. But there was no flinch.

'So is it to be today? So soon?'

Despite the dull pain that filled his head, Davey had finally worked out what was making both Fingal and Morag act so out of character: Fergus was to propose to Shona today. Clearly, Fingal had come to terms with the prospect of a MacLeod as a granddaughter.

'Soon! We've been waiting 18 years, haven't we? All I know is that he had my Maggie's engagement ring sent over to Mallaig to be sized and that young McCredie brought it back yesterday. So, it looks like MacLeod will be having another free bar before too long.'

Morag had been standing in the doorway for a few moments. She had been held at the threshold by the sight of her husband's hand on his father's arm. She had never seen Davey and Fingal so close and at ease, and had not wanted to break the spell. But now she could only laugh with joy at the prospect of her Fergus married. Davey withdrew his hand, but kept his smile. Sitting back in his chair, shaking his head in disbelieving pleasure, he marvelled at the three of them, all smiling together.

six

The sea barely murmured in the bay. By the harbour, its surface was as polished steel. No cloud, no wind, just the perfect stillness of the early morning. No-one out of doors yet: the little village belonged to Fergus and to the gulls that sat motionless on the wooden spars of the old jetty head, out in the bay: fulmars for the most part, in all their soft innocence. They too were simply enjoying the earth's pause and the soul's quiet it brought.

He had slept lightly, dreamlessly, for just a few hours. It had been early morning before the Buchanans had at last left the Bell, Fergus stealing a long kiss from Shona while their parents had exchanged counterfeit pleasantries on the threshold. But he had not drunk so much and had woken brightly when the first grey light had found its way between the undrawn curtains of his bedroom. He had had no need to note his dreams and he could see no point in lying sleepless on his bed on such a day as this. So he had washed and dressed and slipped stealthily through the front door, so as not to disturb his grandfather before his first pipe of the day. He had walked the short distance to the harbour noiselessly. Finding a large coil of worn hawser, he had settled low into its comfort and, with all of the sea before him, had day-dreamed his way through the events to come.

On the empty air, the first faint sound from McCredie's boat carried far across the water, a gentle thumping hum. One of the fulmars rose silently at the intrusion and wheeled away, while Fergus checked his watch to be sure that it wasn't later than he thought. He still had 40 minutes before he would be disturbed. Relieved, he returned his gaze to the small ring cradled tenderly between the thumb and forefinger of both his hands. It was a slight gold loop, almost drowned by the three diamonds set into it. He remembered that, when it was on his grandmother's finger, the gold had been all but invisible: it was the heavy gemstones that had held his infant attention.

He thought briefly of the old woman, barely present in his memory. She had died years before, when he had been very small, barely walking, and the image of her hand, white like paper, was one of the few things he had left of her. And now the ring that had resided there was to pass to Shona. This had been known and determined long before: it was destined. Neither Fergus nor Shona had understood the meaning of the word before the whole island knew that, one day, they would be married. To the elders of the island, the marriage was simply the union of two families and with it the end of centuries of feuding. Fergus knew this now, but he had not known it when he had fallen in love with Shona: even before his adolescent lusts had risen, he had known that she and he were two halves of a whole.

Even so, Fergus was beset by anxiety that morning. He knew that this was no marriage of convenience, of politics and alliance; his heart told him that she was all he had ever believed her to be, that their love was real and enduring. He even liked her parents, although he knew he could never admit that to his father or his grandfather. She was beautiful, kind and clever. He loved her. So why did these doubts crowd in, this morning of all mornings?

He turned his mind instead to how he would propose. His plans were specific but not elaborate. There would be scope for spontaneity, of course. Even so, he had been preparing for the when and the how and the where for years. Since he was 16, when he had first found his tongue inside her mouth, out by the old Dun at the western end of the island, he had known where he would propose, where the sun would be and how the light would hit the sea and the ruins of the ancient church: the previous year, on exactly this date, he had spent the day there, watching the sun and the shadows move, timing their precise positions and the effect they had on the landscape, on the stones. He rehearsed once more the plan he had spent so long constructing, imagining Shona's delight, sinking deeper into the coils of rope.

The sun was higher now, and the spluttering of McCredie's boat more distinct. Fergus opened his eyes. The gulls had left and a light morning breeze ruffled the sea's surface. Some wisps of high horse tail cloud flecked the eastern sky. The *Tern* was close enough now for Fergus to make out the shape of McCredie in the little wheel house. Soon the letters would arrive, and sometime after that they would be in the hands of their rightful recipients. Then he would be able to begin this day, the most important of his life.

— ⊙ —

Shona smiled the smile that she kept for times like this. It was the same smile that had greeted Fergus when she had opened the side door to him at the Bell some two hours before. It had been early in the lunchtime session and Mr MacLeod had been invisible, beyond the curtain to the public bar. He would have been polishing the glasses that had sat in the machine overnight while he chatted with the eager customers sitting at the bar, customers for whom the comfort of the pub held greater appeal than the content of their mornings. They drank beer and murmured their world-weariness towards their indulgent host. Mrs MacLeod was in the kitchen, preparing simple lunches for the guests to come. Fergus could hear the clatter of crockery in a sink, arrhythmic percussion to her tuneless humming.

No words had been exchanged and the young lovers had simply kissed, just in the shadow of the doorway, out of sight of the street and at a safe distance from those inside. Shona had then smoothed her skirt before unleashing her best smile for the first time that day.

It was not a false smile. It was sincere and it was heartfelt. That she knew how it should look, how to tense her face to form it, how to recognise the pull of muscle and of skin, did not diminish its honesty. It was a simple awareness of herself, of how she appeared, nothing more. The smile was a genuine representation of how she felt upon seeing Fergus that afternoon. All the more so now that they were away at the far western end of Hinba, alone together. The village was some four miles back along the shore, and here there were no human witnesses, only the sheep and the rabbits, the sharp-eyed eagles drifting high above the blazing waters.

Within half an hour of setting off, they had left the village far behind, lost behind the slabbed hills that stepped down to the coves of the south coast, the sandy nooks notched into long slabs of harsh black rock. The road had disappeared soon after, and they had set out across the open fields. The sheep had kept themselves to themselves, bar their occasional bleating carried on the wind. Only the rabbits kept close, and their hurried movement they made the turf seethe, as they darted through the moss and derelict heather, not yet recovered from the previous season. Another hour of walking brought them to very end of the island.

'Why've you dragged me out to this old sheep fold?'

'You know why. And it's not a sheep fold anyway. It's an old village or something, from before the Vikings. The Irish, St Columba, you know? See that over there? That's what is left of an old kirk. They say this is the site of the first monastery in Scotland.'

'You mean Mr Galbraith and that sister of yours say. Anyhow, it looks like a sheep fold to me. So why did you bring me here?'

Shona scrunched up a smile, tilting her head and swinging her hips into a twist that left her seeming both knowing and naive. She had been here before, of course, on a school outing to visit the ruins that had so excited Mr Galbraith. Shona had not had much interest in St Columba, but the stone cross that still stood taller than her beside the low walls and the jumbled stone of the old church had fascinated her. Some six years later now, it still did. At its base, a scoop had been worn into the stone, cut by something long since lost, leaving only a bowl in which the rain lingered. On the face of the cross itself, the carving looked like endless, knotted braids of hair, twisting in and out of themselves, and Shona felt for her own braids before she remembered that they were long gone, that she was now a woman, no longer a girl.

In a single movement, Shona wrapped Fergus in her arms. She breathed deeply, her nose nestled in the corner of his neck, then slowly pulled away to look at him. Her own excitement was reflected back to her in his eyes and involuntarily she ran a hand through his hair, soft like spun gold. A longing sigh escaped her, and she felt her head shaking gently.

'What's the matter? Did you not want to walk out here? Was it too far?'

His sudden anxiety closed his face into seriousness. Shona laughed to let him know that nothing was wrong, that he had done nothing wrong, that there was nothing about him, nothing, that was wrong. The smile again.

'No, you numpty. I love it out here, you know that. And there's nowhere on this island that's too far to walk! I was just sighing like a big contented cat in front of the fire. How lucky we are, to have found each other, out here, in the middle of the sea, miles from anywhere. Charmed, that must be it. Maybe I have a fairy godmother. Or maybe you do?'

'The nearest I have to a godmother is Mrs Robertson, and she wouldn't take to being called a fairy, I don't think. She's a very practical lady is Mrs Robertson.' Shona laughed once more, her hand covering her mouth, fingertips pressed lightly to her nose. He loved the way she laughed like that, the way the gentle pressure raised tiny ridges on her nose: a coil of silken cord tightened deep within him.

During the late morning a crust of thin grizzled cloud had collected over Hinba, and it had lingered all the while during their walk out along the island. Fergus had grudgingly conceded that his careful preparations had underestimated the island's fickle weather, but just at that moment, as if he did indeed have a fairy godmother, the last of the cloud slid off to the east and the sun broke unexpectedly onto the earth. Its sudden brightness blinded Fergus before the warm light settled, casting shadows and saturating the surroundings in deep colour.

This was surely a good omen: the plans that he had laid the year before were falling into place. Pulling away from her, his hand trailing out of hers at the full extent of their arms, he sprang up onto one of the large, low, ancient slabs, spreading his arms wide in dominion, in an embrace of his beloved island, as if calling his ancestors to witness this moment. Out at sea the terns flashed across the surface, wheeling and arching before crashing beneath the waves in search of fish that gleamed silver in their beaks as they broke the surface and found the air once more. Fergus watched them for a moment, half remembering something, before turning back to Shona, smiling. She in turn was looking up at him, smiling, hands clasped across her chest as if in prayer. He felt that all of history was pointing at this one moment.

Fergus hopped from his stone to another, and then another, turning Shona until she had her back to the sea, was facing north-eastwards where the sunlight hit the cross and the remains of the doorway to the ruined church. She was standing where he had stood, exactly one year ago; was seeing, as he had, the way that the shadows lifted the knot-work of the cross to a perfect intensity and clarity, that the sunlight coaxed from the grey stone of the doorway a pinkish warmth. He stepped down onto the grass before her, breathed in a little of the air, just as he had planned, and dropped to his knee.

Shona accepted the ring offered up to her, as she had known she would, as Fergus and as everyone had known she would. Even so, her heart had begun to race a little when Fergus had dropped from the last stone to face her, his wide eyes sparkling with latent intent. By the time he had retrieved the ring from his hip pocket, her ears were full of surging blood and the rush and suck of the sea below the cliffs. She could not tell if it was his hand or hers that shook as he slid the sleek golden band onto her finger to a perfect fit. The three diamonds glinting in the spring sunshine still thrilled her, even as she had known that they would.

They remained like that, she standing above him, for several minutes. The wind toyed with Shona's hair, buffeting her occasionally such that she would sway gently; the dampness of the grass spread across the right knee of Fergus's jeans and he could feel a chill numbness eating into the joint, but he did not move, just watched, waited.

Shona had not yet said yes.

There was no need, of course: they had been betrothed since childhood; his grandmother's ring was on her finger. Yet Fergus still waited, with increasing impatience and concern, for Shona to answer him, to confirm in soft, excited tones that she would marry him. That was how he had envisaged the day as he had planned it over the years and months. He waited, the sunlight breaking around the form of his soon-to-be fiancée like a halo.

'I love you, Shona MacLeod, and want you to be my wife. I choose you. No matter what anyone else thinks or says, not your father nor mine, it was me, Fergus Buchanan, that chose you: do you choose me too?'

Shona's abdomen twisted, so slightly that had Fergus not been at waist height he would not have noticed it. She let out another little sigh and a smile broke across her face. It was a different smile to any he had seen before: broader, with a flavour of delicious mischief.

'Yes, Fergus Buchanan, I choose you. And I will marry you a thousand times over, in defiance of my father and my mother and all of Hinba if needs be.'

Fergus was on his feet, arms clasped around her. The warm wriggle of her lithe body reignited his ever-present desire and, as he pressed his lips to hers, his hand strayed lower down her back until it reached the flowing curve of her hip, her buttock. Knowing that he would be stopped, that Shona would pull away, chide him, he fumbled at her skirt, pulling the pleats of cotton upwards. Finding the warm smoothness of skin, he was able to run his palm up the back of Shona's thigh until he reached the hem of her underwear. He had never before got as far as this and he hesitated, feeling Shona tensing, and instead, ran his palm gently back down her leg, the skirt dropping back into place in his wake. He let out a little groan as his hand brushed back over the bow of her before finding its way to the small of her back. Shona pulled him closer, almost purring.

'Soon, my love, soon. We'll be married soon.'

seven

Cameron MacLeod did not like Fergus Buchanan. For a start, he was a Buchanan. That there was no love lost between the families was well known, of course. You could not stay long on Hinba without learning of the centuries of loathing. But to Cameron MacLeod, the contempt he felt for his neighbours was distinct from that felt by earlier MacLeods.

True, his own father had brought him up to dislike the Buchanans, had versed him in the ancient slights, in the unworthiness of their hold on the office of post master. Young Cameron had carried his distain dutifully into the little school room, where he had sat close by the ten year old Davey Buchanan. He had played his part in public, pretending to be at odds with everything the little prince did or said. But later, between the end of school and tea at the Bell, he would go off with Davey and the other boys to smoke and throw stones down on the beach. He had laughed with him. He had become friends with the enemy, such that he began to believe that the hatred of his father and of his grandfather was mistaken.

As the boys had grown a little older, they had become even closer: perhaps the secrecy of their friendship had bound them more tightly together. By the time they were twelve years of age, they would sit on the beach together after the other boys had left for home, talking about the future, about the world across the water. On the way back into the village, after dark, they would throw stones against the front doors of their neighbour's houses, and hide to watch the occupant's rising ire as they were repeatedly disturbed from their tea.

For some reason, they particularly delighted in terrorising old Mr Duncannon, the island's mechanic. His house, isolated up on the cliff road, was set amongst outbuildings crammed with machinery and the twisted outcrops of rusted metal which made for excellent hiding places. After a few weeks of persecution, the old man tired of the game such that he began sending his young son to the door instead. Alec Duncannon was a bright, sociable boy, who would often join the other boys down on the beach after school.

Since he understood the nature of the prank better than his father, he knew where to look for his hiding classmates and one night spotted Cameron. In rebuke, he had called out his name, loudly and clearly in the darkness. Startled by their discovery, the two miscreants had raced away into the night, tearing down the lane back to the village and their mother's food. On the way, they had passed Mr Robertson, walking up the lane from his cottage, pulling a handcart through the darkness.

It must have been him: Robertson must have been the one to break into Duncannon's shed and to steal the tools. Hundreds of pounds worth of Duncannon's tools. His livelihood, indeed. Had they sent the police to search Robertson's house, Cameron knew they would have found the stolen items. But they didn't. Instead, Fingal Buchanan accused the MacLeod boy, who had been seen by the house and who had been known to have been persecuting

Duncannon for weeks. There was no sign of the tools at the Harbour Bell or in any other place that Cameron MacLeod might have hidden them, but this did not trouble the islanders. Fingal Buchanan, the post master of Hinba, had declared him a thief, and it was simply assumed that the boy had thrown the valuable belongings into the sea, in an act of wilful vandalism. Cameron had looked to his friend to provide him with an alibi, to explain that, yes, the two of them had pestered Mr Duncannon but had not taken the tools. But Davey had been too afraid to admit to his father that he had been consorting with MacLeods and had stayed silent. All the while his father was beating him with the old belt that hung like a threat from the kitchen door, Cameron had cursed both Fingal for his cruelty and Davey for his betrayal.

In the circumstances, it was inconceivable that Cameron MacLeod could have any warm feelings towards the young Buchanan. Where others saw an easy charm and open generosity, Cameron viewed Fergus as self-satisfied and condescending. He had been spoiled by his mother and his father's weakness had allowed the boy to become indulged, soft. He simpered about the island, carrying his entitlement like it was a burden rather than a privilege. No son of a MacLeod would behave like Fergus did. He was 20 years of age, but with the face of a baby, his red hair soft and long like a girl's. And then there was the way he spoke to MacLeod, as if he were his social better: he patronised MacLeod, made an effort, made allowances. What was more, adding insult to still-smarting injury, this young Buchanan had his hands all over his daughter. It made him sick to think of it.

And yet, and yet. He could not object to the betrothal. If he put his foot down, Shona would mither and his wife would blame him for the mithering. Whether Shona had feelings for the boy or not was unimportant: simply being told what she could or could not do would raise a storm in his daughter. Maybe they had spoiled her too, he thought, polishing the last of the lunch time pint glasses from the washer.

It was of no matter, anyway. He could live with the whining and the tears of his women, of course. No, the real reason for his mute acceptance of the match was that the whole island saw it as inevitable and desirable. An end to the feuding. A joining of the families. To stand against the marriage would be to turn his face not only against his daughter and therefore his wife, but also the people of Hinba. They would still come to drink his whisky of course, but there would be whispers and gossip, false smiles at the bar and cruel words behind his back. He had no choice but to make the best of it: the Buchanans would get their hands on the Bell, but only at the expense of the MacLeods getting a share of the Post Office. It would not be long before a MacLeod, albeit one called Buchanan, would be Post Master of Hinba.

'What time do you think they'll be back?'

Chrissie MacLeod had walked into the empty bar unnoticed, her hair and face set for the evening. More make up than usual, and a new dress from the catalogue, her second of the week: she would be ready to greet the good news when it came.

'I don't know, love. I don't know why he had to take her all that way to ask her anyhow. And he might have asked my permission first. I suppose some young people these days don't hold with manners in the same way.' To sweeten his bitterness, Cameron leant across the polished sheen of the bar to kiss his wife on the cheek. Pulling away he admired her momentarily. Plumper yes, and there were lines around her eyes, in the corners of her mouth, but she was still the sweetheart of his own youth. He remembered the day they

themselves had become engaged and it helped to steady himself for the loss of his daughter.

Chrissie MacLeod smoothed down her skirt and, hips swinging ever so slightly on her low heels, she walked to the door to unbolt it for the evening's customers. At the stroke of five thirty, she pulled open the door, glanced up and down the empty street, then withdrew into the warmth of the bar, dragging the heavy curtain around its hooped rail to mark the boundary between worldly cares and convivial comfort. She turned and caught the last of her husband's smile.

She loved this time of day above all others. The bar was open but empty; there was just her and her man, with an evening of unknown possibility stretched before them. There was no work to do, no serving, nor cooking, nor cleaning, only the boldness of dominion, the fruit of their labours to be savoured in restful peace. Today, of course, today would bring much more excitement than any other evening and she was torn between wishing the quiet time away and luxuriating in the anticipation it allowed.

She strode across the room to where Cameron stood and threw her arms around him. He seemed a little shocked – this did not often happen these days, it was true – but he was soon squeezing her into him as fervently as she was squeezing him into herself. She did not know if his eyes were also shut, if he was also smiling, but she chose to believe it, completely.

The sound of the side door brought them both back to the world and they broke their embrace seamlessly. Chrissie smoothed her skirt again and pushed her hair gently upwards, encouraging it once more to defy gravity; looking in the mirrored panel behind the optics, she rolled her lips inwards to perfect her lipstick. By the time Shona and Fergus appeared in the bar she was ready and beaming, while Cameron was perched on a stool at the far end of the bar, pretending to read the newspaper.

'Mam, we've got some news...'

Shona was clutching her fiancés hand, as if she were afraid that if she let it go, he would float away on the wind. For his own part, Fergus was staring down at the floor, suppressing an excited, idiotic grin. Both parents held their places, to give the youngsters space to make the moment their own, but looked on with encouragement.

'... Fergus has asked me to be his wife and I have said yes. We're to be married!'

A little squeal punctuated this last, and Shona began to quiver excitedly. Chrissie threw wide her arms and pulled her only daughter into a huge embrace, as Cameron strode across the room, his hand extended towards Fergus. Fergus took it gratefully, no longer afraid of the father's reaction, certain now that his failure to ask MacLeod's permission had be forgiven or simply overlooked.

The men shook hands for longer than either was comfortable, waiting for the mother and daughter to break their embrace. Eventually, they did and Cameron had a chance to hug his daughter and congratulate her while Fergus was pulled into the softness of his future mother-in-law. But the boy pulled away a little sooner that Chrissie had expected; she studied his discomfited face for moment.

'Of course! You must go and fetch your parents, so we can toast this engagement properly!'

Chrissie shooed him away, towards the curtain at the front door, through which he slid into the gathering dusk, past familiar faces made unfamiliar by the knowing smiles, the unexpected slaps on the back and pecks on the cheek.

His mother, father and grandfather were seated around the kitchen table when he clattered in through the back door. Mugs of tea sat undisturbed, no longer steaming, in front of them, as if the three of them had been in a trance until enlivened by his entrance. They knew of course, but they waited, smiles suppressed, until he had been able to deliver his news. He apologised for having gone to the Bell first, explaining that Shona had been insistent, had claimed precedence. Only Fingal accepted this with less than grace, but even the old man nodded, muttered *'Of course'* through his beard.

Fergus shook both the men's hands before his mother hugged him tightly. While his father clasped him more formally, uttering congratulations and unneeded advice, Morag dialled the Glasgow number in search of Mary. His sister answered almost immediately, did not need to be told the reason for the call, and Fergus imagined that, even in the city, his news was already known. She wished him well, offered her congratulations, and said that she hoped to see him soon. As he put down the now-disconnected phone, his grandfather thrust a glass of whisky into his hand and raised a toast in Gaelic to the happiness of Fergus and Shona, and to the continuation of the Buchanan line.

By the time the Buchanans reached the Bell, there were already some half dozen customers, alongside the MacLeods. As they entered a toast went up, and then a cheer when Fergus obliged the party by kissing the blushing Shona in full view for the first time. Others followed into the pub until the whole of the island was present to witness the engagement. Even Duncannon was there, unobtrusive by the door. Only the school master, Mr Galbraith, was missing.

eight

The staccato wheeze of old McCredie's boat had long ceased to bother him. That he had been unable to take the larger and more comfortable car ferry was something of an inconvenience, but his appointment with the dentist, much overdue, did not fit with the Caledonian MacBrayne schedule. Galbraith cast back to the wheel house, where the little boat's pilot hid behind his pipe smoke.

McCredie lived in Mallaig, but spent most of his time afloat. When the weather was good enough he would spend days at a time away from home, moving people, livestock and goods between the islands and Mallaig for whatever recompense he could extract from his clients. His boat had seen better days, but in good weather provided a reliable and reasonably direct means of transportation to and from the mainland. Yet there was precious little covered accommodation on board, aside from the smoke-filled wheel house, and on rainy days this made the three hour crossing from Mallaig somewhat claustrophobic. But there was plenty of space on deck and when the sun was out, as it was on this occasion, it was easy to find a little space for your thoughts.

Galbraith stood on the deck, half-way to the prow, his eyes fixed on the point where he would first see the jetty that stood near the mouth of the bay that formed Hinba's harbour. Landfall was still some two miles distant, and only a handful of the buildings in the village were yet discernible. He could make out – or believed he could make out – his own school house, the bleak grey rectangle punctuating the green of the island. The blue above Hinba was streaked with a rack of exuberant cloud, stacked at a precarious angle.

The gentle breeze left him unmolested, but his knees braced against each tiny dip of the boat on the torpid sea. As far as he could, he stood steady with his jaws locked together while his tongue darted about the exaggerated alterations of his newly cleaned and repaired teeth. In his bag, he had sausages, as well as some library books and a bottle of wine from the Co-op. And he had the page torn from the waiting room magazine. The thought of the news he bore for Hinba, for old man Fingal and for the Reverend Drummond in particular, caused him to tense yet further. They would not like his tidings, but hear them they must.

From behind came a shout. McCredie's head hung out of the wheel house window, his mouth moving in an exaggerated fashion. Then it disappeared inside, immediately to be replaced by an outstretched arm, the index finger unfurled towards a point off the starboard bow. Galbraith followed the line of the old man's arm and peered into the glistening blue. Seals; nothing but seals. The same seals that Galbraith saw from his kitchen each morning. The school teacher felt a wave of irritation at the intrusion, yet he watched the beasts for a while, speculating on their own disinterest in him and their irritation at his intrusion, his disruption of their fishing trip.

He ran his tongue over the new addition to his mouth, surprised again by its smoothness. He was pleased that he had opted for gold in the end. What other material was fit for a crown, after all? The sudden collapse of his molar, its majority swallowed along with the Mint Imperial into which it had become embedded, had forced the impromptu visit to Mallaig. It was fortunate that it had occurred during the spring holidays, although he would ideally not have missed Shona MacLeod's birthday celebration. On an island as insular as Hinba, it was wise to stay on the right side of families, especially ones as important as the MacLeods.

Still, he was pleased to get back to the mainland. Much as he did not regret his decision to relocate, he did miss the possibility and freedom afforded by uninterrupted dry land. If he were a seal, no doubt he would feel differently, but the ability to head off and keep walking for as far as your feet would carry you, without the ever-presence of this great briny barrier, had much to commend it. Where he grew up, not only had there been effectively limitless land in all directions, there had also been the mountains: land you could not only walk across, but also up.

But the Highlands had not been where St Columba had decided to begin his mission, so Hinba was where Galbraith lived. And the teaching was easier here: only a handful of children, all of them well-behaved, terrified of incurring their parents' displeasure. Of course, teaching a class of such mixed ages brought its challenges, but none were insurmountable: the older children could effectively be drafted in as unpaid teaching assistants. On some days, he had barely had to do any actual teaching, leaving him free to continue his reading.

During the drier months, Galbraith would often take the whole class on the long walk out to the western end of the island where the old Dun sulked amidst the sedge. The prehistoric fort dominated the skyline above the stone ruins of the monastery, which St Columba had established in the sixth century, making his uncle, St Ernan, its first Abbot. The monastery was the site of the island's second, more elaborate, cross from the era and, much like the broken stone above the village, it had at its base a worn bowl. Such bullauns were fairly common in Ireland; each had held a turning stone, to be used both in prayer and in older rites. They had been brought to the islands by the Saint, forming a bridge between Columba's origins and his destiny, between the old lore and that of the Cross. Galbraith had known that St Ernan's precious bullaun stone must have been lost somewhere on the island; it could not have swum away.

On the pretext of teaching the children about the history of the island, Galbraith would use the excursions and field trips to conduct his research. Sometimes he would encourage his pupils to dig gently in the soil around the ruins, in the hope of uncovering the stone or at least some passion for the past. Yet in all the years that he had led these excursions, had enthused about the history to his charges, only one, Mary Buchanan, had ever become seriously interested. That she was now at University, studying the sagas and the histories, was his proudest professional achievement thus far. She would write sometimes, asking after his research, enquiring about some forgotten detail of the history, of the topography of the island, and Galbraith would feel the warmth of vindication for days to come. Mary in particular would be saddened and enraged by the news he had to carry to the people of Hinba.

Galbraith looked up from his thoughts, out towards the island. He had to shield his eyes from the sun which was now low in the sky behind Hinba. It would soon be dusk, and he hoped McCredie would bring him to land before nightfall, wondered how the old man would himself find his way back to Mallaig through the darkness. When the sun sank beneath the horizon, the vastness of the ocean became yet more immense and unfathomable, a dark enclosing curtain, an impassable boundary between life on the island and that which lay beyond.

— ⊚ —

The Reverend Drummond was congratulating the happy couple when Mr MacLeod broke from his close conversation with Davey Buchanan to announce that a formal engagement party was to be held in three days' time, on the Saturday night, there in the Harbour Bell. Everyone was of course invited, including friends and family from the other islands and even from the mainland. The older Mr Buchanan responded with thanks and offered, on behalf of his daughter-in-law, to provide the buffet for the event, since MacLeod was so generously opening his bar once more. In conclusion, he raised another toast to young Fergus and his lovely bride-to-be and drained the whisky from his glass.

It was at this moment that Galbraith emerged through the curtain that masked the darkened street. He clutched his little leather suitcase and a carrier bag bearing the name and logo of the supermarket in Mallaig. He looked anxiously around the room, at first unnoticed, until Morag Buchanan gathered him up and led him to the bar, exchanging his suitcase for a glass of whisky.

'So you're back from your excursions, young Galbraith? There's been some developments here in your absence. A birthday, of course, but you'll have known about that. And now a proposal.'

Fingal had spotted the teacher across the room and, bored by the company of Mr McCulloch, had decided that tormenting Galbraith would be more entertaining. While he held out his empty glass to Chrissie MacLeod behind the bar, he kept his gaze fixed on Galbraith, who accepted the scrutiny dispassionately. He knew he was still seen as a new-comer, an outsider, despite his fifteen years in the community, and knew to take the old man's snide condescension as the price of not being born to the islands.

'Congratulations to you Mr Buchanan, and to you Morag. That is the most welcome news. I am truly sorry to have missed it, and can only curse the inconvenience of dentistry. But there have been developments on the mainland too, and not such ones as to warm the heart, I'm afraid. We must talk. Later, naturally, once the celebrations are complete. Now, I must congratulate the happy couple, and offer my belated birthday wishes to young Shona.'

Not until later, when all but the two families and the Reverend had left the Bell, did Fingal call out to Galbraith, asking that he put him out of his misery. Morag went to stand close by her husband as Galbraith opened his little leather case with a click, his eyes clouded with weary determination. Looking up from its contents, holding a torn page from a magazine, Galbraith addressed the room, although his eyes were on the Reverend Drummond.

Drummond was a well-fed priest who had started to lose his hair as a young man. Now that he had reached his fifty eighth year, only the merest wisps of white down clung to his temples. His crown was polished pink, its sheen glinting in sunlight and lamplight alike. But he was fleshy enough to have avoided deep wrinkles and sags and, despite his disappointments, his eyes still twinkled with something like mischief. As Galbraith spoke, however, his sparkle dimmed.

'This is a page from the catalogue of a Glasgow auction house. The catalogue was one of the few diverting items in the waiting room at Dr Laughlin's surgery, and I found myself flicking through it as I

waited for the anaesthetic to take effect. Dr Laughlin really ought to provide more interesting reading matter for his patients, but on this occasion I am glad that he did not.'

Galbraith sniffed, with a wriggle of his nose. He had to push his glasses back into place before he continued.

'I reached this page, page one hundred and twenty four, and there it was. Bold as you like.'

He smoothed out the page onto the table and indicated the top left hand corner. All eyes fell on a small photograph of a lump of worked stone, marked into four segments and looking like a hot-crossed bun. It was hard to see how big the real stone was, as there was nothing in the image against which to judge, but despite the blurring of time, the carved cross was clearly discernible. The eight of them took it in turns to inspect the page while Galbraith polished his glasses in his handkerchief. When it was his turn, Cameron MacLeod then read out the picture's caption: Lot 326: St Columba-era cursing stone; c. CE 574; St Ernan's Monastery, Hinba. Res. £3000.

'They've been found in Ireland, of course. But this is the first to have been found on Scottish soil. And on Hinba!'

Galbraith's voice rose to a broken squeak, which hung in the air for a moment while the others picked through their bemusement. The Reverend Drummond was the first to realise the significance of the matter. Much as he loved Hinba, he knew that his parish was something of a backwater; the stone would put the island on the map and transform its status within the Church immeasurably. Standing slowly, his chair legs scraping the flagstones, he walked to the bar and stood leaning there, his back turned to the others.

His shoulders crumpled with a small sigh. A moment later, his back straightened and his voice boomed out as if he were giving a sermon.

'You all know what this means, of course? Someone has taken this holy relic from the island and has sold it. Sold it for thousands of pounds, it would seem. This wee stone, cut during the very beginnings of Christianity on Hinba. From the very beginnings of Christianity in Scotland itself!'

'Aye, it is criminality, pure and simple. Who do you think could have done this to us? Could it be someone on the island?'

Davey looked around at his neighbours, half ashamed to suggest that one of their own could have betrayed them. He waited anxiously for someone to propose a more palatable explanation. That it was Cameron MacLeod that came to his rescue surprised him.

'It must have been that couple that had the old McHuish cottage last summer. They were from Glasgow or some such. I didn't take to them. Something untrustworthy about him, and she was no better. They spent a lot of time out by the Dun, if you remember, walking and picnicking?'

'That's true, aye. And he kept asking about the ruins, about the history of the island, now I think of it. I thought he was just curious...'

'And we thought he was just humouring you, Galbraith. Anyhow, I think we know who stole the thing. The question now is what do we do about it?'

The old patriarch had stood up and was leaning on the table, his balled fists balanced before him. MacLeod was nodding gently, lost in thought and deliberation, while his wife simply looked perplexed. Fergus stayed silent, catching no-one's eye, waiting for the kerfuffle to blow over, so the he could get back to celebrating his engagement.

'Fingal is right. We need to act. We can't let this pass. We're going to have to fetch the thing from Glasgow, either from this holidaying thief or from whoever he sold it to. I've spent fifteen years looking for that bloody stone, for the benefit of the island of course, and I'm not going to be robbed blind by some outsider strolling in.'

Shona fidgeted in her chair. This evening had been to celebrate her engagement, but now the attention was only on this lump of rock. What did it matter that it had been taken? She kept her eyes lowered. She knew that, if she should catch Fergus looking at her, she would not be able to contain her giggling. To keep her face straight, she examined in minute detail the condition of her nails. They were unvarnished, but long and even, the whites forming perfect crescents, as if she was wearing a French manicure; the cuticles were healthy and neatly puckered. She pictured how they would look in a mauve nail polish, or maybe a crimson, if that was not too much.

'What do you mean, fetch it back? Theft? We never even knew we had it! Would never have known, if Mr Galbraith hadn't been flicking idly through that magazine while his mouth went numb. At least now he can stop traipsing over the moor at every spare hour, looking for a relic of the saints: we know where it is now!'

Fingal looked sternly from Morag to Davey, his face barely containing his displeasure. It was impossible to tell whether he was more angered by Morag's outspokenness or at his son's failure to control it. Both shamed the family and, at this moment of crisis, that could not be allowed. Once again, he had to carry the honour of the family, of the whole island, and his worries for the future were only stilled by the thought of his grandson.

'Stuff and nonsense, Morag. Were you not listening to Galbraith and the Reverend? The stone is part of the island's history, and its rightful place is here. It's a matter of pride. There's nothing for it; young Fergus will go to the city to fetch it. Won't you, my lad?'

Fingal's crooked smile fell on his grandson. At least one of the Buchanans would not let him down. Fergus had said nothing so far, keeping his counsel and following the discussion as it had developed. But now he looked up, startled, suddenly at the centre of the matter. He was unsure how this had come about but realised quickly, under the old man's gaze, that there was nothing to decide that had not already been decided. He nodded mutely, while his mother began to object. Davey cut her off with a show of awkward authority.

'Morag, it's only to Glasgow, for pity's sake, it's not to the ends of the earth. And he'll be staying with his sister, so no harm will come of him. Besides, he's a grown man now, almost twenty one years of age. He'll just go to the city, find this man and explain. And, if there's any trouble, Fergus can just call on the Police to sort things out.'

'No Police. It's best we sort things out for ourselves. Or are we now the kind of people that run to the authorities with every set back? As Fingal says, it's a matter of pride.'

Even Fingal looked at the publican in disbelief, but could not disagree. That the matter had already escalated so far unnerved him almost as much as the realisation that it was his old adversary making the weather. Before he had recovered sufficiently to weigh the implications, Shona's anguish exploded into the uneasy lull created by her father's intervention.

'But we're to be married! He can't just go running off to the city for no reason! He has responsibilities! To me!'

Her mother put an arm around Shona and blew shushes into her ear, while her father looked quizzically in the direction of a still startled Fingal. Slowly, the question settled in the old man. If the island was in need, then it would be a Buchanan that rose to the challenge: Fingal nodded his agreement with increasing vigour. From behind them, at the bar, the Reverend Drummond cleared his throat.

'So it is decided. Young Fergus will set out as soon as possible to retrieve the stone and bring it back to us. It'll need to be after the engagement party on Saturday, of course, but as soon as possible after that. I'll talk to McCredie tomorrow and make sure he is available to take him across on the Sunday. Lad, the whole island is depending on you. I know that you are more than a match for the task. Mrs MacLeod, please, a whisky for the boy!'

nine

Fog. Thick and pale, the colour of misery. It drapes all before you, stretches higher than you can imagine, engulfs the world to just beyond the edges of your vision. Only at its base, where its greyness blurs into the ground, does the world become real.

The smothered grass leeches its greenery, but it is solid at least. Defined. It is trustworthy enough to carry your weight, at least for a short while, before it too disappears into the flat, grey wall. So you fumble forward into the unseen life that surrounds you: only in the darkest corners of your mind do you contemplate the possibility that the fog is not a mask but an ending.

That a world is concealed by the greyness is only a little less terrifying than the alternative. Such opacity is the haunt of monsters and wraiths. This certainty has been buried in your imagination for centuries, since the time before the Cross, before fire. So your footing is unsteady, each step an act of unimaginable courage. And yet you move forward into the unseen jaws that lurk beyond the curtain.

The grass becomes cross-hatched with sedge, until its softness is replaced entirely by its darker, starker cousin. And then the water begins. Flat darkness that extends into the flat greyness. The sound of a crow cracks the damp stillness of the day and a milky sun cuts a pale disk in the sky.

To your left and to your right, there is only a thick line of sedge; you dare not look behind you and before you there is only the water of the moat. Through the fog, you can hear the thin lifting song of your princess, cascading from the castle ramparts like babbling spring water. You are so nearly home, and yet the water stands between you and your rest.

You set off to your left and for hours your only company is the sedge and the water and their monotony. The voice follows you on your circumnavigation, the bitter sound of hope. She is walking with you, unseen, unreachable. In the mind's eye of your mind's eye, you try to picture her, but the fog clouds her sweetness, veils her beauty. But her ever presence drives you on in your endless circling of the castle.

Hours pass, days. And then you remember you can fly. Rising smoothly to a few feet above the sedge you propel yourself uncomprehendingly across the moat. Within moments the sedge has vanished into the fog and there is only the flat greyness around you and the flat dark water beneath you. You move steadily forward towards the voice, expecting the castle's walls to break from the fog at every passing minute. But they never do.

When the voice stops, you no longer know whether you are gliding towards the castle or back to the shore or simply around in circles. You no longer care. Without the voice to guide you, there is no point in your journey, no destination. You simply hang above the limitless water, maybe moving, maybe not.

You forget how to fly.

Into the dark water. It closes above you, wrapping its darkness around you in an instant. It is still, it is heavy and silent, and it is cold. It is so very cold.

ten

A sheet of solid grey cloud had closed over the sea. It stretched to the horizon, beyond the smudge of the distant mainland. It was an angry grey. Its relentlessness choked the world with infectious foreboding. It was not yet raining, but that would surely come. It was inevitable. Fergus cursed his luck: after the last days of clear skies and unseasonable warmth, he had had to set off today of all days, to make the crossing to Mallaig in the chill and certain rain. That he felt queasy after the night's drinking only added to his many miseries. That he had had to leave his Shona, even for a few days, was the first among these.

'What are you reading?'

Mary was standing behind him on the deck, her cagoule zipped up against the tugging wind. She was still well used to the imprecision of the sea, and swayed with the swell, perfectly at ease. Fergus looked up at her, then down at his lap where his notebook lay open at the last entry, dated Thursday the twenty sixth of March: the morning after he had become engaged to Shona, after Galbraith's return and the decision to send him after the cursing stone. He closed the book and shook his head, as much to shake himself back into the present as to indicate that he had stopped reading a while ago.

His sister had come across from Glasgow on the Saturday morning, in good time for the engagement party that had become his farewell. She had not been the only one to venture across to the island. There had been cousins from Eigg, his mother's brother's children, now adults too, as well as crofters from Rum, and fishermen, and of course McCredie. Almost one hundred people had squeezed into the Harbour Bell to toast the happy couple and to drink and dance the night away, blurred by hazy warmth. Only Fergus, Shona and Morag did not smile without reservation. And Mary, of course.

It had been kind of her, to come all that way. She had said that she would not have missed it for the world, that there was nothing in Glasgow that could not wait. She had smiled broadly when he had opened the door to her, but there had been something like anxiety in the hug she had thrown around him, and she had squeezed him harder than had been strictly necessary. And that was before she knew about the stone. In those first tens of minutes, she had had only his happy news to concern her, before her grandfather had begun to describe the island's complaint.

It was no surprise that she should react as she did. She had been earnest and solemn even as a little girl. It was as if the disappearance of the stone were some personal affront. Fergus had never understood her interest in Galbraith's obsession, nor why she had felt the need to leave Hinba, to disappear to Glasgow, in order to pursue it. But he was grateful now for her offer of help, both once they got to the city, but also to travel with him on the journey there. It would simply be more pleasant to travel in company, and would save time and complications. He had never been on a train before.

After everyone had embraced and told each other how much they were missed, Fingal Buchanan had sat down with his grandchildren at the kitchen table to set out the whys and the wherefores of what needed to be done. Davey had sat to one side, silent and nervous, while his wife stood at the sink and washed dishes emphatically.

There was a problem. In his haste to remove the page unseen, Galbraith had failed to note either the name of the auction house or the date of the catalogue. Neither appeared on the smuggled page. As Fingal, Galbraith and the Reverend had talked into the night, the oversight had become apparent. While Fergus and the women had sat at the bar, attempting to remember that this had been a celebration, his father had looked on incredulous as Fingal had taken the error calmly, indulgently, reassuring Galbraith that it had been an understandable mistake, that no real harm had been done; there couldn't be that many auction houses in Glasgow and, besides, the thieves had been on the island only the previous summer, so the catalogue could not be so old. The attempt by Cameron MacLeod to complicate the matter, with his speculation that maybe the catalogue had not in fact been for a Glasgow auction house at all, to suggest that he should perhaps ask some contacts over there to assist the boy in his difficult task, was brushed aside by Fingal. Galbraith's insistence that his memory for such things was exemplary settled the matter.

Perhaps in recognition of the burden they had placed upon the young couple, Fergus and Shona were left alone in the bar after the others had gone to their beds. Mrs MacLeod had even left a measure of whisky in a glass in front of Fergus before she retired. For some minutes the room fell into a slow silence, rocked only by the sound of their breathing, falling and rising harmoniously. Both stared at their hands, entwined on the table, and lost themselves in their own thoughts. The heavy clock above the optics ticked and tocked its way through the passing quiet, until Shona broke the stillness some sixty minutes later to announce she was tired and wanted her bed. They kissed briefly, awkwardly, before Fergus shuffled out into the darkness beneath the cloud-streaked moonlight and the weight of his unexpected duty. The clunk of the door's lock snapped at his heels.

He did not go straight home. For March, the night was mild and still and he had wanted to feel the clean clear space of Hinba around him. He had walked down to the harbour to watch the celestial light play across the sea's surface. There had been no sound other than the water's hush, its gentle slap against the wooden uprights of the jetty. Eventually, the air's unnoticed chill seeped into his flesh and he stopped fighting his yawning tiredness and turned back towards the houses of the village. For the first time in his life he was seized by the thought that his time on Hinba was not limitless after all.

He had woken that morning haunted and cold. His bed clothes lay on the floor and his pale nakedness was marked by goose bumps. Even before he began his recollection of his dreaming, he knew that he had passed a troubled night, and it was with trepidation that he took up his notebook and pen. Even so, it was some time before the foreboding he felt had been joined by the memory of its cause: his imminent departure for the mainland and the city. He had completed his morning round in a state of distraction, accepting the congratulations of well-wishers with cordiality rather than enthusiasm. Galbraith's conspiratorial bonhomie irked him, and even Mrs Robertson's delight had given no solace.

As usual there had been no mail for Duncannon, but Fergus had continued up the lane as far as the hermit's gate nonetheless. He had leant on the stone wall, staring into the jumbled yard for maybe twenty minutes before Duncannon appeared, back from the beach below. He wore a length of hawser, rescued from the surf, like a feather boa. In his right hand he carried a broken plastic paint tub like a bucket. He simply stood and gazed at Fergus, until the boy raised his hand in greeting. Only then did Duncannon smile and wave in return. But he did not approach: he continued to stand in the yard, watching, waiting.

'May I come in, Duncannon?'

His shouted request had surprised even Fergus, but he opened the gate without being bidden. Leaving his bicycle on the verge, he walked purposefully into the yard, but with no inkling as to what he should say next. Duncannon had only ever shown him kindness, but it was a kindness of an undemanding sort. There had never been any expectations attached to the generosity and Fergus had never felt the need to generate false enthusiasm in return. The pair had maybe passed fewer than 100 words together, and yet it felt then that Duncannon was his only friend.

'Well, there is no need to ask, is there? It's this trip that's troubling you.'

Fergus pulled up abruptly. His friend's gaze rested on the far horizon, as if scouting the journey the young man would make. For what seemed like the longest moment, Fergus hung equivocal, his face betraying his confusion.

'Not much gets past Duncannon.'

He did not shift his eyes from the sea, and he spoke in little more than a whisper. Fergus surmised that if you spoke as little as did Duncannon, it must be easier to hear what goes on around you and, satisfied that this insight explained sufficiently Duncannon's precognisance, he mumbled his confirmation. The man and the boy had then stood for some minutes staring at the sea, only the wind audible above their breathing, their heart beats, before Duncannon spoke again.

'It's different over there:' His unmoving gaze indicated the mainland, and Fergus knew this without turning to see. *'They're less forgiving, less willing. It will be hard for you, to be away from Hinba, as much as to be there. Wait here.'*

Suddenly dynamic, Duncannon strode across the yard towards his house, climbed the seven stone steps to a green door, and disappeared inside. Fergus realised that despite the hours he had spent up here, alone or with Duncannon, drinking tea and not talking, he had never been invited inside, no matter what the weather. He wondered what Duncannon's kitchen would look like, whether it would be clean and orderly like the tool shed or chaotic like the yard.

He had lived here alone for so many years, ever since his father had died, when Duncannon had been just 14 years of age. Old Duncannon had fallen from the low cliff one night, his body broken on the rocks that backed the beach; the boy had found him there, they said, but he had waited for two days before he had told anyone. No-one had asked him about what had happened and he had offered no explanation, beyond that given into the confidence of the investigating police officer, over from Mallaig. Ever since that night, Duncannon had spoken about himself only in the third person, as if describing a stranger, a being disconnected and apart. All of this had been before Fergus was born, before Davey had met his Morag, before even old MacLeod had died: to Fergus, Duncannon's isolation was a constancy, an eternal truth of the island.

Duncannon returned in a few moments, clutching a small parcel, wrapped in yellowing newsprint. For the first time during their conversation, he looked directly at Fergus, looked into his eyes themselves rather than the convections that circled about him. And he kept his eyes steady, relentless as he pushed the package into Fergus's hand. The boy accepted meekly, without resistance, struck by how deeply the world's vastness sat in Duncannon's eyes.

'It is something for your journey. Duncannon wants you to have it. To keep you safe, to remind you, to help you to return; it is important that you return. Only when Fergus Buchanan brings back the cursing stone can things be put right on this island. It was your grandmother's.'

Duncannon nodded at the package as he said this last. Then he was gone, his eyes lost again in the open spaces of the island, watching for the things that Fergus did not see. He had picked up his broken pail and, raising his left hand over his shoulder in farewell, he trudged off towards his barn without another word. The door clattered behind him and the bolt shot across, locking away his unlikely treasure along with his secrets.

— ⊙ —

Mary had left the deck, retreated to the shelter of the wheel house against the rain. While she talked to old man McCredie, told him about the city and the land, Fergus sat on the deck and turned the pendant in his fingers. He could feel its time-smoothed edges and the faint trace of the engraving: *To hold me close against your heart, Peg x.* The copperplate script was elegant and spoke of a long lost past, of deep sentiment.

He wondered once again how Duncannon had come to have it. It seemed unlikely that such an object would have been found amongst the detritus of the beach. Much less that Duncannon would have recognised it as belonging to his grandmother: everyone, including his grandfather had known her as Maggie. And surely, in any case, since it was clearly worn by someone else, a loving gift from Maggie Buchanan, it would be more accurate to say that it belonged to his grandfather, to Fingal. Fergus did not want to believe that Duncannon had stolen the pendant, but that seemed much the more likely explanation. Perhaps that was how Duncannon really managed to make a living: not magically from the rubbish he collected, but by stealing the valuables of his unsuspecting neighbours. Perhaps this was why he had decided to say nothing to his grandfather about the pendant. The accusation would have set him into yet another rage against Duncannon and, in the absence of proof, he wanted to protect his friend's reputation. He would ask about it on his return; the matter would keep. He slipped the gold back under his shirt and stared out into the closing drizzle.

To relieve his melancholy, Fergus tried to think about Shona. She had held him closer than ever the night before. While the islanders and others had caroused late into the night, they had slipped into the hallway and kissed among the coats hanging from the rack, lost in the half darkness. She had allowed his hands far greater freedom than he had expected and, so long as they stayed outside her clothing, she let him explore her form without constraint. Yet this had not satisfied his ardour and, when eventually they surfaced, gulping air tainted with stale gabardine, he had burned with incoherent desire.

Through the thin wall behind him, Fergus had heard a peel of laughter and the scraping of furniture on the stone floor of the bar; then the wheezing of Mr McCulloch's accordion had begun, soon joined by the shuffling and stamping of dancing. Shona had untangled herself from him, was smoothing her skirt and pushing her hair back into shape, asking him something, with tender concern. And he had told her that, of course, he would save himself for her, for their wedding night, that the mainland would not tempt him, could not. And he had curled his fists so tightly that his fingernails had cut into the palms, had almost drawn blood, such was his need to regain control of his flesh. And Shona had smiled her best smile and stroked his cheek with the palm of her hand and had then led him back into the bar, slipping in unseen, hoping that their flushed cheeks would be unnoticed among the dancers and the revellers.

His bag was getting wet in the now-persistent rain and Fergus decided that there was nothing for it but to join Mary and McCredie in the wheel house. He picked up the old holdall and rolled his way back along the deck. It was a small bag: he had packed only a few changes of underwear, a spare pair of jeans, a couple of t-shirts, a sweater, his wash bag, his book of UK postal codes, his schools atlas and the notebook; that morning he had also packed some pens, a spare notebook, and the roll of twenty pound notes that had been given to him by his father.

Fergus had also dropped into his bag the package of sandwiches that his mother had brought down to the harbour and thrust into his hands before enveloping him in the most encompassing of embraces. His father had simply shaken his hand, squeezing into the confines of palm and fingers all the things he could not say. His grandfather's embrace had come with two pieces of advice: trust no-one and hurry back. The Reverend Drummond had offered his prayers, since the boat was leaving before his sermon that morning; Mr Galbraith had been agitated, gripping his hand too tightly as he wished him good luck and a speedy return. Shona's final, parting kiss had embarrassed her parents, and they could only wave hesitantly from the jetty. McCredie had engaged the engine and waited while Fergus slipped the lines to allow the little vessel to peel away from Hinba. As the small farewell party stood at the brink, waving and shouting to the receding *Tern*, Fergus had waved back, his arm around his sister, from the foredeck.

As the *Tern* rounded the headland and left the little harbour behind, Fergus had taken one last look back to the island and was sure that he saw a figure standing on the low cliff above the eastern shore. While it was maybe a mile distant, Fergus believed that he could make out the face of Duncannon, certain that he was smiling, looking directly at him, even though that too would have been impossible. The thought of it made Fergus look back once more, over the grey sea to where Hinba should have been. But the island was lost in the thick cloud, along with everyone he loved. Everyone except Mary, of course, and he felt again a rich thankfulness to his sister for her presence. The simple fact of her being there, visible and shouting unheard from the wheel house window, made him feel more confident in his journey and in his quest, despite the gnawing anxiety over what was to come. Mary leant fully out of the door and bellowed again to be heard over the rain and the cascading surf.

'Only another 5 miles until Mallaig, Fergus! We're soon on dry land!'

part two

Into the City of the Dead

THE CURSING STONE

eleven

There was still an hour before the train. They had been sitting in the café for forty five minutes already and still there was another hour to go. Outside, three women stood under umbrellas chatting, the slow business of the day running its easy course in soft spoken exchanges. When two of them headed up the hill and the third slid into the Co-op, Mary turned her attention once more to the café's interior. A clutch of tourists sat around a pine table, scouring maps and guidebooks for something with which to occupy themselves during a damp Sunday. She sighed and tried to drink what was left in her cup, forgetting that the tea was now long cold.

The slowness of life up here, away from the city, could kill a man. Mary had almost forgotten how deathly the waiting could be. Ordinarily, a trip home was a sufficient reminder, but this time there had be the excitement of the engagement party and of the fuss about the cursing stone. The drama had been invigorating; even the plans for the wedding gave unfamiliar momentum to life on the island. But once they had boarded Mr McCredie's boat, the slow wallowing of time returned. Even here in Mallaig, nothing happened very quickly. Indeed, it was possible to sit idly in a café for almost two hours without thinking anything was being missed.

Mary was pleased to be heading back to Glasgow and the life that she had discovered there, as she had known she would. While she missed her family, it was in the city that she had begun to live: she couldn't wait to share it with Fergus.

Her impatience had solidified almost as soon as they had stepped off the *Tern* at the east harbour, picking their way over the decks of still sleeping yachts and fishing boats. Reaching the steady quayside, they had waved their farewells to McCredie who had not even bothered to tie up his boat. Sunday trains meant that there would be a long wait and they picked their way through the plastic crates stacked around the quayside without urgency. The rain had not abated and had, if anything, deepened. The town was shrouded in dampness and the pitter-patter pocked the otherwise calm harbour. Above on the hillside the colours became more vivid, all ochre and rust gilding the deep charcoal of the granite crags.

She had insisted on a cup of tea in An Cala, to hide from the rain. In the forty five minutes that had elapsed, they had talked about the passage of time on Hinba and in Glasgow, about studies and essays, about their grandfather and neighbours, about the engagement, about parties and student demonstrations. Mary had explained the hardships of the modern student and Fergus had accepted them without question, offering only bewilderment that she should choose to endure it. Eventually even this meagre conversation had thinned to nothingness, and the brother and his sister had fallen into silence.

When they had been at school in Mallaig, too young for the pubs, each had been a regular in An Cala. It had been over four years since Fergus had been inside, and yet the café felt as familiar as his mother's kitchen. During those years, he had lodged through the week along with several other boys with Mrs McLeish at her boarding house around the bay. All those nights away and he never once got used to sleeping off the island. It was at Mrs McLeish's that the dreams had started. At first, they had only crept into his bed on the mainland, but little by little they found him on Hinba too, and he had started to record them then, once he realised that they would accompany him through all his nights.

Mary had left the school only a few months before, once her exams had been safely completed, so the café held less mythical significance. For her, it was just a café, one more café in a world full of cafés against which she could compare An Cala. Similarly, Mallaig was not the limit of her encounters with the world, but merely its beginning: it had been the gateway to her one and only family holiday, when she had been eleven years old. And while Fergus and his father had taken from the trip only a confirmation that they need never look beyond Hinba for their satisfaction, for Mary the scale of possibility in the world, even seen from just a few tens of miles from the island, had awoken something that had grown until, that autumn, she had started secondary school in Mallaig. There, she had embraced the newness and possibility of the village, perched on the very edge of the mainland's abundance, just as much as Fergus had resented its imposition on his island life. All through her school days, she had known that she could not return to a life adrift in the empty ocean.

Mary surveyed the tea cups, suddenly certain that mundane distraction was needed to fill the conversation's lull. But there was no sign of the girl, or anyone else that might fetch them fresh tea. She looked over at her brother. He was becoming good-looking, Mary decided. His features were sharpening from their adolescent blancmange. His complexion remained flawlessly smooth, downy still despite his now daily adventures with a razor. His lips were full and soft, but his jaw was straighter, a firm line upon which you could build a thousand romances. His eyes still sparkled their vibrant blue; his red hair, a blessing Mary had always been pleased to have avoided, was evermore strawberry blonde than angry copper. He was becoming a man, and a handsome one. Mary prickled with pride.

She had always known, of course, that her brother was special. The first child, the rightful heir. Mary's accomplishments were important to the family, but Fergus had never had to accomplish anything to be important, neither around the island nor in their home. It wasn't that he was stupid or lazy, or complacent or selfish. Fergus had the sweetest of natures: he was kind, helpful and hard-working. But it was only once she had reached Glasgow that she realised that she had, at one point, resented him hugely. It seemed comical now, with her life, her future, among the books and ideas of the university, among the people and possibilities of Glasgow. She no longer begrudged him his little kingdom, since she had the world.

Only the dimming of affection from her grandfather still saddened her. When she had announced her intention to apply to the university, he had lost even the relatively small store of love he reserved for her. While her mother had fussed over her in joyous, vicarious excitement, Fingal had slowly shaken his head and shrunken from her. He had been unwell the day she had left the island, all her belongings stowed onto the *Tern*, and he had not been able to make an appearance at the jetty. It had been Mr Galbraith who had instead gushed and enthused and babbled as she stepped off the island and into her future. It was her old primary school teacher who wrote to her, asked her about her progress, her reading. Her grandfather would appear on the phone once a month to gruffly ask if she was healthy and was behaving herself.

The girl appeared from the side door next to the kitchen. She carried the sour tang of nicotine and damp wool in with her. Mary waved over to her and caught her eye.

'I'd like another pot of tea, please. How about you, Fergus?'

'Aye. And one of those cream cakes, if I may.'

Fergus nodded towards the glass-fronted counter, under which lay a tray of oversized biscuits, an arrangement of flapjacks and a plate of chocolate éclairs. The young woman nodded and turned to the hot water urn, clanking the tin teapot against the spout. Water and steam fizzed and gurgled into freedom.

'What's so funny?'

Mary had been suppressing a giggle and, now discovered, she could control it no longer. Once she had regained her composure, she took a final swallow of cold tea before replying.

'Just you, with your éclairs and your 'if I may's. Such a well-brought up young man!'

'So I take it you'll not be wanting any of that wee cake then? And manners cost nothing, young lady, or have you forgotten that, living in Glasgow?'

Fergus winked then smiled at his knees. Normal relations had been re-established, he the big brother, she the contrite sister. It felt so familiar and comforting. Mary flushed with the certainty that she could rely upon his wisdom and strength, that even the weakness it implied on her part simply felt safe. She relaxed into her role and asked the question that had been bothering her all day.

'What's the plan, Fergus? I mean, we don't even have the name of the auction house. There's a lot of auction houses in Glasgow, you know.'

'How many do you think? There can't be that many, surely? Anyhow, we'll just ask at the first one, see if they recognise that catalogue page. And if not, I've got all week: I reckon I can knock on every door in Glasgow in that time, if needs be.'

Mary gave her brother a look but said nothing. In the silence, Fergus slid the neatly folded page from his coat pocket and spread it carefully across the table top, studying it closely as if he believed he could find an unnoticed identifying mark, if only he stared hard enough.

She watched him, and looked in turn at the page. It was true that Bonhams, the only auction house she knew of in the city, would probably recognise the design of the catalogue. And they may get lucky – maybe their first port of call would be the one they sought. But most likely Fergus and she would spend valuable vacation time traipsing around the city, working their way through a list of addresses that they had assembled from an internet search. Of course, they might be able to work it out from the websites of the auction houses themselves; they might recognise the font or colours. Mary brightened: it might not be so bad.

'Why do you care so much, anyway?'

His question surprised her. It was something that would be more appropriate for her to ask of him. After all, he had never shown any interest in the island's history, had laughed with everyone else at Mr Galbraith's enthusiasm. She had long shared her teacher's passion for exploring the traces of St Columba on Hinba. She had decided to devote three years to studying the subject at the university, so that she had a better understanding of the story of her home. And that stone was a rare artefact, wrapped in myth as much as scholarship: to hold it and trace its lines would bring to life an entire semester. Of course she cared.

'I mean, you hate Hinba. Couldn't get off it quickly enough, didn't care that your leaving hurt granddad so much. So why so interested in helping him now? Is it because of Mr Galbraith?'

'What?'

She was genuinely disoriented by his questioning, his sharpness; didn't understand what he meant by hurting her grandfather, or hating the island, much less what Mr Galbraith had to do with anything. She could only repeat her one-word question, blinking, shaking her head. Less a question than a challenge.

'Galbraith. Everyone knows that he writes to you, and that you write back. He makes no attempt to hide it. And I do deliver the post, you know. You had a crush on him when you were a girl, didn't you? Always hanging around him, sucking up to him, long after you'd left primary school? No shame in that, everyone has a crush when they're that age. But I've never liked the way that he seemed to take advantage. I know nothing is going on, what with you living over in Glasgow and everything, but I just wondered what was in all those letters...'

Mary was angry now. Her own brother, accusing her of, of what? She straightened in her chair, pushed her lips together tightly. Fergus recognised the face and stopped speaking, his explanation petering out into embarrassed silence.

'Sixth century religious art; the routes and settlements of the Norse

explorers; early Christian monastic life; reference books for course work; that bloody stone! That's what's in those letters, you idiot. Do you think that... I can't believe you'd think that; how long has that one been festering in there?'

She tapped her fingertip angrily against his head and he shrank into his chair, hoping that his meekness would be enough to placate her. But Mary had not finished.

'Mr Galbraith was the only person - the only person - who encouraged me to follow my own path. To study, to read, to learn about the world. About Hinba too. You and dad, and granddad especially, were always laughing at the things that were important to me, wanted me to be something that I didn't want. Mum, she was pleased when I said I was going to university, but only because it meant I'd see something of the world, not because she thought studying was anything important. So, no I didn't have a crush on Mr Galbraith, I had a supportive teacher, who provided me with the self-esteem that my family didn't seem to think I deserved.'

Fergus started to shape his apologies, but his sister had still not finished.

'And another thing: granddad wasn't hurt by my leaving, he was upset that he hadn't got his way this time. It was me that was hurt, by him washing his hands of me, of his own granddaughter, because I wouldn't bend to him quite as easily as you...'

It was Mary's turn to stop, to realise she had gone too far. The tourists were watching, disturbed by her raised voice, and she could feel the colour flooding to her cheeks. She turned to face them and glared until they returned indignant to their guidebooks.

THE CURSING STONE

'Taking account of your family isn't being weird, Mary. It's normal. Sometimes that means compromises, and maybe when you're a little older and a little less self-absorbed you'll realise that.'

She was beaten. The heat in her cheeks had started to mass behind her eyes and she was pleased to see the girl coming with the pot of tea and the éclair. The siblings sat quietly, politely, dressed in cordial smiles and thankyous, while the woman set out the crockery so carefully that the clinks of china on china were dampened to whispers. The hush accentuated the disturbance of moments before, and Mary felt the girl's eyes as a judgement. She was relieved when they were once more alone.

'We'll leave it there, shall we? Unless you want to continue the discussion? Just to say that I apologise for what I said about you and Mr Galbraith. That was wrong of me and I am sorry for jumping to conclusions. Sorry Mary.'

His blue, blue eyes ached with kindness. Mary could not, could never, be angry at her brother for very long and she sighed a weary smile to let him know that everything was still good between them. Fergus gave her a wink and bit deeply into the éclair. They both watched the gout of cream that burst from its startled side tumble towards the floor.

twelve

The train did not move. The little speakers whined, and a weary voice explained that the train would be held at Fort William while the replacement driver was found. Fergus explored his seat for the comfortable spot, while Mary muttered that she didn't see why the driver that had brought the train from Mallaig could not be persuaded to finish the job.

That first train driver had left promptly enough: finally driven from the café by boredom and a surfeit of tea, they had ambled over to Mallaig's small stone station ahead of time, where thankfully the train that had been waiting at the railhead overnight opened its doors just as they arrived. Within minutes the doors had slid shut again and the train had pulled out. Fergus had watched the cloaked islands slide away while Mary had chattered about people they had both known at the school that hung above them on the hillside.

As the open sea vanished behind them, Fergus looked out at the changing landscape. Presently, the train plunged into a tunnel and, when it broke again into the light, a valley opened up below them: a chain of lakes stretched down to the vanishing point. By the

THE CURSING STONE

trackside, a brick fire place and chimney were all that remained of a long forgotten cottage. The window filled with yellows and browns, granite grey and autumn's rust, the ruby remnants of dead heather; the deer on the hillside blurred into the season's palate, lost among the pale browns of last season's bracken which clustered in defeated clumps.

The rhododendrons at Glenfinnan station brought a surprising display of deep and solid green. Some of the plants had escaped the bounds of the manicured station precincts and brought a little of the Himalayas to the Highland valley. Just as vivid was the passenger that had boarded there: a girl wearing a blue and white striped jersey, and blue cotton slacks. Her wavy blonde hair was swept back into a short pony tail, and the remains were held in place by a thin white Alice band. Her face was composed of calm innocence and blue, serious eyes. She took up the seat facing Fergus across the aisle; only when she returned his gaze did Fergus realise that he had been staring at her for some time.

'I think she fancies you.'

Mary had breathed the words into his shoulder with a practiced discretion. It took a moment for their meaning to solidify. Fergus's first reaction had been to smile a bashful smile, to ask his sister if she really thought so, but he had caught himself in time and instead dismissed Mary's silliness. Still, the thought was an appealing one: she was pretty. Almost as pretty as Shona.

The train had picked its way through rocks and gorse and pines, past a ruined castle by the river, and an equally ruined go-cart track, until the wide expanse of Lochaber opened on the trackside. Low, grey houses crowded in on the landside and young silver birches lined the track. The mountains receded behind the low pebble-dashed houses that had clustered around the train as it made its way into Fort William and stasis.

'Is this normal? I mean, for trains?'

Before Mary had a chance to accept that, yes, this was far from an unusual state of affairs on the railways, the carriage jolted into motion and the weary voice above them returned to explain that they now had a driver and as a consequence would be able to continue their journey. The voice was able to specify by how many minutes they were now delayed.

As the train pulled out at last from Fort William, the girl in the Alice band changed her seat so that she faced the new direction of travel. Fergus felt a slight twinge of regret, before he hauled from his bag the tinfoil package that his mother had given to him and pealed open its silvered skin to reveal two more tinfoil packages; one he held out to Mary, impatient. She took it with a shrug and watched while Fergus tore into his own like a fox in a chicken coop. She remembered childhood mealtimes, the frantic scramble of the men to devour whatever was on their plates, to be first in the queue for seconds. She had tried to compete until she decided that she had better things to worry about.

Absently, she gave the last half of her sandwich to the empty-handed Fergus and pulled a hesitant book from her shoulder bag. She found her place within its pages and so indicated that that was her for the remainder of the journey. Fergus was surprised that the book was not some stick-dry academic volume, but was instead a supple, garish paperback. He realised of course that Mary was not simply her studies, that she too must have an interior, emotional life. It was simply that Fergus had never seen it; or perhaps more accurately, had never noticed it.

Following her lead, he retrieved his copy of the most recent edition of *The Postcode Atlas of Great Britain and Northern Ireland* and started to flick through its familiar pages, alighting at Glasgow. His index finger slid down the list of codes as he interpreted the characters, building concrete, breathing places from numbers and letters, tracing their adjacencies and connections in his mind. He saw Mary's Hall of Residence in its proper context for the first time since she had written to him that first week she had been away, and he had taken her postcode from its return address and placed it within the mental map he carried within him. He felt her eyes on him, knew without having to look that her expression was one of soured incredulity. He wondered when they had become so different, he and she, wondered if it mattered, if difference was the same as distance, as estrangement.

The world outside the train's blurred window was a sodden grey. They had left the town behind them now and the landscape felt comfortable, familiar. Less and less attention was paid to the booklet that lay limp in his lap, and Fergus was drawn into the slow drama outside. He stared emptily at the smear of green and brown that enclosed sections of the track, until it broke into the more stable clarity of the wider vistas. The constant shifting of the shapes beyond, married with the rattle and jolts of the carriage, was irresistible and Fergus's mind wandered aimless, as it did sometimes out on the moor, or when he stood on the low cliffs above Sgorr nam Ban-naomha, watching the waves and the terns perform their constant dance.

They were out into open country by now, back among the glens. But the mountains soon stepped back and the trees fell away, thinning until they vanished completely. In their place, the vastness of Rannoch Moor appeared, its full extent lost in the low cloud. Soon there were only streams and pools and the rain-filled air, a fluid world suitable only for herons, moss and the tangled wire of long abandoned fences. Patches of snow clung on in the gullies and creases, and last year's bracken bled rust onto the slopes of hummocks, islands in the peaty ocean. On a small rise, an abandoned house stood in the midst of the mire. It lacked a roof and windows and doors, but the stonework was still crisply defined, as though its inhabitants had left only recently, taking every stick with them.

Deeper into the gloom, the moorland cascaded in every direction towards lakes that collected under the bounding mountains. In the midst of this nothingness, the train slowed to a halt. The world was silent, save for the sounds of steel settling and the hesitancy of Mary's sleepful breathing. Fergus peered out into the greyness, but aside from the small platform and a sign reading Rannoch, there was only a thin road that ran to the station and simply stopped, no longer sure where else it might go. They appeared to be as far from civilisation as it was possible to imagine. Even on Hinba, the constant movement of air and sea, the cries of the seabirds above and the expanse of the distant horizon meant that he felt less isolated than in this closed and muffled enclave.

The sudden imposition of the door's mechanism startled Fergus. The sigh of its opening, and the trill of the beeping that followed, announced the entry of their new fellow. Quite how he had materialised mystified Fergus. There appeared to be no buildings nearby, certainly not a settlement: it was as if the old man had simply condensed from the mist. His waxed coat and lank white hair dripped sufficiently to suggest that he was in fact made of the drizzle that had filled the earth since Fergus had left Hinba.

Tall and lean, the newcomer carried an old leather suitcase, small but evidently heavy. This he placed with great care on the rack above the seat across the aisle from where Fergus and Mary sat. He was close enough that Fergus felt some of the spray when the old man removed his coat and hat; both were placed just as carefully onto the rack, and in the same movement the suitcase was taken down again, before being placed on its owner's lap once he had taken his seat.

He left the window seat vacant, so he was less than a metre distant from Fergus, facing him diagonally across the suddenly too narrow aisle. He spent a moment with his eyes closed, as if in prayer or meditation, or in grateful relief. The man was clean shaven, but the nicks and grazes on his face suggested that this was both a recent and an unusual development. A slow swallow moved down his throat, his Adam's apple sinking like a crease being smoothed from his neck by an invisible hand: a vivid, fluid cut just above his collar threatened to stain the white cotton at any moment.

The train jolted into motion and the old man's eyes opened. Fergus looked away, stared at the back of the seat in front of him, then out of the window which was filled still with indistinct greys and browns and greens. The desolation of the emptiness without filled him with a welling disquiet and he turned back into the warm brightness of the carriage. The old man was looking intently at the suitcase, which he bookended with his hands. Fergus considered the etiquette of the situation for a moment, before disturbing the old man's solitude in any case.

'It's a miserable day out there today, isn't it? I bet you're glad to be indoors at last?'

The man looked up, his watery eyes finally finding their focus. His was face was set in stony weariness for a long moment, before it softened, as if remembering the warmth it had once had for other people. A weak smile appeared and his eyes creased into themselves.

'It's not so bad, although on a sunny day the moor is magnificent at this time of year. You can see clear across to the mountains, still under snow, and the spring flowers are just beginning to dress the peat in pinks and yellows.'

Fergus found it hard to see any of this in the opaque drabness beyond the window. But he had been out on the moorland of Hinba in bad weather, when its beauty was sheathed in rain or sea mist, and he found that he could paint the colours of spring at home onto the canvass of drizzle that cloaked Rannoch Moor.

'My wife, God rest her, loved the moor in Spring, after the snow and before the midges. Never wanted to leave, said they'd have to take her away in a box. Which is what they did, in the end, of course. Me, the bank might get rid of in other ways. It depends.'

The old man patted the little suitcase at this and Fergus was sure that he saw him wink. He did not want to intrude on the old man's grief any further, but was overcome with curiosity and could not contain a quizzical look at the case.

'This? Oh, these are some old books I've had for a very long time. They belonged to my great grandfather originally. A set of Walter Scott first editions. Taking them to Glasgow to get them sold. Worth a packet, I'm told.'

He dropped his voice at this, and looked around the carriage suspiciously, horrified that he had said too much for his own good. His tone now hushed, he continued, never questioning the trustworthiness of his young confidant.

'Yes, well. A little. Enough to sort out some debts, in any case. If I don't get myself robbed before I get to McAteer's tomorrow, that is.'

Seeing the confusion on Fergus's face, the old man snapped open the locks on his little suit case and carefully removed a magazine, which he offered across the aisle. On its cover was a photograph of an old wooden clock, the face of which was ornately shaped in engraved gold and silver. Curled black pointers indicated that the photograph had been taken just before eight o'clock. It was unclear whether it had been the morning or the evening, and of course assumed that the clock was running correctly. Across the top of the cover Fergus could read the words *McAteer's Auctioneers – Summer Catalogue.*

'Page forty seven is the start of the antiquarian books section. I have some of the editions listed on page forty nine. As I said, worth a packet.'

Beyond the window's glass, the moor became more stable, the ground firmer and forming into low hills. Stags and deer stood to watch the train as it passed, before running on in skittish enthusiasm. The trees reappeared and the mountains gathered. Fergus took the magazine and flipped through it looking for the right page, all the while wrestling with a sense of inexplicable familiarity. The tiny images of objects, the strange abbreviated captions, the colours and typeface, all nagged at him, but it was not until he reached page forty, midway through the Rarities and Miscellany section, that the noise in his subconscious broke through into conscious recognition of the torn page in his pocket.

— ⊙ —

The spires of Helensburgh prompted Fergus to wake Mary, to ask if this might be the beginnings of Glasgow, but Mary simply shook her head with a smile. The train ran through well-tended fields and it struck Fergus that the grass was greener here than on the island. The approach to Dumbarton announced their final crossing into the city. The town was ringed with towers, within which families lived stacked one upon the other. Pulling out of town, there were more houses being built beneath a small mountain split in two by quarrying. Presently the train reached the outskirts of Glasgow. There were what seemed like hundreds of towers here, spreading across the horizon. Looking out onto the trackside, there was so much debris in the fences and hedges that Fergus wondered what could have carried it here, if not the tide.

thirteen

'Can you spare a little change there, pal?'

Fergus stopped and could only stare at the man facing him, blocking his path. He was large and solid and in plain sight, but Fergus could tell little about him from his appearance. He may have been anything from twenty five to sixty years of age. His face was a mask etched in greasy lines and brittle bristle; his body was lost in the bulk of sweaters and scarves and lumps of fabric squeezed into an oily overcoat. The hand held out, cupped upwards, might have been made of plastic, so lifeless and inert was it. His other hand clutched a can of lager so tightly that its metallic blue dimpled a little under his waxy fingers. Fergus could not even be sure if the fellow had two human feet, since one leg ended in a plastic carrier bag, tied at the ankle.

Perplexed, he sought explanation from his sister's face. Mary had at first tried to continue onwards, circumventing the man as if he were any other obstacle on the street, but she had been held there suspended beside her frozen brother. Aware that he was watching her now, she tilted her head onwards in silent encouragement to continue.

'Just a couple of quid, pal. Just to get something to eat. It's a miserable day out here.'

Fergus and Mary had emerged from Queen Street Station and into the dull light of Glasgow's drizzle. As they had crossed onto George Square, the beggar had appeared, blocking their path. He did not intend to let them pass with their consciences undisturbed.

Fergus failed to heed his sister's signal, so Mary reached out to her brother to take his hand and break the spell that held him. But Fergus stuck to the block-work pavement. Mary tried a new tack. Looking directly at their challenger, she shook her head.

'Nah, sorry pal. Got no change on us. Sorry.'

She spoke with a practiced weariness and reached again for Fergus's hand, but he remained immobile, transfixed by the beggar's sharp eyes. To emphasise her calm disinterest, she shrugged her shoulders. The beggar's gaze turned to her, and he allowed himself a small mocking smile.

'Well that's no bother; I'll take notes just as well.'

As he spoke, Fergus noticed spots of rain water spring from deep within his coarse beard. Through the bristle, there was the twist of a mouth, the creases of a grin, of a small triumph. His eyes glinted with fresh confidence, flashing like a knife in dirty sunlight.

Mary was at a loss. Short of grabbing her brother and dragging him away, there seemed little that she could do. As if releasing a jet of irritation, she hissed his name. This seemed to rouse him, but not to movement.

'I think we do have a little cash, yes – let's see what's in here.'

Fergus pulled his fist from his jeans pocket, and the beggar flinched fractionally before he saw that the boy was clutching a handful of change. A small pink tongue tip traced over an oily, bristled lip, the eyes fixed now on the glimpses of copper and nickel between Fergus's fingers. The palm opened revealing a mound of coins. As the boy sorted through them with the index finger of his left hand, there were flashes of gold. The total amounted to maybe eight pounds. Mary, looking on in disbelief, wondered why her brother carried so much loose change.

'Aye, I think I can help. Two pounds, was it? Do you mind much if I give to you it in fifties and twenties? What's your name, by the way? If I'm going to be lending you money, seems appropriate that we should be acquainted? I'm Fergus, Fergus Buchanan.'

Fergus poured the coins into his left hand and extended his right courteously. The beggar, looked at the hand and back at the face, and then wrinkled his nose with a sniff.

'Look pal, I only want a little cash for something to eat. I'm not looking for friends. You're fucking weird, going around introducing yourself to strangers. I don't want to be acquainted. If you're not going to give me a couple of quid, you can get out of my way and stop wasting my time.'

Mary spotted her opportunity, and grabbed her brother by his extended hand and pulled him around the beggar. Once free, she continued to drag him across the square.

'Yeah, you fuck off, you bastard stuck-up skinflints! Too fucking grand to give a man a chance at something to eat? Un-fucking-believable!'

By the time they reached the other side of the square, Fergus had slipped his hand from Mary and was walking alongside her, stride for stride. While they waited for the lights to change at the crossing, Mary smiled up at her brother, grateful for the glimpse of the humanity that seemed sometimes to be the price of living in the world.

'You alright?'

'Yeah, I'm fine. Why wouldn't I be? No harm done.'

Behind her, a JCB was tearing apart a building from the inside out; the shrieks of twisted, shearing steel and concrete rose above the roar of traffic. For reasons Mary only barely understood, she embraced her brother and kissed him gently on the cheek. Fergus pretended to be embarrassed by her tenderness, but allowed himself to be held a moment longer.

'No. Suppose not. Anyhow, welcome to Glasgow. Shall we go find a drink now?'

With a drag of her head and a sly smile, Mary led Fergus off into the city.

fourteen

The city wheezed its way into wakefulness, and with it Fergus. Thin light streaked the living room in an indefinite shaft. From the sofa, Fergus watched it crawl, incipient, towards him across the carpet. He was not where he had expected to be. This was not the hall of residence from which Mary had sent those letters and Christmas cards. The return address, neatly printed in her compact handwriting across the back of the envelopes, had signified another place. Fergus was disturbed not only by his displacement, but also by the implications contained within it.

He stretched his feet out over the end of the too short sofa and felt his spine unrolling, his legs straightening with a glorious creaking. His bare toes he pulled up towards him, stretching muscle across shin bone in an ecstasy of pain. The house was quiet yet, even though the noise of traffic outside was an insistent rasping hum. More present and aware, he pulled the sleeping bag over himself, as much to cover his nakedness as to ward against the chill that hung in the air. The sleeping bag was made of blue nylon, pale on the inside, navy on the out. It had been unzipped so that it made a passable impression of a blanket, except that the nylon felt unpleasant against his skin, slick and scratchy at the same time. The coarse fabric of the sofa was another irritant – there was no sheet beneath him. Fergus wondered how he had slept at all, and only his dreams proclaimed the certainty of his slumber. His right hand, a clumsy spider, explored the carpet by the sofa until it found his notebook and his pen. Forgetting his discomfort, he dissolved the waking world in the narrow rhythms of his writing, recounting the adventures of his sleeping self.

'You're awake already. Good. Can I get you a cup of tea?'

Fergus was still writing, propped against the sofa's arm, his knees tucked up, the sleeping bag slid down to his waist. His pale torso, hairless and lean, embarrassed him and he covered his chest with his opened notebook like a startled starlet in a sex comedy. But Craig seemed unconcerned and turned towards the kitchen, padding away in just his boxer shorts and t-shirt, shouting over his shoulder a question about milk and sugar.

All Fergus could do was to shout in confirmation, before returning to his task, to attempt to complete his notes before Craig returned with the tea to end, not simply interrupt, the solitude. His agitation however sat awkwardly, blocking his recollections in a way unfamiliar to him. In the end, he curtailed his notes unsatisfactorily and snapped shut the book to scowl at the empty door frame through which Craig had vanished on his way to the kitchen. He could not be angry only at Craig, of course, or even at all, if he were being honest. His fault was unwitting. It was Mary who had lied, who had hidden from her family the conduct of her life in Glasgow.

The extent of her lie was not clear, of course. That she had moved out of halls and into this flat was a certainty. That she had failed to let her family know this was also a fact. But the reasons were not

THE CURSING STONE

yet known; the full nature of the Mary's friendship with Craig had not yet been established.

Craig was whistling merrily in the kitchen, accompanied by the kettle's hiss. Fergus wrestled with his resentment. Mary's move, albeit unannounced, was not its cause; rather the idea that she might be sleeping with this cheerful stranger filled him with an inexplicable indignation. True, this was the product simply of an assumption. He had not seen into which room Mary had stepped when they had said their goodnights. He did not know whether it was the same room into which Craig had previously disappeared, leaving sister to arrange a temporary bed for her brother. He could not, despite his best efforts, recall an instance during the previous evening when the two had touched inappropriately. There was no objective reason to believe that they were sleeping together, simply his own fetid imaginings. To make matters worse, Fergus could not be sure that, rather than morality, his discomfort stemmed from the humiliation that his little sister had beaten him to sexual experience.

'Here you go, mate.'

Craig returned carrying two mugs. One was plain white, almost entirely clean; the other bore the colours of an unknown football team. Fergus took the almost-white cup and the heat stung the pads of his fingers: as soon as the vessel was safely on the small table beside the sofa, he shook his hand in a futile attempt cool them. He remembered that Craig was not Scottish, and wondered how he had forgotten.

He thought back to the previous evening. From the station they had found their way through the tangle of streets and people to an indifferent, anonymous bar. Its blandness was a welcome relief after the sudden maelstrom of the city. They had lingered a while over a pint of 80/, and talked of their immediate plans. He had surprised himself in his enthusiasm to try Indian food, and they had left the pub hopefully, turning through a narrow gateway and out onto a broad thoroughfare. With coy pride, Mary had introduced Fergus to Buchanan Street and watched while her brother absorbed his surroundings.

'They call it the Style Mile. Everyone thought it was so funny. Because I was anything but stylish. All slacks and windcheaters.'

Fergus had kept close to his sister as she navigated the tides and narrows around Sauciehall Street, until they found the restaurant near a wide ribbon of road, criss-crossed by high concrete bridges. There Mary had talked a little about the significance of a bullaun stone, or butterlump, the word wrinkling her nose in pleasure. She'd talked about the time before Scotland, about the coming of the Christians, the traces they left before the Norsemen followed with their own gods and kings. Fergus for the first time could see the way that the writing of the past in the ground brought his sister to life; it was not simply a device to distance her from Hinba and the other Buchanans.

By the time bill had arrived, accompanied by two gold-wrapped chocolate mints, both brother and sister were anxious, for their own reasons, for the morning to come. They had congratulated themselves on their good fortune in finding the catalogue, in identifying McAteer's Auction House so easily. With the last of the lager they toasted the kindness of the old man from the mist.

They took the subway to Hillhead and walked back down the hill, pausing for Mary to point out the building where she took her classes. On Gibson Street, they slipped into a two room bar, with parquet floors and a zinc counter; a huge painting of a Highland cow stood over a glowing fireplace in the back corner and well-mannered music was rolling under the ceiling. He knew no-one, of course, yet Fergus found the anonymity less sterile than in the first bar: some people did know each other, but more than that, the strangers were content to share words and laughter. They had drunk two more pints together when Mary flung her arm in the air and waved it as if from the shore, her face eager, distracted. It was then that he had met Craig.

Thinking back, Fergus was not sure that he could remember the voice his sister's friend had used, and now it was lost forever behind the beer and the noise of the bar. A friend of his sister, that was how Craig had introduced himself. He was another student at the university, a second year, who lived in a tenement around the corner. The pub was local to both Craig and Mary. It was just as near to one as to the other. These gobbets of information assembled themselves slowly in his mind, turning like the pieces of a jigsaw puzzle until they snapped together, building up a picture. But Fergus did not have the full image to compare against, and it was possible that the picture was distorted, incorrect, as well as incomplete. Every so often, he would ask questions in the hope that their answer would provide the piece that would unlock the whole. He had asked these questions as they occurred to him, out of sequence with the conversation around him, and Mary and Craig would pause for a moment to make sense of them, before they answered and then returned to the flow of their own words and thoughts. At last, Fergus understood that Mary lived not in her Hall of Residence, but there was no opportunity to challenge her without creating a scene. In any case, the three of them were intent upon how best to handle the following morning's adventure.

Craig, it seemed, knew of someone that worked at McAteer's and had offered to join Mary and Fergus on their errand. But Fergus has been resolute, stubborn even, in his insistence that he would handle the matter himself. He made it clear that, while he meant no offence, he did not require assistance from Craig: the Buchanans were more than capable of their task. Mary had shrugged a smile at Craig, to confirm an earlier certainty.

'Stevenage. You're from Stevenage. SG1.'

The small fact had found its way up through the slow soupiness of Fergus's memory. That he had announced it so abruptly, almost proudly, seemed increasingly embarrassing in the quiet, awkward seconds that followed in the empty air of the flat. But Craig's immediate confusion eventually broke into a broad grin.

'Yeah, that's right. Well, it's SG4, as it goes, but not bad. And well remembered, by the way, in the circumstances. How's your head? It was quite a heavy night in the end.'

Fergus wanted to say that SG4 wasn't, strictly speaking, Stevenage, but decided instead that it would be better to answer Craig's question.

'N'yah. I've had worse hangovers. I feel fine, I think. A wee bit tired, a little sluggish, but no actual pain anywhere. You?'

Craig laughed, then shrugged his own indifferent state. Fergus drank tea and wondered when Mary would appear. He was increasingly uncomfortable about Craig's half-nakedness, particularly if his sister was in fact sleeping with him. He knew this made no sense at all, but he was nevertheless grateful when Craig, hearing the bathroom become vacant, made his excuses and went to take a shower. Fergus took the opportunity to pull on his t-shirt and marshal his belongings before his own turn with the bathroom came around.

By the time he returned from his shower, Mary was sitting, washed and dressed, in the living room, chatting with Craig and another young man. This other was a gangly youth whose Adam's apple formed a dog's leg in his throat; his neck and face presented an uncomfortably large canvass of pimply skin, through which burst untidy clumps of badly-shaved stubble. Craig looked handsome in comparison.

'Hi there. Sleep well? I was just telling Johnny about our plans for the day. Are you all set? Had your breakfast?'

Fergus caught sight of the bowl of cereal cradled in Craig's hands and he realised that he was extraordinarily hungry. But his urge to get out from the flat and the uncertainty about his sister's relationship with Craig overwhelmed his hunger and he claimed that he didn't really fancy anything. Mary nodded and rose briskly, retrieving her coat from the back of the high stool beside the kitchen counter. As they left, there was no kiss for Craig, just a wave and a non-committal vagueness about seeing her two flatmates later. Fergus pulled on his jacket slowly and nodded a silent farewell as he slipped through the door after his sister.

fifteen

McAteer's stood in a handsome stone building on the corner of two dignified streets in the heart of Merchant City. It was surrounded by placid boutiques, galleries and pavement cafes, none of which appeared to have any customers. It was a quiet refuge from the empty shop fronts and raggedy desperation of only a few streets away, yet never before had Fergus experienced calmness as disdain. With no great enthusiasm, he pushed open the door.

A small bell chinked behind them as Fergus and Mary stepped into the soft warmth of the show room. It was the only sound to be heard, save for their own breathing and the murmur of two other customers, a middle-aged couple inspecting porcelain figurines. The door swung shut with a sigh; sealed once more, the show room absorbed even these sounds into its plush embrace.

A young woman looked out from behind a glass cabinet. Her hesitant eyes lingered over the new arrivals for a few moments, until she was certain that they were not deserving of her most unctuous attention. She smiled and busied herself once more with the contents of the cabinet, content to let the young couple build up their courage before she approached.

Fergus paid her no great attention, so occupied was he by the treasures that surrounded him. Large statues of mahogany and bronze vied for space among glistening dining tables and silk-clad chaises-longues. By the wall was an escritoire, its patina so deep that he imagined he could see all the way back through its 300 years. Beyond it, stacks of heavy supple carpets filled the space as far as the corner; a crowd of oil paintings clung to the wall above. The centre of the room was made up of cabinets containing spotlit objects on glass shelves: glassware, silver and jewels. Fergus thought of the misery that had brought these treasures together in this place. He thought about the old man on the train, his precious books that would soon be swallowed by McAteer's insatiable vaults.

Mary was suddenly alive to a cabinet of smaller, older statuary, some of which was made from the rough stone of ancient times. She set off towards it with determination and incipient rage. Fergus followed, curious as to why the dignity of the dead meant more to his sister than that of the living.

'Is there something in particular that you're looking for?'

The young woman had appeared behind them, unseen. She was plumper than she had appeared, standing behind the cabinet, her features less precise. Her dark brown hair fell onto her shoulders and, as she twisted slightly at her heel, the changing light caught the glints of soft chestnuts that shone with deep, dull reddishness. She spoke with closely trimmed precision, but her self-assurance was unconvincing. Despite her evident breeding, she had not yet lost the impediment of youthful uncertainty.

Her nervousness emboldened Fergus. He explained that he was looking for a particular piece, which had appeared in the previous autumn's catalogue. On the walk across the city, Mary had persuaded him that he should not yet explain the theft: first they needed to locate the stone and too strong a display of righteousness might make the auctioneer uncomfortable. So instead he held out the flattened page of the catalogue and indicated the picture of the cursing stone.

At her request, Fergus let go of the page and the young woman took it. She turned towards a counter near the back of the show room, hidden behind a stuffed bear that stood on its hind legs, jaws wide, spoiling for a fight. Fergus was surprised that he had not noticed it before, but followed anyway. Mary lingered a while, looking for familiar shapes among the stones in the glass cabinet, as if identifying a corpse.

Fergus stood, uncertain, while the assistant took from beneath the counter a heavy book, its worn spine bound in insulating tape. She dropped it gently onto the desk with a dull thump, then opened it carefully and flipped through the pages, running her index finger down a column of numbers at the left-hand margin. In a few moments, she stopped, smiled and tapped her finger on the page with satisfaction.

'I'm sorry sir, but that item has been sold. Last November, actually. We occasionally get similar pieces in, and if you'd like to leave an email address, I'd be happy to add your name to our mailing list, with a note...'

Her voice tailed off, aware that her customer's mood had changed. She stood to her full height and began to apologise again, to explain that it was important that, if he was interested in a particular type of piece, he keep abreast of the schedule of auctions, which were available on the company's website. Then she paused, waiting to see what the young man would do next.

Fergus felt his hopes for a speedy return to Hinba sinking with his shoulders. He had been overly optimistic, naïve, he realised. There would be no easy resolution to his search. He sighed deeply and, from across the showroom, Mary looked up, frowning instinctively. She watched her brother's surrender and felt his weariness as he tried to gather his strength to begin again.

He explained to the assistant that he was not looking for similar pieces, but for that specific piece. It was only that piece, that stone, in which he was interested. He had travelled a long way to find it, and while he understood that it was his fault that he was too late, the news that it had been sold was something of a disappointment. He apologised if he had appeared rude. If the assistant could just let him have the name and address of the buyer, he would be most grateful and would trouble her no further.

'Oh, I'm sorry but that won't be possible. It's company policy to protect absolutely the privacy of our clients. I'm sure you'll understand, sir, and that you'd expect nothing less if the situation were reversed?'

The book flopped shut with a heavy thump and Fergus cursed himself for lacking the foresight to read across to the name recorded next to the item sooner. The young woman had recovered herself and felt once more in control of the situation. She smiled and raised an eyebrow at Fergus's still cocked head, triumphant. The sweep of the curtain behind her, however, brought a flinch. A squat, round man appeared at her shoulder.

Dressed in a mossy suit, Mr McAteer glowered for a short moment through wire-framed spectacles. His thin hair was slick to his head and his pink skin seemed too small for his face. It had a sickly, glossy sheen and his cheeks strained roundly. Before he spoke, a small pink tongue slid up across his upper lip and lingered contemptuously; his broad mouth curled malevolently.

'Is everything in order, Miss Carmichael? No problems with this customer, I trust?'

She quivered slightly beneath her blouse as she explained that everything was indeed in order and that the issue had been dealt with. Her eyes pleaded with Fergus for confirmation, but McAteer was in any case unconvinced. With a hook of his head, he sent Miss Carmichael scurrying to the back room and turned to face Fergus. The buttons on his waistcoat wrestled with his bulk.

Despite his girth, McAteer was a full foot shorter than Fergus. He glowered for a while longer, licking his upper lip, before a deep swallow pulsed down his throat.

'Am I to understand that you were trying to bully my assistant into revealing the personal details of one of my clients? Because that is something that I find unacceptable. Un-ac-ceptable. Am I making myself clear, young man?'

His voice was steady and controlled, but venomous all the same. Despite his lack of height, he glistened with menace. With the stroke of the hand, he cut off Fergus's attempt to counter and continued.

'You might not fully understand this, but trust is an important part of my business. Integrity. Discretion. I will not tolerate your attempts to harass my customers, nor to intimidate my staff.'

The tongue again. McAteer swayed a step closer to Fergus, his stomach resting on the counter, his fingers spread evenly on the glass.

'Now, before I have you leave the premises, you will tell me exactly why you were interested in this piece.'

His fat finger pointed to the picture of the cursing stone on the torn page that still lay on the counter where Miss Carmichael had left it in her haste. Fergus's eyes fell limply to the page and his resolve drained from him. There was no point now explaining that the stone had been stolen; McAteer would not believe him, would think it simply a ploy, a ruse, to circumvent his policy of guarding the privacy of his client. At best, he would simply tell him to go to the police; more likely, he would erupt in anger and throw him and his sister out onto the street, enraged at the impudent accusation implied about this business. Inspiration came from his sister's presence at his side.

'We're students. At the University. In the Archaeology Department. We're doing a project on the settlement of the Small Isles, and we just wanted to talk to the owner. About the bullaun stone. Where it was found, that kind of thing. It would help us get a good grade.'

'Students! My god, do you lot never think? Supposed to be clever, but really… Why would my client want to talk to you, even if it got you a bloody gold star? Out. Out! Back to your books: that's how you're supposed to learn, not by bothering hard working people. Get out, just get out.'

Fergus stuttered an apology and shrank into himself. As he turned to leave, he had the presence of mind to sweep up the torn page and fold it into his pocket in a single movement, all the while watching McAteer's shaking head, his eyes wide open, his mouth ajar, the fleshy stuffing bulging over the ivory studs of tiny teeth.

As he guided his sister towards the door, past the startled couple by the porcelain figurines, Fergus did not know what the next steps were, but he knew that there was nothing to be gained by arguing with McAteer. They had been lucky enough to discover the identity of the auction house so easily; all things considered, this was not a significant setback. A solution would present itself.

sixteen

He wasn't sure about his new flatmate's brother. Craig didn't know Mary well, of course: she had only moved into the spare room after Christmas, when Patrick had decided that University was not, after all, for him and had not returned from Manchester following the winter break. She had enquired about the room and had seemed the most sane and reliable of all those they had seen. Compared with the boy with staring eyes and an aversion to the most basic aspects of hygiene, she had seemed saintly. It had been an easy decision and Mary had moved in before the end of the second week back.

Craig had soon come to like her. She was studious and earnest, with an interest in art and an adventurousness of spirit that shone only slowly through her quiet calmness. She made no great display of her decision to leave the sanctuary of Halls after just one term, taking independence and responsibility as a given. She was sure of her own opinion and aware of its limits: their intense discussions stretched sometimes late into the night, but were never heated, only illuminating. She was one of the most subtle thinkers Craig had met in his short life and they had started to spend time together on campus between lectures, sitting together in the library. Before long, easy assumptions had been made.

Craig found them in the café on Ingram Street. It was as Mary had said on the phone: the visit to McAteer's had not gone well. He was not surprised. The brother, despite his bluster and self-assurance, lacked guile. He had had no clear plan of action and it was obvious that, by simply presenting himself at the auction house and demanding the address of a customer, he was going to fail. Businesses didn't just give out that sort of information and, as much as it clearly pained him, Fergus was always going to have to ask for help. Craig had been in no hurry.

'How's the cappuccino?'

Fergus did not look up in response to Craig's cheery greeting, but continued to turn his cup in its saucer. The flaky remains of a croissant dusted the table. Craig put his own cup on the table and leant across to kiss Mary on both cheeks, before taking his seat and offering his assistance.

With a long, slow breath, Fergus joined the conversation, although his eyes seldom lifted from the table-top. Craig listened as brother and sister gave their own perspectives on what had passed in McAteer's that morning. Mary was calm, detached, but Fergus's hands fluttered as they illustrated the fruitless confrontation that had occurred.

The details were simple. There was an order book, under the counter by the bear, and in it were the details of the client that had bought the stone. It was a straightforward task really, simply a matter of getting to look inside that book, without the knowledge of the irascible Mr McAteer. All that was required was the right kind of diversion, at just the right time.

'Or, better, how about someone on the inside? You know, someone who works there?'

— ◉ —

He knew where he would find him. There had been no need to call, and it would have been pointless in any case: Joe did not answer his mobile, even if he was aware that it was ringing. Yet despite his studied elusiveness, Craig knew that on that particular Monday afternoon, Joe could be in one place only. So he had left Mary and her brother to their own devices and walked up High Street as far as the cathedral. There, in the heart of the old city, he had passed through the gates to the Necropolis and into its narrow lanes.

The morning's cloud had lifted, tugged away by a nagging wind, and the sky was bright even as the air still held its chill. As he climbed the steep path towards the highest point, he felt the compression of the city's streets fall beneath him and the air buoyed him upwards. The only activity was that of the unseen workmen hammering at wayward masonry and, aside from a prim dog walker and the dead, he had the cemetery to himself.

Joe was sitting on the steps of the domed mausoleum of William Rae Wilson, on the very brink of the hill, his back turned to the bustle below. The wind caught his hair, toyed with it briefly before dropping its waves in bold constructions. Joe did not resist: he was intent upon his sketch of the faceless woman perched on the neighbouring tomb, within which three generations of the Holdsworth family lay unmolested. The statue, a woman holding an anchor, her head covered by a cloth, was carved from a white stone which contrasted with the grimy honey of the main structure.

Craig watched Joe for a little while, knew not to disturb him especially when he wanted a favour. Instead he took up his place on a low wall and looked out across the city, down onto the nearby hospital and out over the receding tower blocks and cranes. Above him, rising through a copse of obelisks and crosses, John Knox watched, unmoved, as the sun inched down a ladder of cloud. Craig breathed in the ageing afternoon. The low hum of the city pulsed, but could not smother the gentle chatter of the birds or the scratching of Joe's pencil. The only other sounds were the occasional intrusion of the wind, rattling the trees that were about to unfurl their greenery.

Joe moved his pencil with a light fluidity, working the graphite with his thumb to capture the shifting tones of the woman's shrouded head. He had a thing for graveyards, for death, for the long departed ghosts of the city. He had been raised among the lush, light villages of Oxfordshire, but had been drawn to the heaviness of the city as much as to its Art School. He had set about making sketches of the relics of the merchant families that had made Glasgow almost as soon as he had arrived, trying to capture the transience of permanence and the absurdity of our attempts to remain present beyond our time. While Craig knew him best from the bars and clubs of the city's night, during daylight hours at least, if he wasn't on Renfrew Street, he would be at the Necropolis with his pencils.

Remind me, when do we start to get proper evenings again? This light is pathetic.

Joe was sitting slumped against the mausoleum, his pad abandoned in his lap. His expression was lost in the fast gathering gloom but the frustration it conveyed was apparent in any case, the irritation at another day passed and the work still not done.

Soon, I think. Let me buy you a beer. Cheer you up. Craig let a shiver run through him, his shoulders shaking beneath his too-thin jacket, and he wondered at the imperviousness of the coatless Joe.

'Yeah, why not? But give me another ten minutes or so. Here.'

Joe threw a packet of tobacco over towards Craig; it fluttered for a moment like a sycamore seed, before dropping to earth a little short of the waiting hands. Retrieving the wrap, Craig rolled a tight, thin cigarette between marble fingers that soon sought out the lighter. Sparks spluttered before a shallow dome of orange flame settled into being, and Craig's face puckered to suck in the smoke, the thin crumple of paper pinched between thumb and forefinger of his left hand. The smoke swelled in his chest and he allowed his head to race ahead of itself a little before he let it go in a long release.

The day's light was seeping cautiously into the ground. Soon the dusk would animate the grain of the granite and the cemetery would become a place of primal fears. Craig wanted to be away to the safety of electric light and the conviviality of the pub.

'Make me one of those, will you?'

By the time the cigarette was rolled, the sun was all but done and Joe had begun stowing his things in his satchel. Craig wondered if the bag was an affectation or a simple continuity from Joe's childhood: his background certainly allowed for him to have been to one of those schools. When he was sure he had left nothing under the dusk, he joined Craig on the wall and took the cigarette and a light from his friend.

'So, anyway. You didn't come up here to watch me sketch. At least I hope not. That would suggest that you're either more dull or more needy than I took you for. Desperate to see me were you? Or after something?'

'Actually, there was something I wanted to talk to you about. Are you still seeing that girl? Elspeth?'

Craig had heard Joe talking about his girlfriend, the diffident convent girl who fought a constant battle against the roving hands of her muculent employer. He had never met her, but knew that she was studying fine art and worked in the auction house during the vacations and on weekends, since she lacked the familial resources of either Joe or even of Craig.

'Well, I'm happy to give it a try, mate. But she'll never go for it: she's terrified of the old man. Why do you care anyway? It's not like you know this bloke anyway.'

Craig watched the orange glow of his cigarette rear and recede three times before he answered. The monuments silhouetted against the sky crowded around him in anticipation of his confession.

'It's the sister. My flatmate. I sort this for him, and she'll be…'

'Grateful? Come on, you old dog. Before they lock us in.'

— ◉ —

It was properly dark by the time they reached the auction house and the sky as washed peach with the sodium glow. McAteer's stayed open until 7.30pm and they had a little time yet. Hopefully the owner would be distracted, unguarded, at this late stage of the day, already half-living his evening plans, whatever they might be. Craig and Joe exchanged a glance to steel themselves before they clicked open the latch and the door swung easily inwards.

The jangle of the bell startled Elspeth Carmichael. She had hoped that this day had already run its course. It was not how she had imagined studying. At her sixth form, she had delighted in learning without obstacle. Her parents made sure she had been provided with the physical comforts of a happy if modest life, while the Sisters had permitted her the space and means to explore all of western art and literature. The School of Art provided that too, more so, but the collapse of her unnoticed mundane support had affected her unexpectedly. She had been surprised to discover how distracting earning money could be, even without the intrusions of her lecherous employer.

At least for now he was out of the way, confined to his office in conference with an older gentleman, discussing the prospects for a cache of antiquarian books. The client had arrived as dusk had flickered on the street lights. He had reminded Elspeth of her own grandfather shortly before his death: refined and kindly, yet also insubstantial, ethereal, scarcely able to bear the cloak of resignation he wore. She had watched him shrink into McAteer's robust handshake and disappear behind the curtain with a mixture of relief and regret. The client's sacrifice at least secured her own release. Until now of course, with the arrival of yet more visitors only twenty minutes from the end of her captivity.

Her despondency evaporated at the sight of Joe, which once more promised release. He could only be here to see her, maybe to distract her from the dying minutes of the day. Even the presence of another only brought the flicker of a frown to her face.

'Hello you! To what do I owe this pleasure?'

She embraced him briefly, brushing her lips on his earlobe, before withdrawing coyly. His friend, she noted, had turned to look across the room rather than to invade their intimacy and she was grateful for this. Despite the three months she had known Joe, she had still not reconciled herself entirely to the physical manifestations of affection, much less their being viewed by others.

Craig was introduced and the three of them stood awkwardly by the glass-topped counter. He smiled at the frozen rage of the bear, its demonstrative impotence. He asked the girl if it had a name but paid no attention to her response, since he had spotted the big blue ledger beneath the glass of the desk. He cast a look towards Joe then began to circumnavigate the bear, as if to get a better understanding of its shaggy bulk.

Joe took Elspeth by the waist and guided her towards some paintings hung beyond a bank of glass cabinets on the far side of the show room. Certain of his seclusion, Craig took up the ledger and flipped swiftly through it to the page on which last November's sales were recorded. The looped letters of the clients' names slid beneath his finger, all fixed in flat blue ink, until he reached the purchaser of lot 326. Craig allowed himself a small smile of triumph, a private recognition of his own ingenuity, and searched his pocket for pen and paper.

Craig did not hear the whisper of the curtain behind him, or feel the eyes narrow and sharpen, the breath solidify in the throat. Only the creak of the floor board alerted him to the fact that he had been discovered. He scrambled through all the words in his head, searching for an explanation that might prove both plausible and innocent, but none had been found before he heard the sharp inhalation that announced his imminent sentence.

'A moment, Mr McAteer. There is one further matter before I go.'

Behind Craig, an old man raised his now empty leather briefcase to his chest and, unseen, turned on the spot and disappeared once more behind the curtain, there to detain the auctioneer. While Craig did not understand why he remained unmolested, he needed no further invitation. Gently he closed the ledger and sidled back around the bear, and into the show room. In moments he had found Joe and Elspeth, with whom he exchanged some hurried words before slipping through the door and out into the street.

The bell's final resonance greeted Mr McAteer as he emerged into the showroom with his new client. The books would fetch a tidy price and he calculated the likely commission they would yield, assuming the right buyers could be alerted: a good afternoon to make up for the annoyance of the morning. But he wondered who else had been in the shop and, more to the point, where his assistant might be. He shrugged and shook the old man's hand and bade him a safe journey. Turning, he noticed that the sales ledger was not in its proper place, but instead was laying openly on the counter. McAteer considered the possibilities, running his tongue over his lower lip in concentration.

'Miss Carmichael! I would be grateful for your attendance please!'

McAteer waited for a moment, but no answer came, save for the clank of the bell above the door once more. His client departing, no doubt. But where was his assistant? From under the shadow of the stuffed beer, the auctioneer peered across the empty showroom.

seventeen

A sudden rush of colour blurs the window, as the bus swings through curves with audacious fluency. The landscape, settling into focus, is familiar but cannot be placed in time or space. You have been here at some time, or will be in the future, and yet the golds and emeralds and rubies that fill the window are more vivid than they ought to be. You can taste the warmth of the day in their iridescence.

The bus is more a van than a bus. It is small, with maybe fifteen seats. There is a name for it but bus will do just fine. Your fellow passengers are children but, while you are not a child, there is no difference in size or age between them and you. You know them and they know you. There are no strangers here. Behind you, you are certain that Shona is staring through the window, watching the thousands of rabbits hiding among the purple heather that clots the carpet of pink and white and yellow flowers filling the valley. The yellow flowers look like buttercups but they are not buttercups; they are larger and their stamen wave at you like kelp.

The bus has gone and you are with your classmates among the plants of the valley. You remember that this is a school trip, a botany expedition, or something very like a botany expedition. There is no teacher and instead your sister, or someone who looks very much like your sister, is taking the class. With a long black stick, a rod made of some material you do not know, she pokes at a bundle, a heap, a mound that is cupped in a hollow. Birds circle overhead, soundless. One drops onto the bundle and begins to tug at the fabric wrapped around it, and the person that looks like your sister stops prodding it and stares at you expectantly. All your classmates are staring at you now, and you search their faces hoping to find the girl whose name skips away from you. She is absent and you doubt she was ever there at all.

There is only the bundle and you. Everyone else has gone, like the girl. Even the rabbits and the birds have left, and the flowers too. There are only rocks and sedge now, everything in shades of grey and you notice that the bundle itself is grey. You should look inside the bundle, peel back the fabric to reveal what is inside, but you cannot, will not. And there is no-one to make you. You want to leave, but you are fixed to the spot: you are caught between your desire to run and the duty to approach the mound before you, wrapped in grey flannel, the same grey flannel as your school uniform.

The bundle has the form of a boy, of a man, of a body, of someone you recognise. But still you won't approach it. The vacant eyes stare across the beach, an expanse of pebbles and boulders, stretching to a distant, silent ocean. Behind you is the valley, from where the ghosts of your classmates' laughter reach down to you. But you are fixed, despite your desire to fly to them. There is only you and the bundle. An old man, unknown, familiar.

eighteen

Thousands upon thousands of books hung heavily from the swollen stacks, pregnant with every dream ever dreamt. Fergus ran his eye over the spines of those nearest to him, carelessly. Faded fabric bindings and dog-eared dust jackets succeeded in making the contents utterly unappealing. He gave up and instead sat on a black metal kick-stool at the end of a run of stale volumes detailing the geomorphology of the West Highlands. The books teetered precipitously above him.

Mary had already been gone for longer than she had promised. It was not only boredom that made him restless, although it was certainly that too. Of course, she had to attend to her studies, but there were things he needed to do, especially in the light of what Craig had found the night before. However, there was no sign of her and Fergus could do nothing but wait. He looked along the shelves in front of him and started to imagine them as fragmented basalt cliffs, like those that clung to the eastern end of Hinba.

He thought again of Jamie McCulloch. He hadn't thought of him for over eight years, not since their second year at the school in Mallaig. Whatever closeness had been between them had worn to nothing once they had left the inescapable proximity of the island. Jamie had made friends among the mainlanders, had left Fergus behind, while Fergus had let him go. There had been no falling out, simply a drifting apart. Jamie had not returned to Hinba with Fergus. As Mary later would, he had chosen to stay in Mallaig until he had the qualifications to get into university. Unlike Mary, he had chosen to study in England. In London. Fergus was impressed by the efficacy of his subconscious.

The low hum of the library swallowed the footsteps, so Fergus did not hear Mary approaching. Yet the gentle pressure of her palm upon his shoulder did not startle him, and he simply turned his head to smile up at his sister. Three short days together had mended the fracture between them and they were as they had been as children, before either had left the island, when they had each other and their family and there had been no space between any of them, when the island had seemed like the whole world to both of them.

'I'm ready. Sorry. I wanted to get this and they'd put it on the wrong shelf...'

There had been no shushing, nor scolding looks, but Mary dropped her voice to a whisper before she held up the slender volume: *Pilgrims in an Atlantic Landscape – Archaeological traces of the beginnings of British Christianity.* He took the book gently and flipped open its dusty beige cover. He did not need to look at the record of borrowers to know that it had been lost on the wrong shelf, unmissed, for some time: the pages reeked of neglect and disinterest. That Mary had spent so long tracking it down seemed an unusual indulgence, an over-elaboration of the situation at hand, but Fergus refused to begrudge his sister: in her own way, she had joined him on his quest.

'I thought it might give you a bit of background. On the bullaun stone. They're from the old religions really, and were just absorbed into Christianity. Like Christmas trees. And Easter bunnies. They were used for cursing people, as well as praying. You'd turn the stone, in its bullaun, which is what the Irish call the stone bowls like the one on Hinba, you know, at the bottom of the cross by the old monastery. Neolithic they think. Magical, as much as religious. Same thing really, back in the day.'

'Thanks. I doubt I'll have time to read it, before I have to get the train. Assuming I have to get the train. But I'll have a gander.'

Craig had been sure that it was London. He had not been able to write down the address in time, before he was discovered, but he had managed to make a mental note of the buyer's name and he was certain that he was in London. His confidence that a simple internet search would provide the rest evaporated quickly; directory enquiries were similarly unhelpful. It seemed that Nicholas Maltravers was not to be found so easily.

They had slept on the matter, but morning brought no answers. Uneasily, Craig had agreed finally to try again and had set off in search of his friend once more. Mary watched him slip loose of the flat and stride away down Bank Street before suggesting that they fill the otherwise empty hours productively, which is how they had found their way to the library. And yet the distraction had failed to distract Fergus from his concerns. The trail had not gone cold but was tepid at best; he had no confidence that the girl would help again, especially now that she knew that her assistance was asked. Fergus could only fret about his next move, and the inevitable disappointment of his grandfather.

— ◉ —

'Well, that was awkward.'

Outside, the rush of traffic reminded Fergus of how much he missed the sea. Craig had taken a seat on the far side of the table, a pint of lager still clenched in his left hand, and delivered his assessment of his meeting with Joe with daunting solemnity. He had still not fully caught his breath after his rapid walk across the width of the city centre, and he gulped down some of his beer before continuing.

Joe had not been at the Necropolis. It had taken the best part of an hour to find him, in the café across the road from the Art School. His mood was darker than usual: Elspeth had lost her job as a result of the previous night's adventure and was seriously thinking of ending her relationship with Joe as a result. Her absence from her post had led McAteer to decide to dispense with her services; he had no idea that anyone had been searching through the sales ledger. It had been Craig's warning that had prompted Elspeth and he to flee when McAteer had called, and there had in fact been no need. They had left with the old man that had been in McAteer's office and, as they slipped into the night, it had been he who had confirmed that the auctioneer had seen nothing untoward, had in fact been distracted by the unwilling client. Craig had not been discovered and it had been his panic that had robbed Elspeth of her livelihood.

'So that's that then.'

Fergus thumped his palm onto the table, making the drinks and the other customers jump a little; the barman looked over with concern. It was plain that even if the girl were inclined to help – which seemed doubtful – she was no longer in a position to do so.

'No, not at all. The strangest thing. Joe was obviously really pissed off with me, but when I mentioned Maltravers' name, he just laughed. Seems he's some upscale art dealer. Sorted Joe's parents out with some saucy statues from Cambodia a couple of years ago. A bit naughty. Contravened all sorts of export bans, Joe reckons. Sounds like he's your man.'

Craig smiled wryly and winked at Mary, who smiled back her gratitude. Fergus was too relieved and thankful to object or even to notice. Only once their excitement had abated and their friend had been toasted, did Fergus dare to ask for further information. Craig was happy to provide it.

'Yep, he's got a gallery down in Mayfair, on Half Moon Street. That's W1J, if it helps.'

Craig slid a piece of paper across the tacky table top towards Fergus. But while his fingers pointed towards her brother, Craig's eyes were fixed on Mary.

nineteen

'Hello? Can I help you?'

'Mum, it's me, Fergus.'

'Oh, sweetheart! It's so lovely to hear your voice... Davey! Come through: it's Fergus on the phone! Well now, how've you been? Has your sister been taking good care of you?'

'Aye, everything is fine. Mary is fine. Glasgow's not so bad. I miss you all, of course. And the island...'

'Shona is fine. I say that... she's pining for you, of course, can't wait for you to get back. Is that why you're ringing? Are you coming back now?'

'No, I'm sorry to say. In fact, I'll be away a while longer. There's been a complication, but never mind that. She's pining for me, you say?'

'Mooning about the place like a lovesick puppy. She misses you. We all do. Why have you to be away longer? I don't understand, what do you mean, a complication?'

'Well, you see, the fellow that took the stone away from the island, he sold it to...'

'Yes, I know, at the auction house. I know all this.'

'...he sold it to a man in London. So, I'm going to have to do down there to fetch it back.'

'London! No-one said anything about you going to London. It's too much. I really think you should just come home, let somebody else take care of it. Davey, Fergus says he has to go to London to fetch the bloody thing. London!'

'Mum, calm yourself, it's no big thing. I'll just be there for a couple of days, tops. Mary's going to put me on a train and I'll be back before you know it.'

'What's that? Hold on a second, love... Uh-huh, right, of course. Fergus, your father wants to know if you've got enough money. It's a long way and it's expensive down there, he says.'

'Tell him I've plenty. I've barely touched the roll he gave me; I've just been using the cash from Mr Galbraith and the Reverend, and that's not gone yet. It'll be fine. I just need to sort out somewhere to stay down there. Which is the other reason I called. Do you have Jamie McCulloch's number?'

'Wee Jamie McCulloch? I haven't seen him for years, and you two used to be such friends too. I see his father, of course, in the Bell every now and then, but not Jamie. He's gone away I think.'

'Aye, he's in London, studying. So, if I had his number I could maybe...'

'Of course! I'm sorry sweetheart, it takes a minute for me to catch up sometimes. I'm sure we could get Jamie's number from Neil… yes, your father says he'll see him in the Bell this evening. We'll get it and phone you in the morning, is that OK?'

'That's perfect mum. I mean, I'm sure Craig could help out, suggest someone I could stay with, but…'

'Who's Craig? I don't think I've heard of a Craig…'

'Craig is a friend of Mary's, here in Glasgow. I mean he's from down there, Stevenage, but he's at the university with Mary.'

'Is our Mary courting and hasn't told us?'

'I don't know, to be honest. I thought so, at first, but I'm not so sure now. But whatever he is, he's a fine lad, really. Anyway, that's for you to talk to her about: not my business.'

'Fingal, I'll explain later, Fergus is on the phone now… OK, well, tell her to expect some questions when I call back in the morning!'

'OK, will do. She'll be delighted, I'm sure. Anyhow, I'd better get on. I want to call Shona, and I'm using all of Mary's credit as it is.'

'All right, Fergus, I'll let you get on. And we'll speak in the morning, OK. Take care of… What, was that? OK, Fingal, I'll tell him… Fergus, your grandfather wants you to know that he's very proud of you; the whole island is, he says. Me, I just want you home safe. Promise me that you'll do nothing daft down there. It's just some lump of old rock. Not worth getting into trouble over.'

twenty

The train slid out of the station and across the river. Along its bank, the jumbled face of the city assembled to offer a final glance to the departed. Swaying slowly, the train picked its way between the high-rise blocks and litter-clogged gullies, but within a quarter of an hour the route scythed through gentle hills and farmland; a bare, broad-backed landscape punctuated by sheep and streams, familiar and comfortable. Fergus watched the world race away from him, the shrinking towers on the horizon serrating the sky just as the mountains of Skye did when he stood on the beach below Duncannon's place.

He clung to the paper cup, fearful that the still-hot tea should be upturned; yet the train at speed swung through curves with audacious fluency and his tea stayed safe. It was afternoon already; the morning had sped away from him in a whirl of plans and goodbyes. The day had started early with the sound of Mary's phone from her bedroom, followed by twenty minutes of murmured, then barked, conversation. When Mary emerged to hand the phone brusquely to Fergus, she had glowered, her mouth twisting to contain its rage. She stood over the sofa, arms crossed, while Fergus took down the address and phone number of his school friend. Mary had glared at him as he had offered his love and wishes to the people at home before hanging up.

'Why did you say that to mum? Do you have any idea what sort of hell you've created for me? Why on earth did you say I was seeing Craig? That's just messed up; you're just messed up!'

She had been incandescent and had not noticed Craig standing within the frame of his bedroom door, had not seen his face fall, nor recover, and only his cheery greeting and the offer of tea had diffused Mary's anger. Fergus had squeezed her hand when he returned the phone and they had turned their attention to preparing for his journey south. There had been no time for anxiety until now, when he was safely underway, installed on the train.

Fergus contemplated another cup of tea, but instead nudged his ticket around the table, astounded that something so small could cost so much. It had required all of the money that remained within the crisp, white envelope that the Reverend had pushed into his hand early on at his engagement party. Fergus didn't know whether there had actually been a collection, but the awkward speech made by first the teacher, then the Reverend, implied that the envelope contained both the hopes and gratitude of the whole island. And now it was gone, exhausted. Fergus would need to rely on the roll of notes given him by his father.

Imperceptibly, the train crossed the border. At Carlisle, few passengers boarded or disembarked and still no-one joined Fergus at his table. He stretched once more into the space allowed him, his feet under the facing seat, and he ran through his plan once more. That Jamie had been so open to his visit had, with hindsight, been a surprise. They had not spoken for years; a call from out of the blue and a request at short notice ought, Fergus reasoned later, to have been an imposition. No matter, he had a bed for the night. Jamie lived close by the Elephant and Castle: Fergus rolled the imagery around his head, allowing himself a small smile that broadened with the thought that Mannion House was in SE1, close enough to W1J that, assuming all went well in the morning, Fergus might be able to take a return train by the end of the day.

Another station. This time, a new passenger boarded Fergus's carriage. He was heavy-set, fat even: the checked cotton of his shirt strained at the point where it disappeared under the waist band of his jeans. He slung his holdall onto the rack above Fergus's head.

'Is this free?'

He indicated the seat opposite Fergus with a dip of his head, and was already sliding in between chair and table by the time Fergus had completed his acknowledgement. Fergus did not feel much like talking and, although such unfriendliness troubled him, he was thankful when the newcomer, having settled, busied himself with his mobile phone.

After Penrith, the mountains rose in the distance to the west, some still snow-topped, growing ever-nearer. Soon they were joined from the east by the Howgills, which closed to form a narrowing valley. The train burst from a tunnel to reveal a landscape that for a moment gave Fergus to believe that he was already on his way home, nearing Mallaig. But soon the earth flattened and the fattening sun to the west broke the day dream. Disconsolate, Fergus stared through the ghostly reflection of the man in the window, whose eyes seemed to stare directly, fixedly into his own. In them, Fergus could see only distance, a still sadness, a looking deep into the past in search of what was lost and far into the future, but not far enough, in fear of what is to come. The open country rippled beyond the grimy window, laid out in grand scale. The landscape revealed in its sparse farmsteads and hamlets the tentative grasp of humans on the surface of the world, even here.

Arrival at Preston shook the sleep from his lolling head. The man was gone; he stood with his bag by the end of the carriage, waiting while the glass door slid repeatedly into his shoulder. The landscape had disappeared completely and the train was indoors, under a vast roof, surrounded by walls. The day's light was beginning to fade and the electric lamps of the shops and cafes within the station burned with an angry phosphorescence, the glare smearing into the gathering darkness. People milled on the platform, clustered at the doors, as the entire carriage emptied save for Fergus. Old men in rain coats and young women in light cardigans all danced an anxious dance as they waited in line along the aisle, fearful of being stranded, unable to disembark. Fergus watched as his fellow passengers filed out from the train and into the swirl of the station.

No sooner had the carriage emptied than new neighbours began to funnel in. There were more now, and most carried bags: tiny suitcases with wheels, rucksacks and holdalls, larger cases with ribbon tied to the handles, surreptitious labels of ownership. As the train filled and the doors were piped shut, a young woman smiled at him. She had a rucksack on her back and was holding a small red plastic plant pot, home to two seedlings.

'Is it alright if I sit here?'

Again, his new companion indicated the seat opposite with a tilt of the head, but this time she waited for his agreement. Placing the plant pot gently on the table, she began to wrestle her rucksack onto the overhead rack. Fergus watched her for a moment too long, such that she had all but secured it by the time he had got to his feet offering help.

'Thanks, that's really kind of you. Think I've got it though. Ought to – shouldn't carry a bag I can't handle on my own, I always say. I pack it, I carry it. But thanks. That was sweet of you, anyway.'

The smile again, but broader now. Fergus was still standing next to her, useless. Another passenger, with a brittle 'Excuse me', pushed past, hurrying along the aisle towards an empty seat.

'I don't know why everyone is in such a rush. They change the train crew here. Going be sat here for a bit yet.'

With that, she slipped off a leather jacket, embellished with padded elbows, and threw it up onto the rack next to her bag. As she slid into the seat, Fergus thought that the jacket, along with her boots, made her look as if she rode a motorbike. But no helmet would comfortably fit over her hair. While it was cropped in closely to about an inch above and behind her ears, the rest was still long and was pulled up into what his mother would call a top knot. This created a sharp V at the nape of her neck, while a short, severe fringe connected the groove above her ears. Inside the V, the top knot was dyed red; not red like copper or carrots or ginger, but red like her lips. She looked up, directly into his eyes, and Fergus felt ashamed. But instead of scowling, she smiled once more, holding his gaze.

'Which side do you want?'

He did not understand her question. She pointed first at the aisle seat and then the one beside the window, her amusement playing on her face.

'I was on the window side, but I don't mind really. Whichever you feel more comfortable in. Your choice.'

The train jolted into life and Fergus grasped the seat back to maintain his poise. The smile rose again, this time for herself. She slid over to the window seat, taking the plant pot with her: the seedlings trembled with the trains gathering speed.

'What are they?'

Fergus was sitting now, nodding towards the red plastic pot.

'Tomatoes. Well, they will be. My mum, she grows all sorts at home. Proper green fingers she's got. Thought I'd try to grow some down in London. You been home for the holidays too?'

Ruby leant in closer as Fergus explained his purpose in travelling south, her eyes flitting over his face as he spoke; wide brown eyes that drew Fergus into ever-more animated explanation. She laughed in pleasure when he said 'butterlump' and grew solemn when he recounted how Miss Carmichael had lost her job in his unwitting service. She asked questions without fear or conceit, prompting him gently to colour the landscape of Hinba for her, so that she might smell the breeze upon the heather.

By the time he asked her how he might get from Euston to Elephant and Castle, had asked whether that was somewhere near where she lived, the evening had encased the world beyond in a slippery darkness, streaked with points of yellow light. Their reflections looked across at them, exaggerated, uncertain.

'Not really. I'm in Stepney. It's convenient for Queen Mary's. Nice too, in an east end kind of way.'

'*Queen Mary's what?*'

Ruby failed to smother her laughter and Fergus's confusion turned to hurt. Her hand rested upon his for a moment, a reassurance, an apology. It was the merest of touches, yet Fergus could weigh the time it lingered, feel the warmth of its arrival and the chill of its departure. Then it was gone, and Ruby was telling her own story as gravity shifted in the approach to Milton Keynes.

— ◉ —

Ruby walked with Fergus up the long ramp from the platform. The wide, bright space of the concourse was filled with people moving under the distant roof in seemingly random agitation. Ruby led him through the crowd with weary assuredness. When they reached the top of a set of stairs descending beneath the concourse floor she stopped.

'*Right then, Fergus. This is the tube. Get yourself a single zone one ticket and take the Northern Line down to Elephant. You'll have to find your own way from there: I'm not a south London sort of person. Remember, the Northern Line. The black one. And it's the Bank Branch you want. That's important. The Bank Branch, southbound. There'll be signs.*'

He counted each instruction into his memory, so that he would not misplace a single piece. The swirling city was too unstable to be without these certainties. Fergus lurched with a sudden giddiness.

'*You're not coming with me? At least as far as the train?*'

'*Sorry, but I take a bus. Goes straight to my door. And it's cheaper. But you'll be fine. Just remember Bank Branch. Southbound.*

Northern Line. And good luck. With everything. I hope you find your butterlump and take it back to your island. It's been really nice to meet you. The journey flew past.'

Ruby gave him a brief embrace, her hand fluttering at his back.

'You too. And thanks for all your help. It's been great. Maybe we'll bump into each other again?'

She was walking away by now, but turned to smile over her shoulder, shouting *'Maybe'* back to him. Then she was gone, out into the darkness of the city, and Fergus felt very alone.

He waited for a break in the flow of people joining the escalator until he realised that there would be no break. He slid in as unobtrusively as he could and was surprised that no-one seemed to take offence, even to notice him. The machine was so clogged with bodies that he had no choice but to stand and wait while he sank beneath the ground.

The ceiling was lower here, although still twice his height, and the crush of people seemed more condensed. Steadily he made his way to the end of the queue for the ticket office and only then did he start to take proper notice of the other passengers. Some moved with purpose, while others meandered, buffeted in the slipstream of those more determined. In the middle of all this convection, a woman and a man shared a fleeting kiss before they peeled apart, their eyes already turned towards their separate lives.

Within a few minutes, Fergus had a single zone one ticket in his hand. Warily he followed the flow of people moving towards the yawning tunnel that sank down and out of sight, into the belly of the city. At the barrier, he slid his ticket into the gate and walked into its jaws.

part three

Here Be Dragons

THE CURSING STONE

twenty-one

It is a small village, but it grows around you. Each element presents itself demurely, keeping itself to itself, never quite coalescing into the whole. You know that this is a village but you do not know how close the war memorial is to the duck pond, or even whether the two stand on the same green triangle. You have a memory of its edges, the boundary seen on the horizon as the fields and roads and streams slipped beneath you, the greens and greys and blues blurring as you sped towards the slender spire that punctured the bright sky. The buds of crisp white cloud hung over you then as they do now, here beside the pale grey stone of the church.

People are milling by the doorway to the church. All are dressed in their finest clothes; some are in uniform, others in top hats, in bonnets, wearing long gloves or jackets or waistcoats. These people, congealing by the porch, are strange to you, known yet unknown. In their murmuring, there is a hint of threat, their lost words a cause for unease.

The memorial service is about to begin and everyone is anxious to be inside the church. There is pushing and the crowd seethes as far as the solemnity of the occasion will allow. For every one that manages to squeeze through the felt-backed door, another two emerge from among the gravestones to join the back of the throng, the congregation growing uncontained.

None of the mourners pay attention to you as you slip ever more tightly among them. In the crush of oblivious bodies, you sense antipathy in them even as they ignore you. You are steered, cajoled, and your escort carries, closes around you, covering the route you have taken.

When the bodies surrounding you withdraw, there is the room. The walls are painted to a grey-beige sheen. In the centre stands a table, a long oval of burnished wood. Around it sit twelve figures. The table is set as for dinner, but there is no food, no crockery, no cutlery, no candelabra, no glassware, no salt, no pepper pots; only black silk napkins, one in each place. You take the one vacant seat, sinking into the pale green upholstery that sucks you down into its voluptuousness.

Facing you across the table, a child lifts its head and stares into you. He is followed by all the others seated around you, and the trial begins. You do not know the charges, and do not understand the process. The voices are gibberish in your ears. You know that you are innocent, but can find no way to make your case; your mouth is tight shut, your hands immobile.

All eyes turn towards one end of the table, where a woman, dressed in dusty lace and crinoline, is speaking. Her ivory gloves reach up to and beyond her elbows, and when she speaks, her mouth widens to reveal her toothless gums. At the other end of the table, a man, round as a ball and wearing a colourful school cap and satin blazer, licks his lips as he watches her. Abruptly, a man dressed in uniform begins a fiery response. The sound that pours from his static open mouth simply rumbles, makes the table quake, and yet his meaning is clear in the absence of words.

The general completes his deposition with a sharp salute. The child facing you bangs his tiny fist on the table and the others scurry from the room. As they leave, they throw their napkins into the air and they swirl and spiral in the disquieted air. Now there is only you and the child, who is covered in the black silk shroud. An oscillating sound rises from under the silk, climbing until it becomes an abrupt shriek. You long to cover your ears to keep out the sound, but your arms do not respond.

And then the charm is broken and the hands that had clasped you to the chair have gone. You are free. Hurriedly, you retrace your steps, but you cannot find the door. Once, then twice, you pass your flat palm across the slickness of the room's enclosure, an anxious circuit of the child draped in black silk that crouches still in the centre of the empty room, shrinking, collapsing, until nothing remains except a dark absence on the ground.

The walls are different now. The stones are rough and haphazardly laid, rising far above you to the sky. Unfamiliar plants, gigantesque, twist through the broken flagstones; gnarled vines and angry rasps. Above you, suspended from a bar raised high above the coping of the garden's walls, are twelve grotesques, dangling at the end of elastic lines. They spring and bounce on their leashes, descending ever nearer to you, their faces venomous and their arms extended, hands hooked into claws, talons; twenty four cruel eyes intent upon you.

One is enclosed within in a silvered bubble, studded with long spikes. His armour makes him heavier that the others and he draws more forcefully on his elastic, coming closer and closer with every extension of the line. His dull shouts and blunt syllables cascade down towards you without direction. Yet you see the needle-point of the spikes seeking out your flesh, anticipate the puncture of you milky skin, the oozing of your life blood. The plants can smell it too and strain at their roots; the walls groan with expectation and crowd in, narrowing around you.

Knowing that you cannot run, you instead float upwards, rising between the agitated bodies churning around you. They come so close that you can smell their breath, feel the whisper of air as they pass within inches of you. You hold your nerve, and continue to rise.

twenty-two

For a time, both worlds merged, the fluid and the concrete, and only slowly did he pull himself from the stew of sleep. From the other world, hands still clamoured for him, holding him down, preventing his flight. At last, sticky slumber peeled away to reveal an unfamiliar room. Numb, he waited for the world to find its focus, simply wondering if he should open the curtains. But elsewhere, the shouting continued and, uncertain of its origins, he was wary of disturbing the uneasy equilibrium, much less of drawing attention to himself. Hesitantly, he reached out of the covers for his watch. The movement unleashed a musty aroma into the air, and he swallowed heavily, his mouth clamped shut.

It was seven twenty. Maybe it was too early, but he no longer wanted to stay in the room. Its strangeness was oddly jarring, and the smell was as unreliable as it was unpleasant. He struggled to place it, knowing only that it was organic in origin and that it was something to do with the bedding within which he was still wrapped. Could something have died in there with him?

The sheets belonged to Jamie's flatmate; the room too. As the last wisps of sleep lifted from him, Fergus climbed from the bed and, naked but for his boxer shorts, stood on the grainy carpet, swaying gently. The shouting stopped abruptly and somewhere in the building a door slammed: the air quivered for a moment while the bricks regained their composure. The stillness brought a fragment of relief but soon wrapped Fergus in chill. He took up his clothes to dress.

There was no living room. His bedroom door gave onto a small, dark corridor from which in turn led four other doors. He knew that the furthest was the front door, through which he had entered the night before, shortly before nine. He had found Mannion House eventually, despite the blank looks of the bored man at the tube station. Without lifting his chin from his hand, he had merely pointed in the direction of a map attached to the station wall, over by the entrance. A howl of traffic had greeted him as he emerged beneath the white towers that he assumed must be the castle after which the place was named, and he had picked his way around the edge of its turbulence. He had passed a looming mass of darkness, a fallen megalith of concrete, a remembrance of some distant faith, before turning from the main thoroughfare and into the narrower streets, quiet and poorly lit.

When he had arrived, Jamie had ushered him into his own room to drop his bag, before suggesting that they pop out for a pint and something to eat. The room had been large and comfortable: Fergus realised now that it had once been intended as a living room. There had been a bed, and an arm chair had faced a tidy desk, on which the screen of an open laptop was filled with an explosion frozen in time.

The door nearest to him was the bathroom, where he had first begun to regret Jamie's unquestioning hospitality as he had brushed his teeth cautiously despite his mild inebriation, unwilling to touch the many greasy surfaces the room contained. Only the final door was mystery. However, it was ajar and no sound came from beyond it. Fergus inhaled and passed through into the kitchen.

The room was less unpleasant than he had imagined. There were dishes still in the sink, but the water was relatively clear. Crumbs besieged the toaster, but the table was not tacky to his touch and he dropped his notebook with confidence. While the kettle boiled, Fergus flicked through his recent entries: four short accounts of troubling dreams, to which he would shortly add a fifth. As he wrote the day's date beneath the last entry, he wondered if he would make it back to Hinba before the end of the week. Even if things went well, it seemed unlikely: between Mannion House and home were two days travelling.

Things did not, in any case, feel as though they would go well. The good fortune he had found in Glasgow would surely not continue; he had no real plan for how he would approach Nicholas Maltravers and had no reason to suppose that he would be a man who would be willing to give up such an expensive prize simply because it was the right thing to do. As the tea turned brick red in his mug, Fergus felt an increasing certainty that his assurance to Shona that he would return before the week's end would become the first promise to her that he would break.

— ◉ —

Jamie did not emerge until a quarter to eleven. The sun had risen far enough to clear the neighbouring block and it cast its light into the kitchen. As Jamie entered, he was caught in its beam.

'*You found the bread. Good. Another cup?*'

He flicked on the kettle and, raising himself slightly on his toes, he scanned the top cupboard for a mug, shuffling mismatched crockery on the shelf.

'No thanks, I ought to be off. Track down this Maltravers feller. I was just waiting on you, as it goes.'

Jamie stopped his search and turned. He grappled for a moment with an appropriate reply, before simply apologising.

'That'll be your rounds. Body clock totally unsuited to normal life. No point going until the afternoon anyhow. He'll be in a better mood after lunch. More amenable.'

He resumed his search and retrieved a brightly coloured mug marked with the logo of some company that Fergus did not recognise. His bare feet crunched through the floor's desiccated detritus to the table. His dressing gown broke open as he sat, revealing a pale torso and striped pyjama bottoms.

'I don't know how you can stay in your bed as long. Have you not got classes or anything?'

He had not grown since Fergus had last seen him. Still a boy, despite his years. His smooth, pink skin, hairless save for the thick pile of curls bursting from his head, had accrued no blemishes in the intervening years, no wear, no gravity. Fergus recalled his friend's unwillingness to take responsibility, either for himself or for others, and their slow separation became entirely explicable as if for the first time.

'No, it's the Easter vacation. Don't have any lectures for another week. That's why Phil isn't here. On that, I got a text: he's coming

back early, so I can only let you stay one more night. Still, if you get this stone sorted out today then that shouldn't be a bother, right?'

Four zeros flashed on the microwave as they had all morning, but with new meaning. Time sank into the vinyl floor, stuck in its gluey waves. The optimism he had felt the previous evening had already been replaced by resignation by the time he awoke, but this blow ended any remaining hopes of a straightforward resolution. He was not superstitious, but without the luxury of more time than he needed, it was inevitable that he would fail. His entire endeavour had been nothing more than an artifice to engineer his fall. He was not superstitious, he repeated. This is nonsense. This is not an omen, there is no pantheon of gods to work this kind of mischief. This was simply an unreliable friend being unreliable. It could be fixed.

'I suppose not. Assuming that Maltravers is reasonable, of course, and there is no guarantee of that – you'll remember what I said about the auctioneer in Glasgow? So, if everything gets messy, could I not just sleep on your floor, once Phil is back?'

The chair creaked under Jamie's weight. He pulled the dressing gown across his body and held it there while he took a swallow of tea.

'Well, no, not really. See, my girlfriend is staying this weekend and, well, you'd be a bit in the way, if you get my meaning... anyhow, I'm sorry, but it was short notice, you know. I hadn't heard from you for years, then a call, last minute, to say you're coming to London and need somewhere to stay. I did my best for you, and two nights is better than nothing, yeah?'

Fergus knew he was right, that he could ask no more of Jamie. They were quits now; the debt, such that it was, had been repaid.

It was a debt that could not survive being named, did not exist if acknowledged. And now it was spent and there was no longer any reason at all for them to see each other again, once another night had passed. And Maltravers might be a reasonable man. All might well be well, after all. And even if it wasn't, then there was probably enough money for a hotel for a night or two. Some cheap place; it would be no less comfortable than Phil's room. If needs be.

'Right, let me get dressed and we'll get you some lunch before you face Maltravers. Won't be long.'

Fergus watched Jamie go, the smile still painted across his face, even as he cursed his wasted morning. When he heard the bathroom door bolted, he stepped gently back to Phil's room to pack his few things and study the A-Z.

twenty-three

The city stood on folds of sluggish clays; myriad rivers gnawed their way through it and beneath it. Buildings rose and fell with irrational rhythms and their fluctuations revealed fleeting glimpses of the city's many faces, until new columns of glass and steel, concrete and stone, arose to conceal and to create once more. The streets pulsed with people and with cars, such that the surface of the earth here seemed to shimmer. It was a transient, unreliable place; unpredictable and capricious. The city creaked and moaned under the weight of its own perpetual motion.

And yet, every block, every building and business, every clutch of neighbours, every chamber and doorway could be pin-pointed in its post code. The city had been mapped rigorously into 199 distinct postal districts and, within them, a further 972 sectors were defined. Within each sector were hundreds of smaller clusters, each designated by two letter combinations that completed the full post code, making for hundreds of thousands of unique variations, each logically classified, identified and mapped. The city was knowable, and the most obscure alleys could be located by anyone who grasped the rudiments of this arcane lore. And yet, the E1 district alone comprised some 26,000 postcodes.

Fergus scrolled through the immensity of the number, humbled and frustrated. Weary, he watched the people milling about the square and allowed the wash of late afternoon sun to seep into his skin while he waited. From his bench against the wall, he had an uninterrupted view of the doorway and of the business of the courtyard. Under a clutch of saplings, a couple of young women sold cakes as people made their way in and out of the library. A statue rose behind the cake stall, a silver ball resting on curved legs and topped with their inverse as wings; Fergus could make no sense of it, and looked away, unnerved.

He had found his way here easily, once he had decided that here was where he should be. He was not yet entirely sure that it was the best decision, but as he had stood outside Maltravers' closed gallery, it had been the best one he could make. There had been no note in the window to explain when the gallery might next be open and it seemed reckless to leave himself only one morning to conclude the matter of the cursing stone, before he found himself without a place to stay in the strange city. What if Mr Maltravers was away for a few days? He would need help, and quite probably somewhere else to stay. Rather than calling his sister or making another attempt at convincing Jamie, he had been surprised to find that his first instinct had been to turn instead to Ruby Adams.

He had neither an address nor even a phone number, much less a postcode. He did, however, know that she was a student at Queen Mary University. As in Glasgow and at South Bank, it would be the Easter vacation. Ruby had said as much on the train. There would, he had reasoned, be no classes. And Ruby was more akin to Mary than to Jamie and would likely be in the library rather than in a bar or in bed.

Fergus had been disappointed when the woman at the counter was unwilling to let him in, to search the library, despite his explanation. Her glance towards the security guard had persuaded him that another attempt to convince her would be fruitless. So he had withdrawn, to the square outside, to sit in the spring sunshine and wait for Mary to leave, as she must surely do, if his assumptions had been correct.

That the sunshine lingered still meant his optimism was more easily sustained. But as his wait nudged passed 45 minutes, the diversion of watching the students pause and pass waned. During his vigil, only two cupcakes had been sold, both to the same young woman. Like the vendors, she wore a scarf over her head and a long plain skirt: they had chatted like friends and Fergus supposed that the sale was one based as much on camaraderie as on market forces.

Soon, he was drifting, becoming lost in labyrinthine thought that led at last to Shona. He should call her later in the evening, if he could find a phone: it had been two days since they had spoken. She would be helping her mother in the kitchen, clearing up the lunchtime things, while her father would be polishing glasses in the bar, ready for the evening session. He thought of her face, assembled her features carefully, piece by piece, and searched for the feelings that she awoke in him. Slowly they rose and raced through him and he settled into contented reassurance. He imagined her thinking of him as she wiped clean the counter, and pictured their thoughts of each other rush across the great distance between them and entwine. Their conversation played out in his imagination as though the sounds resonated on real air, as though her declarations were the autonomous signals of her true feelings, not projections of his own longing. Her joy at his eventual return he experienced viscerally.

He smothered his smile, suddenly conscious that he was grinning like a fool; he could not be sure that he had not been talking to himself. Self-consciously he scanned the faces of the people that still circulated in the red brick square, looking for any sign that they had witnessed his embarrassment. But no-one paid him any regard, almost as if he were invisible. Unnoticed, like Duncannon. Duncannon on the beach. Through his shirt, his fingers searched for the pendant that hung around his neck and absently traced its outline. In Glasgow, before boarding the train, he had asked Mary what she thought it might mean. She had turned the trinket in her fingers with the same incomprehension as had he. But while he had speculated as to how Duncannon had come into possession of something belonging to his grandfather, Mary had been puzzled as to who might have been gifted with her grandmother's affection in that way. The two questions returned to him now, blending into a larger conundrum. Suppose that the pendant had not belonged to his grandfather, but to another; suppose that his beloved, saintly grandmother had become embroiled in some sordid liaison: even if such a thing were true, the mystery of how Duncannon could have come by the piece remained. Fergus wanted so fervently to believe that his friend was not a thief, and yet it seemed unlikely that he could have found it lying on the beach. The only other possibility, that the love token had been meant for Duncannon, was scarcely believable. Moreover, even if Duncannon were a thief, or an unlikely lover, none of that explained why he had presented Fergus with its proof.

'I thought it was you. You gave me a right fright - are you stalking me or something?'

The sun had dipped behind the building across the square and, while dusk was still some little time distant, the women under the tree were packing their cakes into Tupperware tubs. Somewhere,

Fergus had lost the best part of an hour and, had Ruby not spotted him, it would all have been in vain: she would have slipped unseen into the swirl of the city. Fergus touched the pendant once more, to thank his grandmother for her watchfulness.

'Me? No, I was just passing, you know? Bit of a coincidence, really. Fate, maybe.'

His relief at finding her, his pleasure at the sound of her voice, the sight of her welcoming smile, washed through Fergus and he winked as he finished speaking. She laughed, and her laughter emboldened him. He stood to level the terrain.

'Honestly? I was looking for you. And I didn't know how else to find you. So I've been waiting here a couple of hours, hoping you might pass. Knew you would. Something told me.'

'Well, that's very clever of you. A bit creepy, but clever all the same. Anyhow, you've found me now. What's up?'

Ruby settled on the bench next to Fergus. His story fell out of him with ease, and he related all that had happened with a fluidity he had not expected. All the while, Ruby watched him attentively, her body turned in to face him, her right leg hooked under her left knee, her right elbow over the back of the seat, her hand cupping her face. The ripples of her steady breath reached out across the space between them. Somewhere on campus, a clock struck five times and he paused to soak up the bell's warm tones. The square was largely empty now and the remnants of the fifth chime lingered in the stones.

When the air had cleared, Fergus tried to continue, but his fluency was spent, and there was only Ruby's breathing and his discomfort left. He had set out the situation objectively, but could not ask, with cool blood, the question that his circumstances necessarily required. His hands sought to mould his words, like kelp in a languid sea. He could no longer look into her face and so instead watched no-one leave or enter the library.

'Look, if you want to stay with us, you only have to ask. We've got plenty of room, if you don't mind a sofa. It's not a problem, really. No need to stress about it.'

Her right hand balled into a loose fist and bumped gently against his shoulder, and there was her smile, her eyes bright and round, a little laugh to fill the silence he had left. His pride mended quickly with his relief and soon he was thanking her as well as he might with dignity intact. The matter of the cursing stone and the elusive Mr Maltravers still remained, and while Fergus had neglected it in his anxiety about where he might sleep, it was this that most concerned Ruby. Even if he could be found, a more sophisticated approach would be needed if the collector were to accede to the demand for the return of the stone.

Wordlessly, Ruby unhooked her leg and stretched it back into life before trusting it with her weight. She reclaimed her back pack from the bench and, at her command, Fergus rose yet more easily than the straining bag. He followed her without question, feeling the texture of dependence wrapped around him like a blanket, his fate entrusted to this strange woman.

She led him from the square and deeper into the campus; he no longer knew which way was north, nor the meaning of the signs that marked the way. The weightlessness of his ignorance made him giddy, and he felt a spiral of effervescence run up through his spine: for this moment, everything no longer depended upon him.

While he watched Ruby unchain her bike, he imagined himself walking behind his grandfather and Mr Robertson across the island's moors, where rolling grass and heather rippled out to the open seas and the rabbits wormed their way into the heart of the earth; he thought about the sunshine on his face and the sweet June winds; about the time before he had been sent to Mallaig, when the island was his and open and light, and whatever worries he had were left each afternoon in the classroom with Mr Galbraith. But now Galbraith, and even his grandfather, had tied him to the cursing stone and its weight fell upon his neck.

'It's the old Jewish cemetery. What's left of it, anyway. You're probably standing on some of the rest of it. I guess in time, when everyone has forgotten about the people here, when no-one cares, they'll build on it.'

Ruby's bike had been chained to a rail beside a wide gravel expanse between awkward buildings made of metal, brick and glass; the space was littered with grave stones and tombs. The rows of low, flat, grey stones stretched away from them. Fergus wanted to count them, but the graves became lost among the greyness of the gravel, a confusion of dead stone. That some had significance, while others did not, seemed remarkably arbitrary. He imagined the cursing stone lost somewhere in the expanse, and the weight of his duty returned.

'Pub? We need a plan of action and I think a pint might help.'

twenty-four

With each gust, the wind scooped up the noise of the traffic and stirred it into the tops of the trees. Their branches were already vivid with new growth, their leaves still bright with innocence, and the daffodils that gathered around them in the park nodded with delight, safe behind their bars from the fevered motion of the street. Buses and taxis bustled in the road, while the pavements throbbed with the incomprehensible dance of rush hour. People scurried in every direction, but a few minutes of observation revealed that they moved with detached purpose, as if on tracks that brought them close to each other but guarded them from collision.

The blur of faces, and the constant shuffling out of and into the way of harried commuters, meant that Fergus could learn little of the people with whom he shared the morning. Among the movement, however, a handful simply stood, like him, conspicuous in their immobility: they handed out newspapers, or checked their phones; others expectantly scanned the faces of the crowd around them. A young woman, pretty, in a blue skirt and glinting heels, stood near the entrance of the Tube station, her anxious eyes flitting between the people emerging from underground to her watch to the street;

every so often, knees together, she would bounce rapidly on her toes, her face twisting into an almost tearful terror.

In those places where there were benches, each was occupied by a solitary person: a woman smoking, her face distant and calm amid the proximate chaos; a man, his arms folded across his prodigious belly, watched the passers-by with disdain; another man struggled to keep the contents of a burger between failing pieces of bread as he forced great mouthfuls into himself, greedily, hungrily. Fergus wondered if he should take up one of the vacant seats while he waited, but each occupant created distinct disincentives. Instead he checked his watch, already knowing that he was still early, and shuffled from foot to foot.

He wanted to go back into the park, of course, but he feared that he would miss Ruby when she arrived. He wasn't sure from which direction she would appear in any case, only that she would not come from the Tube station. When he had suggested to Jamie that he would walk, his friend had been horrified, as if he had suggested something unimaginable, much as he had greeted the news of the time at which Fergus intended to depart. He had not thought to tell his friend that he would be staying in London, and as they shook hands at Jamie's bedroom door he knew that they would not see each other again; their long estrangement now a thing of permanence.

Instead of the sixty minutes that Jamie had insisted such a journey would take on foot, he had needed fewer than forty, including the time spent marvelling at the view from Westminster Bridge. The parks had been his favourite part of the journey, more so even than the sweep of the river and the grandeur of the buildings. He had paused beside a small lake to watch the pelicans stretch the morning light into their wings. There, in the shadow of palaces, a ramshackle man, encased in a greasy anorak despite the spring sunshine, was eating a breakfast of tiny biscuits pulled from their packet. As Fergus passed him, he dropped a couple of the biscuits onto the ground and crushed them carefully under his slack-jawed boot, leaving small mounds of crumbs; he then wafted his hand in welcome to the curious pigeons. Hunger and fear led them to approach with caution, hobbling on their malformed feet. One wary eye was turned to the man, the other devoured the crumbs in anticipation. The man grinned and coaxed them onwards in a surprisingly gentle voice. As the birds ate, he admired his work, washing himself in the company of other living things. Their combined vitality was comforting: Fergus had dreamed of ghosts and, unusually, he had been unable to contain them in his notebook that morning; they had pursued him from his bed and into the street, where they wandered freely, aimless, through his daytime thoughts.

Ruby's touch upon his shoulder startled him more than it should and he turned a little too quickly, his haunted eyes not yet calmed before she faced him. Claiming tiredness, he accepted her embrace awkwardly, her reassurances unconvincingly.

Slinking through the narrow streets, Fergus led Ruby towards the gallery on Half Moon Street. Neither spoke, and Fergus's only thoughts were to wonder at what might be in Ruby's mind. In the canal-side pub the evening before, they had postulated, over the noise of the bar, about how they might approach Maltravers. Despite two pints, there had been no inspiration: he found no advance on the simple idea of challenging the man to return the stolen stone, while Ruby tried vainly to escape the conclusion that it was a hopeless errand. By the time Fergus had accepted that he should allow Ruby to return to her planned evening, it had been nine thirty and their only plan was to meet at Green Park station in twelve hours and then to see what transpired. He watched Ruby ride away along the tow path, and headed to the tube, to return to Jamie's flat at Elephant and Castle to pack his few things and dream.

They reached Half Moon Street, where the day before Fergus had found only darkened windows and a locked door. The sun had not yet cleared the buildings to the east and the roadway and houses that lined it remained in shadow: it was already clear that no light was lit in the window of the gallery. Undeterred Ruby rattled the door in its hinges, while Fergus pressed his face to the glass. He dropped his holdall to the stone flags so that he could cup his hands to get a better view inside. The sparse interior housed a few cabinets, and the walls carried a number of paintings, but there was much less clutter than at McAteer's. There was no sign of movement, nor that any was imminent. Perhaps the trail had gone cold after all.

Peeling his face from the glass, he found himself alone in the street. After the frenetic adjacency of only a few minutes earlier, his isolation unnerved him; then Ruby's absence washed through him, the confusion replaced by concern almost immediately. Maybe she had found a way inside, had shaken the lock loose with her obstinacy? But the door looked as firm as it had always been. Perhaps, her assistance had been a joke, a trick, a raising of his hopes simply to watch them crumble. He scanned the nearby doorways to see if he could glimpse her, sniggering. Or perhaps she had simply had second thoughts, decided that she did not want to help, did not want to have him stay on her sofa, disrupt her remaining days of leisure. Forlorn, he peered once more through the window.

'You won't see anything.'

Her voice was as if nothing had happened, but her face wore a new self-satisfaction; her short, dense eyebrows hovered as she waited for him to provide her cue.

'Where did you disappear to then?'

Her head twitched backwards to indicate the dry cleaner's shop behind her. Fergus followed the trajectory with his eyes, but had still not caught up. His bewilderment was too obviously entertaining and Ruby curtailed her game.

'The guy. In there. He told me that it's appointment only. He was surprised that we didn't know that, seeing as how we're clients of Mr Maltravers. Don't worry: I've got a number. When would sir like to make an appointment?'

His astonishment was struck numb onto his face. After all the difficulty and cost that had been expended in Glasgow to acquire no more than his name and yet Ruby had simply walked into a neighbouring shop and left with his phone number. The secrets of this man that was hidden even on the internet fell open to her. He speculated on what his new friend's capabilities might be.

'How did you manage that?'

Ruby just smiled, her nose wrinkling slightly.

'Well, let's just say I have my methods. Now, if my work here is done, how about we go look at stuff in shops we can't afford?'

She led him back towards the church, sunlight now bouncing from the white stone. They rounded the corner and they also were bathed in its rays. Ruby's hair was aflame, burning red like a torch. She was still smiling, still beyond any questions he might ask.

Ruby pulled back sharply on his arm as he stepped off the kerb. As the car flew past, scything through the space where he would have been had she not intervened, Ruby stared wide-eyed, horrified, incredulous at Fergus, her head shaking slowly. Then the tension broke with a snort. Ruby's laughter was infectious, and Fergus could only giggle with weak indignation.

'We do have cars where I come from, you know?'

Except they didn't. Hinba was home only to a couple of quad bikes and a tractor: the sound of internal combustion was, for the most part, the product of marine diesel and could be heard for miles. There had been a car once, but then MacLeod's old Mercedes had been dragged off to Duncannon's barn, to be dismembered and used for who knew what alchemy. Even before that, the car had stood immobile outside the Bell for three years, until the sea air and winter squalls did for it. The rust had steadily eaten under the paintwork, gluing its gears and other moving parts, so that the awkward carcass would no longer move of its own volition. Even before that, the car had only moved on a handful of occasions: a couple of tours of the harbour-side, and two trips to the mainland.

Despite its immobility, Shona had loved to sit in the back seat of the car and watch, aloof, demur, while the world whirred by to its own rhythm; sometimes she would ask Fergus to sit behind the wheel and take instruction as if he were her driver, and he would comply willingly, happy only to be with her, to complete her game.

Ruby took his hand and led him safely across the road, into a warren of tight alleys and streets bounded by narrow-fronted houses. Beside him, she bounced slightly with each step and, when they burst once more into a broad and handsome street, the brilliant red of her top-knot quivered and shimmered in the returned sunlight.

twenty-five

For all she hated Mayfair, she had to admit that its streets were much more pleasant than Stepney, or even than Preston. As they crossed Berkley Square, the thought of nightingales insistent, she realised that she had never walked through the neighbourhood at any point during her four years in the city. Often she had circumnavigated it, by bus or on foot, but had seldom ventured onto its streets. The buildings and plane trees were much as those around Gower Street, where she had reluctantly discovered London's grandeur as a cocksure student, but here they were more assured, sumptuous. The sunshine lit the greening tree tips as if they were properties on a film set; the blackened bricks of the townhouses bore no resemblance to the stains of industry that discoloured the terraces at home. The place was not simply a square on a board game, but it still felt like somewhere too expensive to linger.

Her mother would understand, even if her housemates would not. Perhaps that was why she had not told them the night before that they were to have a houseguest. Bridget had been out until late, rushing for the door as soon as Ruby had returned, running for the bus, her record bag over her shoulder. There had been no time to tell her, but Matt and Jacob had been in, had eaten with her, had watched the television, described their days, asked after hers, and she had not mentioned Fergus once. They would have taken it in their stride, of course, used to Ruby's lost causes. At least that was what she hoped, what she was relying upon.

But her mother would throw herself gladly in with her daughter's lost cause, would sense the adventure it contained, just as she did. Since her father left them, her mother had encouraged her to explore, always to explore; through those last difficult months of primary school and through the defiant time at secondary school. Always books and learning and escape. University had been the way out of Preston, just as it had been for her mother. Only she had stumbled back there, for love and for the want of other ideas beyond a vague notion of healing the planet. So when Ruby graduated, she had not returned, had left her mother and Alex in Preston, one willingly, the other resistant, and she had conducted the two relationships through train rides and telephones and emails while she embarked on her Ph.D., pursuing her own route to heal the world.

She had been seeing Alex since she was sixteen. Much of the fire had died since they had passed their exams and headed off to their new cities to study and plan. In her heart, Ruby knew that Alex's plan had been their reunion in Lancashire, or Manchester, or anywhere but London; but she had pretended it had not been understood. Another year of long-distance love, while Ruby read books about Cambodian genocide and the slow rebuilding of an ancient society, and Alex tried his best to understand, bound together through history and commitments made in the ever-dimmer past.

'Your hair looks really red in this light.'

They had found themselves among the glossy shops of South Moulton Street, the sun arcing its way towards its zenith, casting its glow along the street. There were no cars here and the two of them ambled carelessly. Ruby had paused to glance in the window of a shoe shop and, seeing nothing that caught her eye, had turned to see Fergus a view paces ahead.

'What? You're one to talk!'

'Well, yeah, but mine comes from a bottle. You're proper ginger.'

It was not a thing that Ruby would say in normal times. The red-headed boy at her school had been teased without mercy. Ruby would make it her business to take his tormentors to one side and explain the genetic composition of the complexion, its scarcity. By the time she had explained that the Viking's fierce thunder god had had red hair, they had invariably become bored and wandered off in search of other distractions. Perhaps that memory had led her to adopt Fergus as a cause.

'No, not ginger. Mr Robertson, my granddad's friend, now he was what goes for ginger on Hinba. Me, I'm what my mam calls copper. My fiancée, she says it's like warm honey, but I guess that's just her being poetic and so.'

The news that there was a fiancée broke the steady pattern of her breathing. It was quickly recovered, unseen, and Ruby stored the niggling puzzle it provoked for later. Instead, she apologised, even though she had caused no offence, and asked if he was ready for a cup of tea. Fergus had had no breakfast once again and eagerly accepted the offer.

'Righto, there's a place just up here. After that, I'll introduce you to

Selfridges, then we can get a bus back east, get you settled in, make some plans.'

Later, she would call the number on the business card that the man in the dry cleaning shop had handed her. She would endure the sound of condescension and let the pampered young woman, who had never had to work for anything, arrange a meeting for the following Tuesday morning at the shop. The young woman would not call it a shop and so Ruby would delight in shaping the word in her mouth and hurling it at her in confirmation of the appointment.

twenty-six

Grey light suffuses the street, blurs its low walls and shallow spaces, the houses that stand beyond them, continuous, opaque. Through the drabness, you glide smoothly, passing each gateway in turn until at last you reach the one that you know to be home. It has been so long since you have seen it, and a thick gloom shrouds it so that you can barely recognise it. But your memories are awakened, fuzzy like the sky, by the black lacquer of the metal gate and the cracked paved path leading to a bright red door beneath its white-rendered arch and you know, without seeing, that this is home.

Yet the windows are blank, closed, shuttered, sheaved, stopped up like dead eyes. The door does not respond to the gentle press of your hand, or the rapping of your fist. There is no light, no movement, within. The still shadows remain lifeless, dappled through the window's distortion. A voice behind you. A woman, her hair white and her face of crinkled alabaster, bloodless lips. You recognise her as your old neighbour, left to watch over your home in your absence. You have been absent for such a long time, and she is grateful at last to return to you your key.

Its heaviness lies in your palm as you pass through the opening door and into the empty hallway. The air is dead. No-one is left. The old woman, too, has gone, vanished into the closing gloom outside. In turn you pass through empty rooms, each cold and lifeless; the colour drained from carpets and curtains, pictures still hanging where you left them on the wall. Despite the comfort of familiar things, the fading light outside and the stillness within disturbs you, makes you fearful, anxious. You return to the hallway and lock and bolt the door against intruders, usurpers, then begin again your tour, securing each window in every room.

Your circuit takes you back to rooms you have already visited and, with growing unease, you find things moved, broken or dirtied. Windows that you have only recently fastened are once more unlocked. In the dining room, you find a pile of chicken bones, neatly stack beneath the table; in a bedroom, the sheets are ruffled, creased, still warm to the touch; in the hallway the locked door stands open, swinging on its hinges. With desperate urgency, you repeat your tour, closing tight all that you can, watching for signs that others might be inside, hiding or hidden.

Night falls in a hurry and the house is dark now. So very dark. And the noises begin. There should be no-one in the house, you tell yourself, since everything has been locked up. It is simply your imagination. You are lost to foreboding, irrational fears, the clamour of night terrors. The darkness beyond is such that you cannot see anything beyond the window glass; your faint reflection, indistinct, surprises you. There should be no light inside; you have lit no lamp. And yet light crawls up the stairs, riding on the indisputable noise, the sound of muffled voices, rising from the kitchen.

You creep to the stair head and see light oozing under the kitchen door. You can hear voices and clanking and the shuffling of feet. Already you are in the hallway, caught between the kitchen and the front door, between danger and safety. But you do not know which is which: the voices in the kitchen might be your family, your mother making dinner, talking over the day with your father, or they might belong to thieves and villains; outside, you might find the kind old woman who has been watching over you, or you might fall prey to wraiths and harpies.

Within an instant of willing it, you burst through the kitchen door. The four men, lost in thick red hair and beards, are making food at the stove, setting the table, slicing through meat, glossy and slick, near the sink. They look around, surprised but weary, then angry. They shout at you in a language you can no longer understand. They wave their arms and spit imprecations at you in a thick and angular tongue. One picks up the kitchen knife from beside the sink and plants it cleanly in your chest, puncturing your heart, its point coming to rest against your spine. You can feel it scratching there, can feel the blood pumping in hot waves out of the hole in your chest and from your mouth. Oceans of blood, seeping out of you, and you are on your back on the kitchen floor, dead.

The men have gone and it is daylight, and you can see your corpse more clearly, prostrate on the lino. The woman from next door is discovering your body, stepping gingerly in the pool of thick black blood that is congealing, cold, around you. The woman is screaming, silent, and it is simply cold, the empty damp coldness of death, noiseless and distant.

twenty-seven

There was a cat: black and imperious, blacker than the mouth of hell. It sat on one of the arm chairs, facing the sofa where Fergus lay. Although seemingly unimpressed by the interloper, it kept its half-closed eyes fixed upon him. The day had come suddenly to Fergus, as if he were anxious to be free of sleep. The jolt of his awakening stirred the cat too, and it slipped from its place and padded across the floor towards the sofa. Fergus could see now that the cat was not entirely black, its feet stained white, as if it had been dipped in milk. His eyes gradually assembled the impression of its slinking approach, such that by the time the animal had leapt up onto his chest, he was at least prepared for its landing.

Fergus was not a great friend of cats. He had never had a pet of any kind, but all the same he could understand why someone would keep a dog. Yet a cat seemed pointless. He thought of the farm dogs on the island, their energy, intelligence and loyalty. Often he would see them on his walks, never far from their owner, always industrious.

There were no cats on the island, not since old Mrs Muir's ratter had disappeared one night a few years before. There had been a storm and Mrs Muir had not been able to call the cat in: off chasing mice or what have you. In the morning, Jerimiah had still not returned, nor the next morning. Mrs Muir's son had been despatched, and he in turn had recruited the island's young people, including Fergus, to hunt out the errant cat. But there had been no trace. Jerimiah had vanished into thin air. For a few nights, his fate was the topic of distasteful speculation in the Bell, but soon he was forgotten, never to be replaced.

The cat stood on Fergus's chest, its four white feet planted close together at its centre. A rumbling rose from it, greater than its size would suggest, and the front paws began to paddle at him, kneading his flesh. He could feel its claws drop and press into his skin, cutting through the thin blanket under which he had slept.

'I see you've met Boots?'

Ruby was holding out a cup of tea for him. She was smiling, happy to be among her own things, in her right place. The cat leapt from Fergus and trotted back to his arm chair, glaring at Fergus with a contemptuous superiority.

Ruby had moved across the room and was kneeling in front of the cat's armchair, clutching his furry cheeks, one in each hand and stroking him under the jaw. Her forehead was almost touching the animal's head as she cooed nonsense at him. Fergus could hear the purring from across the room, and felt faintly uncomfortable. He looked anywhere else around the room and tried to think of something to say, to distract him from the purring. Thinking of nothing, he scrambled instead for his things, uncovering a large picture book on Cambodian religious art, and rummaged through his bag until he found his notebook. Ruby looked up from her cat, intrigued by the scuffed yellow cover, the way the pages broke almost unaided, the supple paper stretch out ready for Fergus's pen. He felt her gaze.

'I write down my dreams. Every morning. Have done since I was thirteen. It's a bit of a ritual, I suppose. Keeps things in the right place, one side or the other.'

He was glad that she asked no questions, even more so when she excused herself, leaving him to his writing. He heard the shower stutter into life, and listened for other noises above the scratching of his pen.

— ◉ —

By the time Ruby returned, he had completed his notes and, dressed in yesterday's clothes, stood at the window, looking out on the grey ghosts of Stepney Green. The blue skies had gone, leaving a thin mist hanging in the chill air of morning. Ruby's house looked out onto a green, fringed with mature trees; between their still-bare branches, he could make out a small grey church; the grave stones that surrounded it, like the church itself, were licked by sheets of mist drifting on the rising air, such that they appeared more or less solid with every glance. Beyond the church, Fergus could see nothing: none of the city or the tower blocks and slabs of buildings that had crowded his walk from the bus stop the previous afternoon.

'It's really foggy out.'

Fergus grunted in response. It was just a morning mist but he was too content to contradict her, enjoying the comfort of the soft solidity of the sky taking the city away, leaving only ambiguity, and the possibility of being elsewhere. The greyness stirred memories of the weight of the fogs that wrapped around Hinba in the late autumn.

'Did Bridget disturb you last night, by the way? She always winds down in the kitchen for a bit when she's finished working. Gets herself something to eat, a cup of camomile, that sort of thing. I left a note for her. Hope she didn't clatter about too much.'

'No, it's fine. I slept straight through. What does she do 'til that time, anyway?'

Fergus had left the mist behind and returned to the sofa. His bedding was rolled into a neat bundle at one end, and he moved this to the floor, under the arm, so that Ruby could sit with him. The cat still occupied the arm chair.

'She's a DJ. Well, that's what she does at the weekends. Rest of the time she works in HR at a law firm in the City. Commercial property, I think. You'll meet her soon – she'll be up in a bit. Needs very little sleep, fortunately.'

Fergus had met the other two housemates the previous evening, but Bridget had already been gone. Jacob had been there when they had arrived, tapping numbers into a laptop computer at the kitchen table, projecting his expected earnings for the next three months, a hopeful, disappointed look on his face; he had gladly curtailed the task to join Ruby in cooking, and they had been eating when Matt appeared, cloaked in the gentle glow of mild inebriation and lycra. Both had asked endless questions about the island and his reasons for coming to the city, and Fergus had held court, happily answering them all, while Ruby shone with satisfaction. But Bridget had not appeared, not even when the wine was done and the four of them slunk off to their beds around midnight.

'But doesn't she have a child?'

He had also asked about each of the housemates and this one fact in particular stood out in his memory. It had seemed odd then, that a child should be raised in this household, but it was odder now that he understood the implications of being a DJ.

'Yeah, but his dad has him on alternate Fridays and Saturdays. Which is great, mind you. There aren't many men of Steve's age who would give up their weekends like that. Even if he was a twat to Bridge. Want some toast?'

The kitchen was as they had left it, save for a saucepan on the stove and, on the table, a plate streaked with orange, the dried remains of baked bean sauce. A spoon pointed to the sink. While the toast cooked and the kettle boiled, Ruby swept the remnants of Bridget from the room and pulled the blind, revealing a small garden, dense with rich greens under heavy dew. The sound of the chair scraping on the tiles made her turn with a start. With her hair down, it looked like any other hair. Except for the colour.

'So what do you want to do? Until Tuesday? I've got stuff I need to do, I'm afraid, so I can't babysit you the whole time.'

She was leaning on the counter by the toaster, the tea cups and the plate. A knife see-sawed on her finger but her eyes were fixed on him, waiting for reassurance that he was not going to be a burden, would prove to be as curious and independent as his adventure had promised.

'Don't know. Since I'm here I might as well see the sights. Plus, I've got to work out a better way of approaching Tuesday. As you say, I can't just turn up and say 'Give me back that wee stone'.'

Ruby had put down the knife and, retrieving a wrap of tobacco from the window sill, was rolling a cigarette. It was the thing that most troubled him about her, but he liked to watch her nimble fingers working the paper, the tip of her pink tongue slide along the edge to close it. If she only did that, not actually light the thing, he would be content with the habit. She moved to the back door, unlatched it and stood half in, half out of the kitchen while she lit the cigarette from a book of matches. The first exhalation was pushed out into the mist with something that sounded like a purr.

'Well, you could say that you're a journalist, doing a piece on the theft of antiquities… god, no, that's stupid, it'll put his guard right up. You'll be escorted from the premises before you can say 'Stupid suggestion.' Sorry.'

The toast popped and, with a shrug, Ruby turned to attend to its buttering. He was not a good liar, but even if he were there did not appear to be a good lie to tell. It would, in fact, have been both simpler and more effective to simply call the police in Mallaig, despite Mr MacLeod's protestations, and let them deal with the theft, if theft was what it was. The longer he had been away from home, the more the disappearance of the stone appeared to be a simple business transaction: there was little legitimate claim he could make to Maltravers, unless he was overlooking something glaringly obvious or spectacularly clever.

'Can you put a slice in for me, love? Christ, what time is it? Feels late and I'm not even dressed.'

Fergus wondered if he should turn to greet the new arrival. He had not heard her enter the kitchen, but assumed that Bridget was standing behind him.

'You must be Ruby's mysterious new man. Hi, I'm Bridget. Sorry I missed you last night. Hope I didn't wake you when I got back. I tried. Honest, Rube, I tried.'

Grateful for the invitation, Fergus twisted in his seat to acknowledge the greeting. He was surprised to find that his eyes were practically level with hers, even though she was standing. Dark eyebrows arched beneath a ruffle of cropped bleached hair. He had to resist the urge to stare too long at the tattoo that peeked above the low, stretched neck of her faded t-shirt; more tattoos, three small stars, were visible at her left wrist when she reached for the mug offered her by Ruby. But most striking of all was a thin red scar that ran horizontally across her throat, about five centimetres in length. Her voice was infused with tobacco smoke and late nights; it had the timbre of a fine rasp on pinewood. Fergus was captivated by her wantonness.

'Does he speak? Or just stare?'

Bridget had given up on Fergus and crossed the room to join Ruby and the toaster. Her loose, blue-striped pyjama bottoms, much like his own at home, disappeared into knitted boots, slippers patterned with Nordic figures and designs. Only Ruby's raised eyebrows and disapproving stare brought him back to himself, reminded him of his manners.

'Sorry. You just startled me. Sorry. Didn't mean to… Sorry. Anyhow, I'm Fergus. Pleased to meet you.'

Fergus was standing, hand extended in greeting. Bridget looked from him to Ruby and back again at the hand, before exploding, doubling, in laughter.

'Fucking hell, Rube. Really?'

He let his hand fall to his side, ashamed, confused, angry. Bridget watched, waited, but soon became bored, turning to the toaster, prodding the slice of bread cooking there with her extended finger, as if she could accelerate the process. Fergus ran through all the things he could say, tested how far they would reassert himself as someone that did not deserve to be laughed at by strangers. Nothing came to mind, each phrase, explanation, challenge or apology only serving to deepen his ridiculousness, so he remained silent, aware that that too made him ridiculous. For the sake of doing something, he sat down once more.

Ruby, smiling, brought him a plate of buttered toast and sat beside him.

'Don't be such a dick, Bridget. I know you're not used to blokes with manners, but no need to make a show of yourself. Anyhow, it's not like that. Fergus is a friend. Needs a place to stay. I'm just helping him out.'

With a wink, Bridget disappeared back into the hallway, toast between her teeth.

twenty-eight

The dragon stared down from its perch, implacable. Its tongue snaked like blood between silvered teeth; a talon raised in warning, guarding the gateway to the City. Fergus lingered a while on the Aldgate traffic island to watch it, to fix its iron-cold eyes with his. The lights changed and he resumed his walk, the buildings rising and closing about him.

The hour since leaving Ruby's house had slipped seamlessly from pastoral quietude to grinding anxiety. The trees and grass and cobbles of Stepney Green had vanished with the leaving of Hayfield Passage, the funnel mouth disgorging him onto the Mile End Road. Traffic roared alongside him as he'd walked westwards, the pavements filling with people bundling in and out of shops and cafes. Soon even the trees that lined the streaming road thinned, replaced by the stalls of a street market. The air was thick with rare smells; unrecognisable products cluttered table tops and paving stones, some under canopies of colourful plastic sheeting.

It seemed to him that no-one in this vast city came from here. More than just those who looked different or who spoke in foreign languages, everyone he had met came from somewhere else. Jamie of course, but even Ruby talked about going home to a place in which she did not live. It was as if this vast, teeming city was a hollowness, an absence filled with the misplaced peoples of the world. If one night everyone was called to return to their grandfather's hearth, as he was destined to do, he wondered how many would remain, what those few would do in all the emptiness.

Ruby had suggested that he start his sightseeing in the City, that he spend the morning roaming its streets and alleys so that she could do some work, catch up with things that needed to be caught; they would meet later for lunch and complete his tour in the afternoon. She had told him which bus to catch but he had decided to walk, to feel the sticky pavement passing beneath him. He knew already that it was only the masking of the horizon behind concrete and stone that made distance here an obstacle.

At Whitechapel, the engorged towers of the City had shaken off the thickest of the morning's mist, and sunlight pierced the greyness, its point almost grazing the pavement. By the time he had passed the iron dragon marking the division between the grimy east and the citadel, shafts of grey brightness were breaking between the tall buildings as the morning sun burnt off the last of the mist; shreds of grey clung to the shoulders of the towers, ghost flags slowly flapping in the convections of air-vents and warming concrete.

Fergus had no idea where he should head; where the sights were to be seen. He knew only that he was to be at the cathedral for one. At St. Botolph's church, he left the swirling traffic behind and journeyed into the lanes and passes, where there were few people to be found; the buildings instead crowded in and over him from all directions. Everywhere was height, constraint.

On every corner, it seemed, gaping holes appeared in the earth, concrete stumps and twisted steels clinging to the jagged edges of muddy gashes, as if the buildings they had previously anchored had been torn from their roots and carried off by giants. Behind painted boards, new leviathans rose, concrete piles pulled up by cranes. Fergus paused at one to read a sign posted on the hoarding of the site: *'We have achieved 27 working days without a reportable incident'*. The '27' was in movable type, and Fergus presumed that it was someone's job to update the tally each morning. He looked at the building rising above him. The site had plainly been here for longer than a month and Fergus found himself wondering what had happened 28 days before.

Two construction workers walked past, dressed in grubby white hard hats and still grubbier yellow jerkins, jersey jogging bottoms and oversized boots. Fergus could not decipher their conversation, but the unfamiliar language blurred in any case into the hum and clank of the day. One drank coffee from a cardboard carton, the other a can of ready-mixed gin and tonic. Fergus looked at his watch - it was ten past nine - and back again at the sign, at the '27', then at the two men who were finishing their cigarettes beside the site entrance. While they smoked, others brought tall and slender gas cylinders out from the hoarding and loaded them onto a waiting truck, bearing the name BOC. One of the carriers looked up and caught Fergus by the eye. They were entwined momentarily, as if held in a suspended city, suddenly silent and still, before Fergus fell back, embarrassed, into the noise and movement of the street.

If the threat of death, however small, hung in the closed air of the city, so too did the pulsing heat of life. It was a mortal city, a visceral city. The winds on Hinba could make it seem as though the islanders were clinging to the rock for dear life; and in the spring when light and greenery burst onto the island, in was a place of fecundity. But death and life came from elsewhere, and the island was simply a refuge from one and the site of the other. Here, the city itself was death and it was life. The buildings throbbed with hissing whines, warm air escaping from their gills onto the street.

Past Bank and along Cheapside, the hard stones of the pavement almost fizzed, and indeed sometimes shook. Women in tailored skirts bustled by, clutching mobile phones to their ears, their incongruous trainers flashing garish in the morning light. The walls of the street were lined with inscrutable stone facades, ridged with the harsh rhythm of windows, or immense glassy behemoths that sat hunched, seemingly dropped into the city from another world entirely. Some of these were vast constructions: almost cities in themselves, almost big enough in which to lose the whole of his island.

— ◉ —

In the shadow of St Paul's dome, Fergus sat among the grave stones. He had some time yet, and the quiet of the churchyard, nestled under trees, was more welcoming than the steps of the cathedral, where it seemed that hundreds of others had also arranged to meet. Although relatively secluded, he was not entirely alone: on a neighbouring bench, a very fat man sat staring straight ahead, lost. He wore a black suit and black shirt, which did nothing to mask the ball of his stomach; his only movement was to bring a fat cigar to his mouth and back to his knee like waves on a beach. More active, a round-faced Japanese woman, in her early 20s, wearing optimistic hot-pants and big sunglasses, strolled in circles beneath a statue's plinth; she was dictating something unintelligible into her phone and held the pink-cased apparatus in front of her, like a saucer, recording her observations in a low voice, calm but enthusiastic; with her free hand she conducted her thoughts with swirls and rolls of her fingers and palm and wrist.

Noticing his interest, she paused, looked over her sunglasses at Fergus, and raised her eyebrows in reprimand. Fergus dropped his eyes and studied his shoes. The black leather was dull and scuffed. He wondered if Ruby had shoe polish, before conceding that it was unlikely. Dissatisfied and resigned, he looked up. The Japanese woman still circled the statue, but the fat man had gone. In his place, a young woman with red hair was smoking a cigarette and talking on her mobile phone. Her face was turned away, but it was unmistakably Ruby: the same shade of red, the same leather jacket and boots, the same shape to her shoulders, her back.

Her voice did not carry on the fuzzy, motor-soaked air, but the circles drawn with her free hand suggested a weary explanation, one often rehearsed, no longer of interest. When she hung up, she sat for a few moments, her head bowed over her lap, the hand still cupping the phone. Then the red of her hair wriggled with her shaking head before falling lower down her back, and he imagined the point of her chin, the extent of her throat. Fergus waited until the irritation had had time to pass, then moved with all the poise he could muster across the tarmac to her bench.

'Fancy meeting you here.'

Her face betrayed the last traces of her phone call, but quickly settled into surprise instead, and then a smile.

'Bloody hell, Fergus. How'd you do it? Have you got sonar or something?'

'Nah, I was just sitting having a quiet time over there, before we met. Nicer in here than out among all those. You're early yet.'

Her eyes lost focus, although her lips retained their sharpness, and when she spoke it was, at first, only a little above a whisper.

'Yeah, I like it here too... And yes I am early. Got my shit together quicker than I thought. You know how sometimes the thoughts just fall into the right order without much help from you? Everything in the right place, no scratching around looking for the right word, the idea that makes it all, just... right?'

He had no idea what she meant. To him, thoughts were always where they should be; the words that came to mind were usually the right ones and, if they needed that much wrangling, they were probably the wrong ones anyway. Instead, he thought about how he approached a piece of wood: sometimes, it would take him weeks of working away at its margins before its true nature would emerge, and other times he would feel its purpose as soon as he picked it up, the salt still crusted into the grain.

'Anyhow, we're here now. And we're going that way. Lunch.'

Ruby pointed back across the churchyard and set off, the little bounce of her stride appearing soon after. Fergus followed, catching her at the crossing on a main road, and as they made their way down the hill towards the river he shortened his steps to match her stride for stride. Conversation did not come easily: he wanted to ask about the phone call, but knew that that would be to pry, would reveal that he had been watching her without her knowledge. It was none of his business anyway. Thoughts bounced inside his head, each apprised for suitability.

'I meant to ask you, Ruby. About Bridget. About that scar…'

They had reached another crossing and, as they waited, Ruby gave him a helpless glance before turning back to face the traffic with a sigh.

'I don't know, Fergus. Really. None of us do. I suppose we all knew not to ask. And the longer we've lived together the less likely it is that we'll ever ask. It'd be weird now. Like we'd just noticed. Honestly, Fergus, it's best you don't say anything. Ignore it. If she wanted us to know she'd tell us. Sometimes it's best not to know everything about someone.'

'But she would've nearly died, a cut like that. And it's that straight that it can't have been an accident. How can you not ask someone about something like that? You said that the bairn's father had been a bit of a bastard… do you think that..?'

Ruby's laugh was as much of release as of amusement. She touched his arm gently with her hand and Fergus resisted the urge to look at it there, her fingers nestled in the indentations created in his sleeve.

'God, no! Steve is many things, but he's soft as muck. Besides, they were still together when I met Bridget, and she had it then. You've met her. Do you reckon she's put up with someone who'd tried to slit her throat? Come on. The light's changed.'

The land fell away towards the water. Above the sky opened up, crisp blue streaked and cross-hatched by high cloud, some grey, some white. Across the river stood a tall tower that rose from a vast brick bunker; between it and them, a narrow bridge curved across the river. Boats plied the river's course, gliding on or wrestling their way against the current.

twenty-nine

The knife was loose in his hand, the handle damp with steam and dish water. Fergus was unused to preparing food and the initial thrill had already worn off. He was only two carrots into his allotted task. He surveyed the irregular disks already sliced. He wanted to ask Bridget to approve his work before he continued, but she was busy with meat and string and herbs. From the living room, laughter, then a swinging of doors and the catch of slippers on carpet.

'How're the workers getting on?'

Ruby looked brighter than she had any right to be. It had been gone three by the time the housemates had returned from the bar, still buzzing, and while the others had gone to bed, she had sat up with Bridget in the kitchen while she prepared her post-performance meal. Fergus had not heard her go to bed before he had drifted into uneasy, dry-mouthed sleep, the product of which had been a flat, monotone dreaming, devoid of anything but grey menace. Outside, the sky was much the same.

'We're getting there. Should all be ready in time.'

The oven door clanged shut and Bridget ambled over to where Fergus stood motionless, queasy. She looked at the chopping board and shook her head in disbelief. Gently she displaced her apprentice and took up the knife herself, chopping at an alarming rate and dancing a little as she did so.

'Go in there and play with the boys, will you? I think I'll be able to struggle on without you.'

The women exchanged smiles, before Bridget returned to the carrots. For a moment, Fergus watched the knife flash in the kitchen's fluorescent light and thought of Bridget's throat, of blood and pain and fear. Ruby's hand on his elbow steered him from the kitchen and out into the hallway.

There were still thirty five minutes before Steve arrived and the house was already tidied; lunch was in hand. Fergus had been surprised that, despite the ending of their relationship and their inability to live together with their child, Bridget was willing to cook a meal for Steve on alternate Sundays and to sit and eat it with him. That Steve was a friend of Matt's provided some explanation of the arrangement, but that raised still more questions. He had decided that they should probably, on balance, remain unasked; that Bridget's life demanded the not asking of questions.

'Morning! Has she dispensed with your services already? Rule number one around here is don't volunteer to help Bridge cook. Best just to keep your head down and wait to get fed.'

Matt's left leg dangled over the arm of the chair, while his right was tucked under him. On his lap wallowed a laptop computer, his fingers poised lazily over the keys. A little way off, the cat sat staring at the imposition. Jacob was by the window, staring out into the lingering gloom: the mist was thicker today and had still not cleared. There was no sign of sunlight.

'Miserable out there. So dark. Can't believe it's gone midday already and I can barely see. In April, too. Doesn't look like it's going to clear anytime soon, either.'

'Jacob, shut the fuck up will you, you miserable bastard? It's just a bit of cloud. No one is interested.'

Matt reached behind him and launched a cushion in the direction of the window. It missed its target and bounced from the glass back across the floor. The cat scurried out of its way, leaping ultimately into Ruby's waiting arms. She said nothing, but scowled; Jacob shrugged his innocence, while Matt returned to whatever he was doing with his laptop.

'You know, your man Maltravers really doesn't make himself easy to find. I mean, there's nothing, no Twitter, no Linked-in, no Facebook, nothing on Google, not even a 192 listing. It's a long time since I've seen someone with a profile as low as this. OK, there's the gallery's site, but that doesn't tell you much. Lovely looking, but pretty useless. Just a contact form and some pretty pictures of old stuff. The address, but we know that already. No association with him, that's for sure. Either he doesn't believe in computers or he's keen to stay very private indeed.'

Matt paused. He was used to being able to find his way around the internet and was really very pleased with himself once again. Certain that the stage had been set for his revelation, he shifted in the armchair.

'But, you see, if you think about things a little differently and approach the subject a little more obliquely, you find out the most

fascinating things. So, your Mr Maltravers is going to become much more well-known when his father dies. Here.'

Fergus took the computer. His eyes flicked over the screen for a moment, before he began to make sense of what was written there. It was an entry in the listings of prominent families of Britain; the main entry was for a Simon Maltravers, the sixth viscount of somewhere in the south west of England, but at the end, under a faint emboldened heading, were listed his wife Frances and only son, Nicholas.

'What? Fergus? What does it say?'

He sat on the sofa and read again the entry, hoping that in so doing the implications would become clearer. Impatient, Ruby poured the cat onto the floor and sat beside him, so close that her cheek pressed against his arm as she read.

'It seems that we are up against a peer of the realm. Don't know if that's a good thing or a bad thing. But it is certainly a thing.'

'What Jake is trying to say is that I am a genius. And that we at least know this Maltravers bloke is real. That's a start, right?'

Silence followed, each trying to determine what kind of a start it meant. The stillness was only broken by the heavy sound of a buzzer from the hallway. A loud expletive and some clattering followed from the kitchen, then a call for Ruby. Matt slid somehow from the armchair into an upright position and over to the window, where he gave a little wave to someone outside.

'Yep. That's them. Early. She will not be happy. Only Steve can cause trouble with women by being early.'

— ◉ —

Steve picked the last piece of carrot out of the dish and dropped it into his mouth. His son sat in his lap, clasping a small metal truck that he ran backwards and forwards across the table cloth. Its engine's grumble bubbled from between Lou's lips. Father and son seemed oblivious to each other, but when Steve tried to slide out from under him, Lou squealed in displeasure at the separation, his eyes following his father's retreat to the sofa before slipping from the chair himself to follow.

Bridget watched them. For the thousandth time the thought arose and nagged until her conviction that it just wouldn't work squashed it back into its lair. She sighed and slowly caught up with the conversation at the table.

'Look, a man like that, he's not going to be bothered by threats, or fooled by any cunning plan. No, his weakness is going to be his fascination with the exotic. So, you just have to make yourself exotic.'

Matt stifled a snigger but this only perplexed Fergus more. He had no idea what Jacob was talking about. Ruby too was quizzical. There seemed to be so few courses of action open to their house guest and the suggestions had become ever more unlikely. Steve had advocated a break-in, but Bridget had made him apologise, to assure Lou that he had only been joking, that burglary was not something good people even considered. At this point, Steve had become disinterested in the conversation and had started chasing the scraps of food left over from lunch.

But Jacob's suggestion, that Fergus should try to make the return of the stone the more interesting outcome, seemed the most plausible by far. Maltravers already had enough money it would seem, and he would likely have enough pieces of ancient stone, wood and metal littering his life; if only a way could be devised to convince him that the act of reuniting the stone and the island were itself part of his collection, then maybe Fergus could return home other than in failure and disgrace.

'It doesn't happen often, but I think Jake could be onto something: you can't buy it, you can't steal it, so maybe you're going to have to charm it back. And the only thing we know about him is that he collects rare things. What could be rarer than you and your quest? Give him a big part in that, let him own that, instead of the thing itself.'

There was a momentary silence and Ruby stared at Fergus with a steady insistent gaze. She was sure now that, if only she could hold onto this slippery idea, something could be done to put things right; restitution could be made. But despite Jacob's nodding and upturned palms, and the murmurs of recognition, Fergus was no clearer about what exactly he should do. While instinctively averse to criminality of any kind, he had much preferred the clarity of Steve's intervention than this jelly-like idea that was seemingly grasped by everyone except him.

While Ruby waited for him to find his own way to comprehension, Jacob grew impatient.

'What you need, Fergus, is a good story. Something about the island and the importance of the stone, something superstitious, something mythical. Or failing that, something historical. It's Columban, yeah? Well, give him an opportunity to be a crucial part in that history. I'll ask my dad, after Evensong, see if he's got any ideas.'

Jacob smiled warmly, then stood; he scraped the debris from his plate into an empty dish and stacked it onto the others; these he carried to the kitchen, before disappearing to his room to change. Maybe it was because he didn't really know what the Tower of London signified, but Fergus had been less surprised than Ruby had expected when he had heard that Jacob's father was chaplain there, and that his son sang in the choir every Sunday.

'It's a bit Temple of Doom, but it might work. Good as anything, I suppose.'

With that, Matt gathered his wrap of tobacco, his papers and lighter and headed off to the back door; Bridget rested her hand briefly of Fergus's forearm before she too withdrew to join her son and his father by the window. She and Steve ignored each other while both played separately with the boy. Back at the table, Ruby shrugged to Fergus and began to gather the remains of the meal. He helped her, as he helped his mother back home, more in a statement of willingness that in helpfulness itself.

thirty

Tuesdays were the worst days, he decided. Mondays at least had a trace of novelty, a sense of new beginnings; Wednesdays marked a midpoint. Without leaning forwards from his slump, he flipped the photos over in the folder once more, hoping that something would reignite his interest. Tuesdays. Only on a day so lacking in energy could the contents of a minor Anglo-Saxon hoard, ripe for acquisition, hold such little allure. He pushed the folder across the desk and spun in his seat to face the cabinet behind him. There was more diversion in the way the late morning light glanced off a simple curve of ebony than in his work. He picked up the female figure from its shelf, felt its smooth suggestion lead his fingers along its length and watched the white reflection move fluidly over its contours. Worth practically nothing, of course, just a few hundred pounds. But it was pretty enough. He felt its weight as he bounced the piece in his left hand. It would make a nice present, for the right person.

His father always said that, with antiquities, aesthetic pleasure was a secondary consideration, especially if one intended to make a living in the field. He held the same views about women: his mother had been a solid, sensible match, and his father had always ensured that his mistresses were kept well away from the ancestral home, much as he did with the art works he actually enjoyed. Nicholas had learned both lessons well. While he was yet to marry Harriet, he had already mastered sufficient discretion to enable him to continue to enjoy the company of women beyond the monotony of matrimony.

Professionally, he had taken to keeping those pieces that pleased him, regardless of value, in his private collections. Like this African woman. He turned its smoothness in his hands once more, and appreciated the angle of her ankle, which suggested she was about to spring into the air, poised. Then there was that Scottish stone. It looked like nothing so much as an oversized and malformed hot cross bun, but he had found it strangely beautiful. Perhaps it was the smoothness of its lumpy surface, burnished by all those hopeful, hateful hands over the centuries; the contradictions it carried, its ambiguity.

It wasn't stealing, of course, to take pieces that had been acquired through the business into his personal possession. He was the business after all: his money, his discernment, had built the business. This gallery, much as this foot-long piece of carved ebony, were his possessions. And the point was to possess them and either to take pleasure in their possession or to profit in their disposal.

This Tuesday had gone on too long, and offered neither profit nor pleasure. With the sudden energy of decision, Nicholas Maltravers rose to his full height and took three precise strides to the slender hat stand in the corner of the office. There he rummaged in the pocket of his jacket for his cigarettes. With a shake of his head, he surveyed the room to ensure he had forgotten nothing of importance, before slipping out of the gallery unseen.

— ⊙ —

Fergus was early, of course. He had woken sharply. His dream still throbbed in his temples, not yet slowed by wakening. As it receded into its own realm, he understood without the need for interrogation that it had been an anxious dream, and that anxiety continued as he recorded his night's adventure in his note book; it continued as he had showered, dressed, greeted the cat, greeted Ruby, and eaten a small breakfast of bread and soft cheese. The tea had quivered in his cupped hands. The weekend's mists had gone and the sky over the green was blue, striped only by the first of the day's contrails. A gathering breeze raked the infant leaves of trees surrounding the church, in premature anticipation of autumn.

He had not wanted to be late, so had taken the tube to Bond Street station and retraced the route Ruby had shown him. He had hoped to lose himself a while, in order to erode some of his surplus time, but it was surprisingly easy to find his way through the broad streets lined with houses jammed together in unbroken rows. Although most of the buildings were as good as identical, there were still landmarks by which to navigate, fragments from when he had tagged behind Ruby's determination: the fright-faced painted lion, rampant in its cornered niche; the slinking fox sprayed across the foot of a forgotten wall.

Without his anticipated detours, Fergus had arrived at Half Moon Street forty five minutes before his appointment with Nicholas Maltravers. The blank glass looked no more inviting than it had four days previously, despite the now present lamp light glowing at the back of the gallery. It was unlikely, Fergus concluded, that disturbing Maltravers earlier than arranged would enhance his chances of success. He reasoned that it would be best to await his appointed time in the café at the end of the street.

He joined the queue which had formed near the counter, welcoming every passing moment that those in front of him consumed. It was only when he was next to the glass-fronted cabinet, containing all kinds of pastries and cakes, that he noticed the woman in front of him. With tidy hair and specific tastes, she was largely unremarkable: a woman like any other in the city. Except for her hand. Fergus was startled by the small hole in the hand that rested on the supple leather of her handbag, which rested in turn on the little ledge that ran along the front of the counter. It was a small but distinct hole, a black absence, a breach in her smooth skin. There was no blood, no gore, none of the sticky inconvenience of mortality. Simply a hole; a triangular absence. His surprise turned to confusion: did she know? Did it hurt? Only slowly did it occur to him that this must be a prosthetic hand, attached to a prosthetic arm. A damaged, prosthetic arm. And then a young woman behind the counter was asking him for his order; it took Fergus a couple of tries to request the tea both because neither could understand the accent of the other, but also because of the questions swirling in his head.

He watched the woman with the hole in her hand carry her supple handbag and her huge carton of milky-sweet coffee from the shop, her hand and its hole hanging unremarkably at her side. Taking his tea, he found a seat by the window and watched her disappear into the crowds on the pavement. He wondered how the hole had been formed, how the absence had occurred; long after she had vanished into the human tide, the crisp shape of the breach stayed with him.

Most of the customers took their drinks with them. Although the café was busy, and the queue never completely vanished, only a handful of others occupied the seats set around little tables and counters. There was more life to be seen on the street, fleeting

THE CURSING STONE

though it was. Fergus watched the faces of passers-by and wondered what it was the drove them to such urgency. Only the tourists, small family groups, took their time in making their way to wherever they were heading. The steps from the tube station discharged an endless stream of people. Many of the men were unshaven, but the beards were smaller than at home. Shorter and fussier, they sat uncomfortably on fresh faces and on less fresh faces, but none the less separate from those faces. None of the men wearing them seemed relaxed in their manicured whiskers, which they wore like new clothes, starched, still finding their owner's curves and creases.

When the tea was gone, Fergus set off again towards the gallery. As before, Half Moon Street was empty, without the people and the vehicles that crammed the main street only few yards behind. Reaching the heavy glass façade, Fergus pressed the button by the door and waited. His stomach clenched in anticipation and he rehearsed his story as he waited to be granted entry.

The door swung open. It revealed a tall young woman, her dark hair pulled back in a loose pony tail. She wore a fine woollen sweater, turquoise, with a v-neck; the collar and neck of a white shirt opened to reveal a simple string of pearls that glowed against her skin. She greeted him by name, hesitantly, questioning, and seemed surprised when Mr Buchanan nodded. Stepping back a little, she swept him into the showroom.

'Mr Maltravers has stepped out for a moment, but he shouldn't keep you waiting long. Would you like to wait in the showroom?'

It was unclear what he should do if that wasn't what he would like to do, but in any case Fergus was happy to take the time to seek out his stone among the sparse display. Unlike the showroom in Glasgow, there was no clutter. Where McAteer had crammed furniture, books, porcelain and taxidermy, Maltravers had arranged emptiness, interrupted by twenty or so pieces of stone, wood and bronze shaped into forms, human and demonic. Fergus studied each carefully, and yet it took only moments to be sure that the stone was not amongst them.

He stared into a painted face, a god or a monster, its mouth stretched in a snarl or scream, its tongue curled grotesquely between pointed incisors protruding upwards from blood red lips. But it was the malevolence of the eyes that disturbed him most: wide and startling, they pierced the soft stillness of the showroom, and drilled into his unknown fears. Fergus was relieved when the young woman returned to break its spell and to show him into the office at the back of the room.

'Mr Buchanan, I am most terribly sorry to have kept you waiting. Trupti, some coffee, please?'

The young man had risen from his desk at Fergus's entrance, approaching him briskly, hand outstretched. Fergus had accepted it, been surprised by its cool forcefulness; he allowed his own to be shaken as if lifeless, and was struck by the precision of Maltravers' hair, his flawless complexion. Every feature of his face had been composed into a perfect replica of welcome. Fergus allowed himself to be ushered into a chair, while Maltravers returned to his own, to face him across the desk. His smile broadened. Fergus was as used to people smiling as he was to people scowling, but had never seen a smile so disconcerting: it wrapped around him like a noose.

They exchanged pleasantries, speculating on the weather and the arrival of spring while they waited for the coffee. Maltravers asked about his journey, about his impressions of London, about his family. Fergus was startled by how soon he found himself talking of the things he had left behind, of Shona, and he tried to mask his discomfort by joking about the insecurities of women.

'I think she's worried that I'm going to come home smelling of cheap perfume.'

Fergus offered a meek smile, hopeful that this small lie would convince Maltravers that he was in fact a man of the world.

'Would she rather you came home smelling of expensive perfume? If she has any sense she'd prefer the cheap scent.'

It was not what Fergus had expected and he flushed.

'I think she'd rather I came home smelling of neither.'

'Oh come now, Mr Buchanan. When one goes out into the world, one always ends up smelling of something or other.'

At this point, the young woman returned carrying a tray set with two cups of coffee and a jug of milk. There was no sugar. She set down the tray on the desk, leaning past Fergus as she did so. He felt the air tingle between them and a spiral squirmed down his spine. Maltravers watched her as she left the room, following her movement with his eyes until the door clicked shut. Only then did Maltravers ask Fergus about his purpose in visiting. The story took some minutes to tell. Fergus recounted first how the cursing stone had been taken from the island, then went on to detail the history of St Columba's landfall on Hinba, the founding of the abbey, and the historical significance of the discovery, the centuries through which the stone had been lost, undisturbed among the sedge and heather. Much of this, he summoned up from his memories of Mr Galbraith's lessons and from his sister's breathless enthusiasm; the rest he made up.

'You see, Mr Maltravers, there is an opportunity here to do something truly remarkable, to reunite the stone and its bowl for the first time in over a thousand years. Think of the acclaim you'd receive, being the man who made that possible. It's the chance to be a part of a story stretching over centuries.'

Fergus felt at first that he had delivered well the lines that Jacob had drilled into him, but there was something ominous in the mischief that played around Maltravers' thin smile.

'I'm not really too interested in seeing my name in the papers, to be honest. Nor in a memorial plaque on some island hundreds of miles away. I'm afraid, Mr Buchanan, I rather like your cursing stone – it looks very much at home where it is. Ordinarily, I would be open to the possibility of selling, at a profit of course, but I rather like it. It has found a suitable niche in my home and I would rather miss it, I think.'

The room fell into silence. Fergus could feel the opportunity slipping from him with every moment that passed without a word. It was the wrong thing to do, he knew, but he had to do something.

'If you're not interested in being the hero of the piece, Mr Maltravers, I'm sure the papers would be happy to make you the villain. You know what journalists are like for their David and Goliath stories – especially when it comes to peers of the realm.'

'Really? Threats, Mr Buchanan? Oh, how delicious. Thank you. Today had been rather dull up to now. But I'm afraid I have no *good reputation to lose, you see. In any case, the artefact is in my possession quite legally, bought and paid for; that is all that matters really. I have the receipt of sale here.'*

Maltravers hand rested lightly on the desk, although Fergus could see no piece of paper under it. For too long, he could not look away from the hand, the walnut veneer beneath it, expecting the receipt to appear. He waited for the inevitable conclusion of the interview and, when it came, he made no attempt to resist the invitation to leave.

He found himself on Half Moon Street, alone. His feet took him to Berkley Square and, feeling faint, he took a seat on a bench in the little park, to breathe out his disappointment. A young woman walked passed him with purpose, her hands clutching the hem of her hopeful dress in defiance of the lascivious wind, which had to content itself with running its fingers through the lush grass. Fergus noticed the chill edge of the day for the first time; he looked at the sky, where a fine lace of cloud stretched across the highest part.

thirty-one

Ruby pulled her cardigan around her shoulders more tightly. The kitchen was colder than it had been for several weeks and she wondered which of her housemates would suggest first that they once more switch on the heating. She could hear Jacob and Matt from the living room, their voices excited and serious. Since they had returned home to Fergus's news, they had been eager to hatch a new plan. While their guest spoke with his family in her room, she had withdrawn, irritated by their evermore outlandish stratagems. She was glad that Fergus was out of earshot, and didn't have to listen to the way the problem was being treated as a game. She appreciated the seriousness of the situation, even if the others saw it simply as a puzzle to be solved. It was almost quarter past seven: she should make some food for herself and Fergus.

The cat flapped into the kitchen, as if summoned by the thought of food. Pausing by the backdoor and his empty bowl, he looked up at Ruby and gave a short meow of rebuke. Without waiting for an answer he approached the bowl and ducked his head into it, to ensure he had left nothing uneaten from earlier, then looked back with unblinking eyes. With a sigh, Ruby went to the cupboard to fetch a tin of cat food. The electric can-opener ground through the kitchen's stillness.

She was squatting beside the bowl when the door swung inwards. Over her shoulder, she shot a smile towards the entrant. Fergus mustered a weary response, then slumped into one of the chairs by the table.

'How're things, then? Pleased to hear from you? I bet Shona was glad...'

Her bright chatter stuttered to a halt. Fergus was simply staring at the table, oblivious to her questions. She finished spooning the sticky brownness into the bowl and crossed the floor to sit next to him, her hand on his arm.

'Did your father take it badly, that you've not got the butterlump yet?'

She suspected that his father had been unreasonable in the way he had given Fergus his quest in the first place, and that that unreasonableness continued still. She felt anger and sympathy for her bullied friend. She was on the verge of admonishing his distant task-master, but saw the tear in time. It hung from his eyelash for a slow moment, then tracked across his velvety cheek. She waited, her heart breaking.

'He's dying. My granddad. They didn't say it, but it was in their voices. I could hear it. They just said that he's very ill, that the doctor's over from Mallaig.'

Ruby stifled two or three sentences, buffeting against her closed lips, before he spoke.

'Well, if the doctor's there, that's something, isn't it? I mean, I'm sure...'

But she knew that this old man, on this remote island, would not allow the doctor in unless he was beyond objecting, and her comforting stalled.

'Did you speak to him? Your granddad?'

'No, he was too ill to come to the phone. Asleep, they said. My dad, he said maybe I should think about going back sooner than planned, just in case.'

But that was impossible, without the stone. If Fingal survived, the shame of his grandson's failure would kill him anyway. The disappointment of the morning took on new proportions, and its weight pressed in on his skull. If only he had done better, been cleverer, quicker, more like the man his grandfather believed him to be. He could have been home by the weekend, with the stone, and Fingal would be sitting up in bed, glowing with pride and the will to live. But he had failed; it was better for his grandfather to die without that disappointment and shame.

He felt Ruby's arms wrap around him, her cheek against his neck, felt her mouth move and the word 'sorry' prickle his skin. And he released the tears he had been holding for later, when everyone had gone to bed and he was alone in the darkness of the sitting room in the dead house. He felt Ruby tense against his sobs, containing him in his shape even as he dissolved in misery.

They sat like that for maybe fifteen minutes, until all the crying had been done and there were no tears left. Sensing that calm had returned, Ruby reached out to the counter top and pulled back the kitchen roll, handing him a sheet.

'Here, tidy yourself up. Don't want the others to see you like this, do we? What we need is a plan of action.'

By the time Bridget returned to the house, the conspirators were lost in their plotting. They no longer paid much regard to Lou, who had been running around the kitchen playing monsters, attempting to frighten, or at least distract, Matt and Jacob in turn; Ruby and Fergus were left unmolested, both too intimidating to a four year old ogre. Unperturbed by his neglect, Lou ran boisterously around the table, growling and yelping, breathless and giggling. At his mother's arrival, Lou ran to her, his face now stretched into the broadest grin, rather than how he imagined an ogre's face to feel. Arms flung wide, he launched himself into a hug, his legs swinging free of the earth. Ruby merely looked up and nodded a greeting before returning to her laptop.

She was looking for the home of address of Nicholas Maltravers. Rather, she was trying to establish that his home address could not be found: Matt had decided early on that Steve was probably right, that a break-in was the most direct way to resolving the matter, especially now that they knew the stone was in his house rather than the shop. Ruby had objected to any kind of law-breaking and urged Fergus to listen to Jacob, who had suggested that before doing anything, they determine the actual legal position. But Matt, emboldened with three cans of lager, was resolute; Ruby instead wanted to show that, whatever the rights and wrongs of a break-in, it was impossible since they did not know his home address.

The discussion had become tense. When Bridget put Lou back onto his feet, she noticed that no-one was talking, except her son, whose babble was so familiar an accompaniment to life in the house that it seldom counted as noise. She looked from one face to the other, then decided that everything would be more easily interpreted with a beer. Scooping up Lou on the way back from the fridge, she sat at one end of the table, child on her lap.

'So, who's going to bring me up to speed here?'

'Matt's sulking, because no-one wants to join him on his mad burglary adventure.'

Ruby did not look up from her laptop screen, but she allowed herself a small smile. Bridget looked from Ruby to Matt, expectantly and a little aghast.

'I do. Well, if the legal way doesn't work.'

Even Ruby looked up. Fergus sat quietly for a few moments, with his shoulders cupped in apology, while the others watched in bemusement, vindication or disappointment. Bridget bounced Lou a couple of times to settle his squirming, and Lou in turn grasped a tiny fistful of table cloth, pulling it and several glasses and empty cans fractionally closer. Otherwise, the table was still.

Fergus had taken the duration of the debate to arrive at his decision. He did not believe that the law would help, but nor did he want to commit a crime himself, especially one that would most likely end in failure and arrest; much less to expose his new friends to danger. There seemed, however, to be few other choices.

'But you'll still see my friend tomorrow? Before finally deciding to do something so stupid, I mean.'

Early on in the kitchen table discussion, Jacob had suggested speaking to his friend, a barrister. It had seemed unlikely to Fergus that a self-employed gardener would mix with barristers, but it had been explained that Jacob was rather more elevated than it might appear. His father, chaplain of the Tower of London, was remarkably well-connected; his mother, even more so, and independently wealthy. Jacob's trust fund had enabled him, four year's previously, to buy the house they shared. The simplicity of his life was a testament to his temperament rather than his means, and his social circle beyond the household included surgeons, investment bankers and lawyers. Ruby was fairly certain that, if anyone could find a legal resolution, if would be one of Jacob's friends.

'Of course. I don't want to get any of you in to bother. That's the last thing I want.'

The cat returned, sensing that sanity had re-established itself in the kitchen, and people began to shift out of their seats to make a start with feeding themselves, their children and their cats. Only Fergus and Matt remained unmoved by this return to domesticity, the one regarding the other.

'But as a back-up. Just a back-up, maybe we should find out where the bugger lives.'

Fergus wasn't sure if Matt was talking directly to him or to the room in general, but the groans from Jacob and Bridget suggested that his comment had been for public consumption. Ruby turned from the sink, knife and dish cloth still in hand, and smiled breezily.

'That's the thing though, Matt. You can't – he's even paid to have his details hidden on the electoral roll. And if you can't find him, you can't break-in. Sorry.'

Her hair swished with her turn back to the sink and, in the reflection of the window, Fergus could see her silent laugh.

thirty-two

The man spoke in a friendly but professional way. His round face bobbed in agreement when she in turn spoke, but his eyes remained constant upon her. Throughout their conversation, he sought a comfortable way to sit on the little stool, and with each shift in weight, some curls of hair would emerge from the open neck of his shirt. She had the advantage of a seat on the bench that ran along the pub's wall, under the window, where the lamp light from the alley beyond twisted in the bottle-bottom glass. Yet she also shifted perpetually and, with each new position, she pulled the hem of her oatmeal knitted skirt over her black-stockinged legs.

The conversation was entirely audible, but completely incomprehensible. A looping, almost familiar language, interspersed with guttural rasps. Occasionally, recognisable words would drop from their sentences: 'payroll', 'human resources'; 'profit forecast'. With each English addition, the hidden conversation became less alluring. Not a lovers' tryst then, nor a tale of adventure, but a discussion of offices and work, of bloodless commerce. And yet the throaty depths of the woman's voice, crunching like snow then swooping like a raven, captivated Fergus. As the all-too comfortable embrace of impending inebriation rose slowly from the nape of his neck and cradled his skull, he had drifted from the conversation at his own table. Will had begun to explain the 1996 Act and its implications for the treatment of treasure in England and Wales. At first, Fergus had simply moved his attention from his beer to the beams above, festooned with china jugs from a hundred different places and times, and then to the carpet, tracing its pattern through red and green and gold curlicues.

But when Will had moved on to discuss the differences between English and Scottish common law, he had capitulated to his fascination with the conversation at the next table. The sound it made was infinitely more appealing than hearing that there was possibly something that could be done within the law, but that it would probably take years. There had been a case in the fifties of a carved porpoise bone found on some Scottish island; eventually, at appeal, it was declared treasure trove. But that had taken five years and, while there was precedent, the fact that the stone had crossed legally into England would complicate matters.

Fergus had wanted to bury his head in his hands and wail, but he knew Will was trying to be helpful. It was clear, however, that recovering the stone legally would take years, if it were possible at all. And Fingal did not have years: the law, therefore, could not help. And so Fergus took temporary solace in the meaninglessness of the couple's looping sentences twisting over the babble of voices that rose and fell, clashed and collapsed and rose again, like the cries of gulls on a spring tide.

'I'm sorry, Fergus. But it is worth pursuing – the St Ninian case is encouraging, isn't it?'

Will had already left for the bar, leaving Jacob with the disconsolate, distracted Fergus. The kindness in Jacob's voice drew him back.

He wanted to say that it was not encouraging, that St Ninian was a world away from Hinba and that the stone was not some fish bone, but he was interrupted by the in-rushing chill of night air that presaged the arrival of Matt.

'It's cold out there. The sky's like a slab. Anyhow, what have I missed? Has your barrister solved the case?'

Matt indicated Will at the bar, and winked to Fergus.

'Didn't think you were coming?'

'Well, Jake, I was in the neighbourhood. Sort of. Anyhow, I know where he lives, if anyone's interested. Just over there.'

He looked directly at Fergus as he said this, boyish excitement twitching about his mouth, and he pointed over the shoulder of the Dutch woman, out into the city.

'Are you sure? I mean, isn't he off grid?'

Jacob's calm, dismissive tone betrayed a hint of fear, concern that after he had done so much to re-establish sanity, Matt might just have found a chink through which to re-admit the madness.

'I just followed him.'

With breathless appreciation for his own ingenuity, Matt described his frenetic chase across London, he on his bike, Maltravers in the taxi that had picked him up from Half Moon Street. He barely paused when Will returned from the bar with three pints, and only briefly when he returned a second time with a fourth, to drink deeply for an instant before ploughing on with his tale, until it reached the gates of Maltravers' London home. While Matt drained the rest of his beer, even Jacob hung entranced, demanding him to go on, to reveal the location of their quarry. Matt looked over the rim of his pint, eyes twinkling; but when he next spoke, Jacob raised his hands in exasperation. Fergus did not know where the Barbican was, but he gathered it was a rather imprecise location.

'No, no – I know the exact address, actually. The cab dropped him at Lauderdale Tower, I watched him go in and call a lift. He hit the button for the top floor.'

'Great, so we know which floor he lives on. What do you propose? Breaking in to all the flats on that floor?'

Will recoiled. He looked from Matt to his friend, and back again, suddenly aware that he might be involved in something more than a theoretical discussion of the law and ancient artefacts. Even the Dutch couple at the next table looked over, hopeful for further intrigue.

'Hush now, Jake. No-one is talking about breaking in to anywhere, just that we know his address now. I called the concierge and asked if he could confirm that Mr Maltravers lived in number 412, as I needed to get something couriered to him. Good job I checked, because he's in 411. So now we can send him a Christmas card. Or a writ.'

Pleased with himself once again, Matt winked at the Dutch couple. Disappointed and a little uncomfortable to have been discovered in their eavesdropping, they looked back to their drinks and resumed their own conversation. Fergus rose and offered another round. Will declined, happy to at last be able to escape. He extended his hand to Fergus, and wished him luck, before giving a bloodless hug to Jacob; to Matt, he offered only a nod. And then he was gone, back out into the alley and the cold.

thirty-three

All around is pitch blackness, a darkness so deep that it swallows the room and every living thing that could possibly exist. You wonder how something, anything, could ever be so dark and you strain your ears, your useless eyes, for any trace of your friend. Even a whispered memory of his name. But it and he are swallowed too, lost in this endless pitch. You wonder whether, instead of a room, you are in a coffin, buried in the deadening ground. Your friend, lost along with his name, his face, are absent in the world above, where life is still lived.

But you can reach out your arms and touch nothing. You can feel the pull of gravity where your feet push into the floor. The dead stillness that encases you is a room, and you are standing in it. That much is true, even if you can be sure of nothing else. That truth, and the truth that you are alone. Until the yelp. A strangled yelp that struggles across the room. A human yelp and then the soft noise of something heavy, limp, slumping to the floor. You are not alone.

You call out, hoping that your friend will answer, but there is no reply. Just a dragging shuffle that moves towards you.

You feel the cold metal of a pistol in your hand. You do not know how you came to be holding a pistol, but in your gratitude you forget to ask. Instead, you hold its weight out in front of you and you fire, thoughtlessly, in the direction from which the shuffle approaches. In the flash of combustion, you see a beast, bloodied, coming towards you, its fangs curled upwards in its wide-mouthed grimace. You fire again and again, each time seeing more of the thing, until your indiscriminate firing finally finds its mark and the monster drops to the floor.

There is only silence and darkness for a time, and the sticky smell of decay. You edge around the room, feeling the walls until you reach a door frame, then a door knob, with which you wrestle, vainly. Breathless, heavy, you slide down the door with your back until you are sitting on your haunches, sobbing. All hope of finding your way back into daylight is gone. Time passes, slowly or quickly, you cannot tell, but ultimately and with a heavy clunk, a bright light bursts into the darkness.

In its ferocity, you are blinded still, blank blackness replaced by painful, featureless white. Slowly shapes form and, once your eyes have adjusted, have stopped hurting, you look around, anxious at what you might see. But there is no beast, dead or living, on the floor. And instead of a subterranean cell, you find yourself in a high tower, the surrounding sea visible through the narrow windows. The moonlight dapples its surface.

The lights hum and buzz, fizzing on the close air. Across the room, a door handle turns and the door swings inwards. As the first foot of the visitor appears from behind it, the buzzing from the lights gains intensity, becomes deafening, overwhelming, and the walls, and doors, the unseen man, all fall away, crashing towards the sea.

thirty-four

Finally it arrived. The city had been waiting for a day or two, anxious and excited, ever since the weather man had announced that snow was coming. Snow. In April. It was unheard of, in London at least. Growing up in Lancashire, Ruby had seen snow fall at pretty much any time of year. But not down here.

At first, it was simply a light dusting on the empty pavement outside, like icing sugar on a tray bake. But then it had thickened and darkened until greyness filled the spaces between the falling flakes and the sky closed in around the houses, pushing down on the city, leaden. Ruby stared out of the window, her breathing laboured under an ancient fear. As the street disappeared under an immaculate cloak, she decided that today was a day for indoors.

When she had first arrived in the city, it almost never snowed in London. Not really snowed. Sometimes there would be a bit of a scattering in the morning, but it was almost always gone by lunchtime. Older students, who'd been here a while longer, confirmed the scarcity of snow. But then, over the past couple of years, snow had become an annual feature, then a biannual feature. And this was snow in a northern sense, a close-down-the-city-for-days kind of snow. A snowmen-in-the-park, icy streets kind of snow. A shut-the-schools, cancel-the-trains-and-buses snow that came twice a year, once before Christmas, once in the New Year. Almost regular, certainly expected. It was the new normal.

But not this. Not snow in April. This was still abnormal, unnatural. She didn't understand the science entirely, but Ruby knew that this was one of those freak weather events, a result of global warming. Climate change. Ruby was struck by the power of language, by the smooth elision of 'global warming' into 'climate change', which had happened about the same time that it became apparent that the effects of steadily rising global temperatures would be snow and storms and floods, not the drought and forest fires she might have presumed. Here at least. In Spain and in Australia of course, droughts and forest fires were exactly what they were getting. But in Britain, and in the city, it was snow. In April.

She had been standing, staring from her bedroom window, for maybe forty minutes before she heard the buzzing of the alarm in the living room. Fergus let it run longer than usual; it had been a late night for the boys and Matt had even left his bike in town rather than risk it in the gathering snow and the fuzzy haze of alcohol. She had stayed up until they returned and had taken them to task for putting Fergus in such a state before herself heading to bed, leaving the men to wrestle with toast and water glasses. She thought back to their faces the night before: Fergus had been a mess. A cup of tea was the very least he would need.

Padding through the living room to the kitchen, her greeting received only a grunt in return. Fergus was otherwise lifeless, forearm draped over his eyes while his other hand brushed the carpet. She looked at the outstretched arm, admired its lean solidity, the lines of muscle and sinew that stretched under his milky soft skin. Her mouth curled to a bud as she recognised her voyeurism and, wary of discovery, she slipped into the kitchen.

Bridget was already late, but was unwilling to leave the half-finished cup of tea cradled in her hands. Even though she spent most of her waking life in her work clothes, they always made her look like someone else: still her, but her in a parallel universe, where dance music had never happened and mothers always did the responsible thing. Only the three small stars tattooed on her left wrist reassured Ruby that she had not woken into a dream.

'Please, Ruby, can we have the heating back on? It's fucking snowing. It's bad enough that I've got to go out in the filthy stuff, without having to freeze my nuts off when I'm having a cup of tea.'

She breathed out a tiny laugh and crossed to the boiler, flipping a switch that made the white box stutter into a roar. It was strange that, even though anyone in the house could turn on the heating at any time, they always asked for her permission, left her to operate the machine. With water heating in the radiators, Ruby turned her attention to the kettle, to assembling mugs, teabags and milk in readiness. Absently she asked about what the day had in store for Bridget.

'Nothing special. I think we've got some interviews to sort out, and otherwise... Oh, I think we're going to advertise for a communications assistant, if you fancy it?'

For all her anti-establishment bluster, Bridget had never quite understood why Ruby would choose to be a full time student when she could get a proper job in an office that paid an actual salary, and still allowed for your hobbies: DJing for her, reading about South East Asian genocides for Ruby. While the water tumbled out of the kettle's spout, she repeated her disinterest in the world of financial services with as much humour as she could muster on a frozen morning.

Unseen, Bridget stared at the V cut into the back of Ruby's hair. She was the outsider in the house: Bridget, Matt and Jacob had all been undergraduates together and when Jacob had inherited, it had been a natural development for the three of them to move into this house together. When Ruby, hair aflame, had presented herself at the front door two years later, they had all felt a huge affinity for her and had welcomed her into their household. But she remained, in many ways, a lodger.

Bridget had been most optimistic. Another woman, of course, but also a student, someone who could keep them young. Could keep her young. Matt and Jacob worked for themselves, one designing websites, the other tending to the gardens of London's wealthy, and they were not so mired in corporate life. Neither of them had to wear a suit.

And yet Ruby had turned out to be the most stable, the most mature, of them all. She took care of paying the bills, making sure that there was milk in the fridge, juice for Lou. She was the most grown up of the four, and yet she refused to grow up, insisted on continuing the pointlessness of study.

'What are you going to do, Rubes? After you're done with the PhD? You're due to finish this autumn, right? Do you get to be a professor then?'

This again. It was like living with her mother, except Ruby's mother never asked that kind of question, instead willed Ruby to delay settling, conceding, surrendering. It was well meant, of course,

Bridget's curiosity, but she wondered how many more times, how many more ways, she could say that she did not know, did not want to know.

'And what about you? When do you stop with the DJing? You must be knackered.'

The stamina of Bridget astounded Ruby: that she was able to hold down a proper job, look after a toddler and still manage to run a night at the Old Blue Last was superhuman. And yet she did all of these with dedication, organisation and enthusiasm. She didn't drink much, and Ruby had never known her use illegal drugs. Aside from the smoking and gallons of tea, she seemed to have few vices.

'Actually, I am getting a bit old for it. Don't want to let it go though. It's all that's left of me – if I stop DJing, I'm just insurance and Lou. I love Lou, you know that, but I don't think it's healthy for him for me to just be a mum, and a corporate drone. How's he ever going to find who he is, if I don't know who I am?'

Ruby wanted to say that she would always very definitely be who she was and that Lou's very particular upbringing meant he'd always be a very particular person. But while she tried make this sound less like an accusation, Bridget rose from her chair, to check that her son was ready to go to day care. She paused at the door and turned back to her friend.

'Are you sure you're not shagging him?'

She nodded back towards the kitchen door that separated them from the living room and Fergus.

'Duh, no. Anyways, he's got a fiancée and, if you remember, I've got a boyfriend.'

'Yeah, but neither of them are here are they?'

She winked and swung into the living room, where Fergus was sitting up rubbing his eyes. He looked startled by Bridget's cheery 'good morning' and amused smile, and then the door swung shut. In the momentary silence of the newly sealed room, Ruby was left only with two cups of tea and the fleeting thought of Alex. The distance between them had grown ever greater, even on her visits home, making the relationship more a theoretical construct than a living, breathing thing. Yet even this sepulchre provided an anchor, an explanation for her living so deeply in books.

She slipped into the living room, leaving the ghost behind her, and took tea to the barely functioning Fergus. He accepted it with all the grace he could and sucked in the hot liquid. He had pulled on a t-shirt in the time since Bridget has passed through, but his jeans still hung neatly over a chair-back.

'Do you mind?'

Ruby was at the window and, once Fergus had grunted his acceptance, she drew back the curtains to reveal the glowing world. She wondered if Fergus was watching her silhouetted there and looked out at the whiteness beyond the window. The sky still hung like a threat over Stepney Green and tiny flakes still meandered through the air. But the snow was definitely thinning, slowing down. Tyre tracks cut through its carpet on the street and unseen walkers had left their trace as well. She peered up into the cloud, trying to ascertain if that was actually it, as if she could read in the flat grey the sky's intentions. But the flat greyness remained indecipherable, the sky tight-lipped. While Ruby deliberated over the wisdom of venturing out to the library, fatter snowflakes crowded the air once more, snarling and circling, blurring the familiar street: Ruby decided once and for all that indoors was the best place to be.

thirty-five

The dreams were becoming still more vivid, such that some mornings Fergus was not entirely sure whether he was waking or falling asleep, whether the alarm clock beside his bed was real or simply the signal of the coming dreamscape of the day. At this time, the city also became less intelligible: the longer he was there, it seemed, the less well acquainted with it he became. Navigating its streets and its social mores became harder, not easier as Fergus had expected. Familiarity with its complexities did not simplify the city; it simply made things more complex.

The snow was clearing, but the day still hung slow and greasy, and the melting slush accreted its dampness in small pools that gathered across the patchwork pavement, fragments of brown broken glass. Fergus had left Matt and Ruby working in the house, to take some air, the aches and sickness of the night before having withstood the combination of tea, water, painkillers, fried eggs and apples. Jacob had driven off to Highbury around mid-morning and the living room had become increasingly silent. Despite the damp, being outside had become irresistible.

The goats of the City Farm had refused to be coaxed from their shelters and the gate was in any case locked. On an ordinary Thursday, the farm would be open to visitors according to the sign, but Fergus realised that in this city, snow made any day extraordinary. St Dunstan's had similarly provided only brief distraction, so Fergus headed east, to the canal, to follow its towpath to Limehouse Basin. Much of the snow had already melted and, since lunchtime, the sky had lifted to reveal a murmur of the spring it had interrupted. But the path was still wet and slippery, the air still chill, and Fergus dug his hands deep into the borrowed pockets of Matt's waterproof jacket.

He made slow progress on the treacherous path and his mind wandered into the near future. Victorian terraces and postwar blocks peeked over the towpath wall but along the sunken course Fergus felt almost entirely apart from the confusion of the city. Yet the calm did little to soothe his hangover or to settle his swirling uncertainty: despite Matt's boyish enthusiasm and the absence of alternatives, he could not escape the conviction that his plan would end badly. Absently, he entered the darkness beneath a low bridge.

'Wanna come past, you gotta pay the tax. 'Else.'

With a flick of his head the boy indicated the canal. He was younger that Fergus, but tall and broad and his youth rendered him no less intimidating. Fergus had no recollection of approaching the bridge under Salmon Lane, but by now he was obscured under its span to all but the fish and the boy. And whoever it was that now stood behind him; an accomplice no doubt, greeted with another, friendlier nod.

He did not understand for some moments and his assailant grew impatient. He demanded whatever money the gangly Scot

THE CURSING STONE

was carrying; he in turn claimed he had none, nor a phone, nor anything that the thief would find of value. This was almost true: but while he had used most of the roll of notes that his father had given him, something over £50 remained, the notes and coins stuffed into his jeans pocket. He cursed his decision to bring the money with him, rather than leave it in the safety of the house.

'Are you fucking with me? I warn you, do not fuck with me or I'll cut you. Do you get me?'

Fergus felt an arm wrap around his throat and his own arm twist painfully behind him. Immobilised and suddenly more scared than he had been in over a decade, he waited while his assailant approached, brought his face very close to his own. The boy was shorter than Fergus, and his hard grey eyes were barely level with his victim's chin; Fergus could smell the nicotine on his breath, the sticky aroma of whatever the boy had used to cement his short bleached hair into a little, brittle flick that rose like a fence from his forehead.

With his free hand, Fergus wrestled into his pocket to retrieve the cash. Holding it out in front of him, loose in his upturned palm, he watched the boy's face crack in to an ugly smile that revealed a snaggle-tooth rising from his lower jaw, felt the boy's nail rake across his hand and close around the last of his money.

'See? Easy, isn't it?'

Fergus wasn't sure if the boy was talking to him or to his accomplice, who still held him from behind. He wondered if he should say something, acknowledge the situation, explain that this wasn't easy in the slightest, until he felt the grip around his right wrist tighten.

'It's only fifty quid, so you owe me, right? And I don't want none of your shit next time.'

Were the boy taller, his mouth would have been an inch from Fergus's face, but even so the snaggle-tooth and nicotine were close enough to make him tremble in an involuntary quake. The boy took a step backwards and launched a short punch into Fergus's soft stomach; he strained against his restraint to bend and double against the pain, the dull spreading pain, and when the unseen assailant released his grip, he stumbled to his hands and knees, and coughed and wheezed and tried not to vomit. Through his tears and his hair, he could see four legs walking away out into the light beyond the bridge; he could hear their laughter, its malice and cruelty. Then they were gone, and there was only Fergus, the cobbles and the pain.

thirty-six

Fergus shifted fractionally in the armchair, as far as the slow hot pain would allow. Matt began another iteration of what he insisted on referring to as the plan. Steve watched the slow traces of bubbles rising through his glass of beer, his faraway smile almost obscured by a knot of hair that fell across his face. While Matt spoke, explaining how they could gain entry to the tower through the car park, that Steve had done precisely this on a number of occasions previously, Fergus sought hints about the character of his unexpected guide from the tattoo that slithered down from the sleeve of his t-shirt.

The t-shirt, like the tattered cargo shorts, had once been black, but was now fading into a purple-ish grey. Matt had met Steve one summer, while he had worked as a bicycle courier to save some money for the following term. Steve had not been on summer vacation, had not gone to college; his work had not been an interesting diversion on his way to somewhere else, but was what he did, would do, until something happened to prevent him from doing it and he had to find another way to make a living. Steve lacked the advantages of Matt and Jacob, but found them both amusing; he had found Bridget to be both amusing and alluring and it was through his curious friendship with Matt that the conditions for Lou's birth had been established.

He had been to the top of Lauderdale Tower, and many other buildings in the city, not to steal, but to take pictures of the night-time vistas. These he would post on websites under the pseudonym of Harpy. There was a community, apparently, of similar adventurers whose only reward for risking arrest or worse was to gain access to places that ordinary people never could: abandoned hospitals; the skeletons of new towers; tunnels under the streets, connecting hidden stations and secret control rooms; other people's apartments.

Maltravers' apartment would be empty the following evening: Matt had already called the Half Moon Gallery and been able to elicit from the young woman on the phone that Maltravers would be unable to give an opinion that weekend on Matt's fictitious painting, since he was away at his parents place in the country, as he was most weekends. Not only did this mean that the coast was clear for the next day, it also meant that Fergus would have a two day head start before the alarm was raised. Fergus had no more objections, nor needed further clarifications, but Matt ran through the plan once more, elaborating on the details in excited anticipation until even he had become tired of their repetition and instead raised a toast to the success of their endeavours. Three glasses clinked softly.

'Shall we pop out for a pint, then?'

Fergus winced as he settled back into his chair, certain both that he had no desire to leave the house again that day and that he had not the means to buy a drink. He shook his head but suggested that the others should feel free to do so. Steve pushed himself upright from the suction of the sofa and put his head around the kitchen door to say goodbye to Ruby and Bridget and his son. Lou raced out into the living room, throwing himself at Steve who hoisted him high into his arms.

'Why don't you two come out for a drink?'

Fergus was relieved that Ruby at least declined Steve's invitation, offering instead to watch Lou, and he was happy in the calm of the house once the others had gone, and Lou had been put to bed. Ruby returned from story-telling and, having fetched a couple of beers from the kitchen, sat next to Fergus on the sofa. She studied him for a moment then clicked the TV into darkness.

'It's stupid, you know that don't you?'

At first, Ruby had been vocal in her opposition to Matt's plan, objecting both to its morality and its wisdom. But then Steve had arrived and Fergus had stopped listening, so she had withdrawn sourly to the kitchen, where she had been joined by Bridget and Lou while the men plotted in the living room. All the while she had held her tongue she had wished that Jacob was home, to bolster her objections. But, with Jacob out with friends and Bridget pretending not to care, she had been a lone voice of sanity.

He knew that her raising it now was less an attempt to sway him from the decision, more a simple distancing, a reminder that she did not approve, did not support the plan; that Fergus was about to disappoint her. He was surprised by how much this hurt him. He tried to explain that he had no choice, that he had tried legitimate means, and would have continued with them had the news from home not made things so urgent. It felt as if everything was conspiring to drive him from the city: from the need to return to his grandfather's side to the fact that he no longer had any money. He had run out of time and out of options. Only Matt's plan remained, and he was following it without joy or enthusiasm.

'Look, if it's the money, we can sub you, you know? No need to race away because of that. You'll be missed, whatever.'

He looked close to tears. To comfort him, she reached out a hand and rested it on his shoulder. That he flinched in response was unexpected.

'Are you OK? I didn't mean to... I'm sorry.'

With a grimace, Fergus rested his own hand on his ribs. His eyes squeezed shut for a moment, before his face settled back into its former composure. Ruby was watching him, with concern, with suspicion.

'It's nothing. Just some lads. This afternoon. They took my money, and one of them gave me a whack for my trouble.'

It was as he'd feared. Ruby started fussing over him, gently lifting his t-shirt to inspect the site of the pain. He tried to tense his muscles, for vanity's sake, but the pain would not allow it and his torso sagged under her gaze. Gently she ran her fingers over the reddened glut of pain, exploring its centre with the most tender pressure. His face twitched, but she did not see it.

'Thank god, it's only a bruise. But it's going to hurt. Christ, why didn't you say anything? You've got to report it.'

She leant forward to rummage through the objects heaped on the low table, finally retrieving her phone, holding it out to him like an accusation. Fergus focused instead on pulling his t-shirt back down, gingerly edging the fabric over the gathering contusion. The phone was still there, although Ruby's outstretch arm had begun to waver.

'I don't want to make a fuss. It was only a few pounds, anyhow. And they'll not get it back. Plus, if I call the police, they'll want statements and the like and I don't have the time to hang around for things like that. With what's going on tomorrow evening, I don't think I really need to be drawing attention to myself with the police. They'll be wanting to talk to me soon enough as it is.'

She laughed despite herself and her eyes sparkled, their light dissolving her concern and indignation, the weight of responsibility. Fergus laughed too, less forcefully but with no less relief. It felt good to have her laugh with him, rather than to judge him.

'You've had a crap few days, haven't you love? Come here – I promise I'll be careful.'

Gently, ever so gently, he felt her arms wrap around his shoulders, draw him to her, felt her warmth and softness cloak him from the harshness of the world. His cheek brushed hers, and his skin prickled with questions, uncertainties, and possibilities. He wondered why he had not thought of Shona for days, why he did not want to think of her now, why his own hand was now resting on Ruby's shoulder, why that should thrill him in the way it did. And then the front door slammed and he pulled away with a jolt, muttering apologies.

Bridget was in the doorway almost before the sound of the lock had died. She looked at them, on the sofa, at Ruby's smiling, open face and at Fergus, his flushed cheeks and the way he stared at his hands. She winked at Ruby.

'Sorry if I'm disturbing anything. I just couldn't stand being around Steve any longer, he was doing my head in. Anyway, sorry again. I'll be in my room. With the door shut. So, you know, as you were.'

thirty-seven

The city stretched beneath him under a clearing sky. The nearby towers jumbled like a forest, pushing hungrily into the light; but for the most part the buildings shrank until they formed a long low carpet that rolled out to its hazy edge. It did not peter out, even as it became more frayed, but simply ended. When he drove out from its precincts in a few hours, this border would not be apparent, would be lost in the transition to other towns and settlements, places that were not London. But now, from this vantage point, the end of the city was obvious and distinct.

By the time he reached Dorset, he would become the other person again, the one who was not London. He would again belong to the past, to his family and their land. He would become someone for whom marriage to Harriet Norden seemed plausible, necessary. The crush and hurry of the city would become briefly alien and unwelcome. He would unfurl himself.

The wind that drove the last clouds bit into his cheeks, reminding him that spring still carried the memory of winter. He pulled the cardigan more tightly around him and looked over the parapet to the street below. Life still pulsed, but the vehicles moved with a timid compactness quite unlike the fury of street level; the city's voice was stretched and buffeted on the wind, dreamlike.

His coffee was cold. He was cold. And it was nearly four o'clock. With a last look up to the hills of the north, Nicholas left the balcony and slid the door shut behind him. The sounds of the world became whispers and he stood for a moment in the hush, cataloguing his last eight years in the acquisitions that surrounded him. These relics of himself were predominantly sacred and ancient. There were no works of the secular or the modern, to which he felt no affinity despite himself. Nor was there doctrinal coherence: the symbols of early Christianity nestled alongside the totems of animist fertility spirits; Hindu dancing girls tilted their heads to angry Buddhist deities. Each had been emptied of meaning when it had been bought, but in their totality they seemed to speak of something unintended.

The moment passed and he shrugged. Another look into the cup convinced him to cross to the kitchen and, as he passed the sofa, he patted the hump of a seated bull, carved from polished black stone. The cold coffee swirled in the sink, settling quickly into ragged blotches on the steel. Nicholas refilled his cup with what remained in the little metal pot and swallowed it with one gulp. The cup rattled in its saucer as it met the cool stone of the counter.

At the front door, Nicholas looked again at his watch. He would be at the house in time to change for dinner. Harriet would be wearing a new dress and he wondered if, this time, it would help. He picked up the holdall and slung it over his shoulder, pausing only to key in the alarm code.

— ◉ —

He had seen the three towers of course: their jagged edges rose like bread knives above the city. But the blank starkness of the walls still startled Fergus. They rose from the pavement like a fortress, impenetrable at first sight. Through gaps, he could glimpse lush gardens and placid lakes, and the garlands that hung from the windows of the lower blocks. All this was hidden from the noise and clamour of the city outside, the province of the citadel within.

In the pub, while they waited for Steve to arrive, Matt and he had exchanged broken sentences, each uneasy at the prospect of night fall and their task. Surrounded by dark wood and the chatter of office workers, he had listened to Matt's stories of his previous adventures with his friend into the forbidden places of the city; the thrill of clandestine exploration and the times they had almost been discovered. These stories had not reassured him and he had found himself clutching at the little golden pendant that hung around his neck.

'Is that from your girl?'

Matt had broken off from his description of his night in the condemned hospital, the unfathomable shapes frozen in the sample jars that lined the shelves of the abandoned laboratory, to watch Fergus turn the trinket in his fingers. At first confused, as if waking from a dream, he shook his head, then grudgingly allowed Matt to look, to read the inscription.

'It looks like a love token. You sure you're not secretly seeing another woman?'

His flippancy irritated Fergus. Wordlessly he took back the pendant and returned it to his neck, slipping the metal under his t-shirt. Icily, he said simply that Peggy was his grandmother.

'Sorry mate. Fair enough. Is it your grandfather's then? Like, a good luck charm for your trip?'

His answer stalled on his tongue. His mouth hung open, waiting for words that would make sense, resolve the questions into coherence, but none came. A burst of laughter and shouting broke from across the bar, and the need to speak passed. Both young men turned to the source of the disruption, but only one in gratitude.

'Wankers.'

His venom spent, Matt returned to his story of the enlarged body parts he had discovered in the derelict hospital. Fergus drew deeply of his pint, pleased that this excused him from talking. Instead he listened as Matt moved into the operating theatre, where gowns still hung like ghosts in an ante room. His excitement in the retelling was childlike, an endearing naivety quite beyond a concern with consequences.

The story had only reached the roof by the time Steve arrived and Fergus felt cheated that he would not hear how they had escaped, untroubled, from the building. The three conspirators settled on another drink before they headed off into the darkening lanes that clustered around Cloth Fair. Beyond the ripples of light and sound that marked the way back to The Hand and Shears, the narrow streets were silent but for the echoes of their steps; the houses blind with darkened windows.

The solitude did not last. Emerging onto Aldersgate Street through a narrow passage, the brightness and din of London re-established itself, became a wall. Across the street, the tower rose above them, blacker than the darkening sky. Where before the walls had seemed simply impassable, they now took on a more menacing and forbidding aspect. There seemed no way in, and Fergus hoped vainly that they would have to abandon their attempt. But Steve led them across the road and down a ramp that curved below street level.

In the shadows below, Matt pulled up the hood of his jersey, as did Steve – from a small back pack he pulled a peaked cap, which he handed to Fergus. Once all were obscured, Steve pressed a finger to his lips and indicated that they should wait beside a large metal gate. The minutes crawled, but then there were lights dancing in the darkness and the gate swung inwards. With a purr, a car pulled past them and swung slowly up the ramp. The driver did not see the three figures slip between the closing gates, illuminated by the fading red glow.

The harsh white light of the lift was brutal, and Fergus instinctively pulled the peak of his cap lower over his face. Numbers illuminated and climbed on the panel beside the door, until it they reached 41; the door slid open and revealed the subdued lighting of the triangular lobby. The sound of the closing lift doors sank into the thick carpet underfoot. Three doors led on from the lobby, including one marked with the number 411. But Steve passed by without a glance and led them onto the landing of the fire escape. At the very top of the staircase, he eased open a door to reveal a ladder. With a smile and a cock of his head, he began to scale the last few metres of the tower.

thirty-eight

There was only the single red eye, flicking left and right. Fergus could feel it hunting him, searching him out in the darkness of Maltravers' living room. Nothing else was visible, only patches of blurred blackness on a field of blackness. And the light. He should look away, he knew, let his eyes grow accustomed to the gloom, but he was transfixed by it and so remained locked in the darkness of the apartment.

On the roof top, the lights of the city had provided sufficient illumination. They had been able to pick their way without difficulty through the blocks of metal and concrete that littered the platform atop the tower. The footholds and grips that had made finding the way down onto the terrace possible had been clearly visible. And in the night's glow, Steve had eased open the unlocked glass door that led into the flat with a single touch.

But here, inside, the dancing lights of the external city only deepened the blackness. Fergus could not make out the shapes that threatened to appear from the gloom as his eyes gradually grew accustomed, and so he stood transfixed by the light of the burglar alarm, too afraid to move, to breathe. He felt the swirl of displaced air as one of his companions strode out into the darkness, smoothly, unimpeded; heard the feet slap gently on the wooden floor, heard clicks and snaps, then saw Steve's smile through the stew of grey. The red light had disappeared.

'I thought you'd never done a break in before?'

Fergus had had his suspicions about Steve, even when he had indignantly denied any criminality.

'No, I said I'd never burgled a place before – not 'til now. I've been in flats and houses though, just never taken anything. Never left a trace. I'll reset the alarm when we leave.'

Matt's flashlight flicked on and its beam jittered about the room, casting fleeting shadows. Fergus followed its path to the kitchen, where he lit his own torch. In the corner was a bowl of cat food, half eaten; a small white cup sat lonely on the counter, the only testament to the apartment's human occupation. He understood now the urge to explore, to open every cupboard and draw, and felt queasy at its seduction. He dragged himself back to the task at hand, and into the living room.

'What does this thing look like anyways?'

Matt was by some shelves arranged along one wall, his lamp light licking the artefacts they housed. Frozen faces glared back in their brief illumination, some painted, others in naked stone or polished wood. The shadows contorted his face and form too, as he moved along the cabinet, studying each object in turn. Across the room, Steve was on his haunches staring into the lamp-lit face of a cow.

'It's just a big stone. Like a granite doughnut. But it's got a cross

scratched into the top of it, like a hot-cross bun. I don't know how big it is to be honest. I've only seen a photo...'

Fergus was interrupted by a hiss from the darkness, then a yowl; there was a clatter and a stumbling and an abrupt yelp from Steve.

'Fucking hell! What the fuck was that? Fuck!'

Almost instantly the room lights were ablaze and Steve was sitting on the sofa, clutching his cheek with his left hand. Matt remained with the light switches and swept the room intently, his eyes narrowed, his skin taut. But while a hundred eyes stared back at him, none of them belonged to a living creature.

Steve peeled his hand from his face and winced at the red stickiness that had collected there. His cheek was tracked with four risen scores, each running maybe two inches in parallel. Bulbs of blood swelled under each before beginning a slow descent towards his jaw. Fergus offered his handkerchief mutely; Steve accepted it and pressed it firmly to his face.

'I was just looking at this bull when, wham, something hits me, slices me. It was like a knife cutting me, and then there's all this hissing and squalling. What the fuck man?'

He stared intently at the bull, then looked to the demon with six arms standing behind the sofa with suspicion; in one of the hands was a trident.

'Don't be fucking stupid. It was a cat, mate. A fucking cat.'

Matt was pointing at a large grey cat, back arched, standing in the shadows by the bottom of the stairs. Its tail flicked like a serpents tongue and, while it did not advance, it showed no signs of retreating either.

'I think you woke it up. You probably sat on its tail or something.'

Matt laughed at the absurdity.

'I suppose it's too late to be much use turning these lights off? Can you see it, Fergus? Any hot cross buns among the demons?'

It took fifteen minutes to be sure that the cursing stone was not there. Steve and the cat kept a close watch on each other throughout the search: the cat glared from the bottom step of the stairs, its tail counting out the seconds as they passed. By the end, Steve had to pull Fergus by the shoulder from the study that led off from the living room. They sat disconsolate for a few moments at the dining table, Fergus thinking only of his failure. He shaped his mouth, and then again, but could find nothing to say.

'Hey Fergus! Up here! I think I've found it. Fetch that knapsack up, will you?'

Matt's voice, a little too loud, drifted down the stair way. They had not noticed his absence, lost as they were in their own disappointments, and only slowly realised that he had slipped upstairs to the very top of the tower. Had it not been for the cat, Fergus doubted that he would have noticed the staircase at all. Caution abandoned, he scraped his chair over the floor and, with building speed, ascended. By the top he was taking two steps at a time and was breathless when he reached Matt in the bedroom. He was by the window, gazing out onto another terrace. Fergus scanned the room. Seeing nothing that resembled the stone, he followed Matt's eyes to the circular table outside. At its centre was a stone.

'A big fucking doughnut, right?'

He reached out his hand toward it, but the window held him back. Fergus could only rest his palm on the glass, while a thin tear escaped over his eyelid and glanced off the smooth cheek below. Embarrassed, he gripped his bottom lip between his teeth and tried to contain the relief that the stone released and the unexpected sadness that he now knew would follow.

Steve stood behind them for a moment, then turned his attention to the door. The lock this time thwarted him. He swore, his frustration now as acute as that of the others. Carelessly he took the picture frame from the window sill and threw it onto the bed. The latch squealed and the window complained as he slid it open. His foot on the sill, he was out onto the terrace and to the table in an instant. There he paused, his back to the others; the hum of the city rose on the night air. A sigh, and Steve lifted the stone to his chest and turned back to the window.

'Fuck, that's heavy. Shit. We're never going get this up over the roof. And that little rucksack is going to be next to useless.'

Fergus heard the crush of the wooden window frame as Steve rested the stone there. So close now. Behind him, Matt was rooting through the wardrobe, scattering bags and boxes across the floor.

So close. To have come so close.

From the other side of the open window, Steve's eyes looked straight into his, a mirror of his own anger and frustration. Their hands also, planted gently on the dome of the cursing stone, formed a symmetry, one resting in each of the stone's four quarters. Steve began to say something, but his eyes slipped from Fergus, over his

THE CURSING STONE

shoulder and into the room beyond. A small smile, the hint of a nod.

'I think we've blown any chance of leaving without a trace, but this should be strong enough to carry it.'

Surrounded by the contents of Maltravers' wardrobe, Matt held a large leather holdall, the kind with handles that wrap all the way around the bottom of the bag. It would take the weight of the stone and could be easily carried by two people, one holding each handle. Fergus laughed.

'Aye, I think he'll know we've been. So much for getting away scot-free. Anyhow, shall we go? I mean, let's just walk out the front door. Nothing to lose now.'

'Except it's double locked. And unless you've seen a spare key lying around, we're going to need a hammer and chisel. And for the neighbours to be deaf. We're better having a go at the roof.'

Matt was already at the window, lifting the stone into the mouth of the leather bag. As he did so, his bottom lip protruded in appraisal of the weight, his head bobbling and his eyes raised to the night sky.

'Yeah, I reckon it's ten, maybe twelve kilos. There's three of us, so should be alright. Shall we? I fancy a pint.'

thirty-nine

With every jolt, the bus reopened pain in his abdomen and the ache bloomed. The exertions of hoisting the stone up and over the roof of Lauderdale Tower had ignited the welt bulging beneath his ribs. In the night air, his grimaces had remained unseen, but once on the stairway back to the lift lobby, Matt had raised an eyebrow before taking the leather straps from his hand, carrying the holdall in tandem with Steve, until they had reached the bus stop by the cathedral.

On Hinba, or in any other place Fergus could imagine, they could only have looked suspicious, or at least odd, even in the electric darkness of Friday evening. But none of the people scuttling over the pavement, towards home or towards a bar, gave them a second look, simply rolling their eyes at the obstruction they caused. They had passed the ruins of a church where men with beards and shabby clothes gathered around a bench to share cigarettes and to drink from cans. Emerging into the bright light of a too-pristine square, men in suits stood in little corrals outside a bar, smoking and drinking lager, noisy and provocative. They had skirted the steps of the great temple, still spotted with seated tourists, wondering where next they should head; above them rose two stocky towers and a dome of preposterous proportions, topped with a golden cross that glinted in the lights from below. And then they had waited for the bus to labour up the slight hill and to open its doors to them.

As the bus meandered eastwards, the conspirators said little, content to breathe in the relief of their liberty. Fergus kept the holdall tight between his feet, one leg looped through a handle, and watched his face shimmer in the window. Behind him, he heard Matt on the phone, calling the house, calling Ruby, to give their news, so that preparations could be made, so that Ruby could stop her worrying, could relax, rejoice.

Fergus wanted to ask her if she was glad that it was over, that her unexpected houseguest would be leaving shortly, if she knew either way, happy or sad. He knew of course that, even if it were he talking with her on the phone or even beside her in the privacy of the house, after the others had turned in for the night, he would not be able to do so. He tried nonetheless to picture her face at the moment of hearing, but his imagination gave him no clues as to whether this moment was a moment for rejoicing, or one for regret.

As the bus moved off from its stop, it swayed violently and Fergus put his hand to his stomach to contain the ache. A young woman swung onto the top deck from the stairs, laughing with whoever was on the other end of the phone line; she sat in the seat immediately in front of him and continued to talk excitedly about her evening. Her head bobbed and her hair danced across her shoulders. Among the tresses, something flashed white, a playing card in a magic trick. Only in a stationary moment, while she paused to allow the other to speak, did Fergus realise that it was the shop tag still attached to the back of her dress. He did not recognise the retailer's marquee and could not make out the price, but he wondered if he should tap her on the shoulder, if mentioning the offending square of cardboard to her would make her happier or sadder.

— ◉ —

Most of the food was eaten, but gobs of sauce lurked in the corners of the tin boxes scattered across the table top; some pieces of brown-blistered bread remained and rice grains clung in clumps to the plates. There were empty cans too – the ones still containing beer had moved with the people to the sofas of the other room. The cat considered for some moments the piece of chicken, painted brilliant red, that had been placed in his dish. He bent forward to smell it, withdrew, then returned, this time extending a pink flash of tongue in exploration. He recoiled, coughed, then slunk into the living room in search of other distractions.

'But the views! Fucking hell, all of London, just stretched out like that. Beautiful.'

Matt's exuberant retelling of their adventure stilled a little at the thought of the lights and absences that had etched the shape of his city from the vantage of Lauderdale Tower. Steve rose to leave, handing the sleeping Lou to his mother; it was very nearly midnight and the story of their visit to Maltravers' flat had been told twenty times. It was time to head home. Fergus received Steve's last embrace before he departed; he thanked him fulsomely for his help and promised to say nothing, should the question be asked. As Steve left the room, his shadow peeling slowly from the door frame, Fergus slumped gracelessly onto the sofa once more. A moment later, Bridget wished him good night from the hall, taking Lou with her, to settle him for the night.

'Well, big man, I'm off to bed too. I'll see you in the morning, before you head off, right?'

Matt bumped his fist gently against Fergus's wavering outstretched hand. He flashed a demonic grin at Ruby, then dragged the dozing Jacob from his armchair.

'I'll throw this one onto his bed. Leave the stuff in the kitchen Ruby – we'll sort it out in the morning, OK?'

Ruby nodded. Unlike other evenings, she was happy to leave the detritus for another time. She slumped onto the sofa next to Fergus, only to rise immediately to claim to cans of beer from the low table.

'Cheers, Fergus. I still think it was madness, but I am pleased that you've got your butterlump back. I hope it helps. With your granddad. With everything.'

Now he could ask her. Now, here, he could ask if his leaving made her happy or sad. He could find the words, rolling loose in his mouth, that might end the ambiguity. Only the cat was a witness to whatever his drunkenness might say to her drunkenness. And his leaving tomorrow meant that anything remembered could be forgotten soon enough, would not matter, unless it mattered. He could ask, could find out how she felt. How he felt.

But he did not ask. Words seemed suddenly superfluous; instead he turned to her curious, smiling face and he kissed her. Or tried to kiss her. It was not clear to him whether what passed between them counted as a kiss; their mouths had met and he had felt the coolness of her tongue against his, but he could not tell how much time passed before he felt her tensing, felt her hands hard against his shoulders, pushing. It might have been moments, or not time at all, but it was over quickly. Ruined. He pulled away in horror of himself.

'Hey, it's OK Fergus. I'm not angry. Just, I've got a boyfriend. And you're engaged. Got to sort that stuff out, before, you know. Up to you, really. But I'm not two-timing anyone, and I'm nobody's holiday shag.'

She stroked his arm while she spoke, and his cheeks reddened all the more at her touch.

— ◉ —

When he had left the house, finally, she had embraced him, kissed him bloodlessly on the cheek, told him it was all good, that they were good, that he should stay in touch. And she had waved and smiled as he had trudged down the steps, the leather bag that contained his notebooks and his few clothes, wrapped around the cursing stone, gently swinging at his side. Matt and Bridget and Lou had also embraced him, told him the same things, but he had not heard them. Only the pressure of Ruby's arms had reached his skin through the back of his jacket, his shirt. As he'd dropped the bag onto the back seat of Jacob's car, had slid into the passenger seat, lowered the window, he had only heard her farewell wishes. He had watched her vanish from the rear-view mirror, as Jacob turned the car past St Dunstan's and past the wary goats.

Neither of them spoke for a long time. The chaos of cars and people, buses and vans swirled beyond the windscreen and Fergus felt the city to be evermore incomprehensible. It was as if he had arrived for the first time and had forgotten the language of the place. As they twisted through the back streets and thoroughfares

THE CURSING STONE

of east London, all he had learned unravelled in drab brick and the debris of the street. Blocks of look-alike flats blurred into one, such that he thought they must be lost in an endless circle, condemned to return and to leave and to return forever. Later, they sped along angry motorways that cut through streets, where front doors stepped out directly into the roar of unforgiving mobility. This city seemed, finally, unknowable.

'This should be fine, Fergus. You know. It should get you home safely.'

He did not have money left for train fares. The idea had emerged last night, looking for all the world like something concrete, reliable. Steve, the man who had made the recovery of the stone possible, had endorsed it, given it credence and validity. He had hitchhiked to Manchester and back only two months previously. All that was needed was to get to a service station on the motorway and find a driver heading as far north as you needed. At the right service station, that would not be a problem. Everyone was sure of it. Even Jacob, who had brooded on the moral content of their actions in Maltravers' flat since their return; even he joined the chorus of approval. Furthermore, he had offered to drive Fergus to a service station the following morning. Today.

'You must be glad to be going home.'

Fergus did not answer and Jacob did not press. The road slipped past them with a muffled roar, but the silence built around them, so that neither could breathe. They had arrived at London Gateway and Jacob had stopped the car in a space among a hundred other cars. He rested his hands on the wheel for a moment, and exhaled.

'Look, I'm sorry, OK? I just think that breaking and entering is wrong; it was stupid and wrong. But, OK, I understand that it was

a last resort. You had no choice. I get that. And I am pleased that you've got the stone. It belongs on Hinba, I accept that. Just don't ask me to cheer your exploits, OK?'

He looked back to where the holdall sat safe behind Fergus, and then at Fergus himself. He waited, his face open, hopeful, but his companion simply looked at the hands resting on his thighs. The finger ends were ragged, the victims of a nervous, dreamless night. Only the slow rise and fall of his chest announced his presence in the car. Jacob touched his shoulder and Fergus accepted its warmth.

'You OK?'

He realised that he hadn't spoken for over an hour and his rudeness appalled him. Weaving together a smile, he looked up.

'Yeah, I'm fine. Sorry. Just all a bit much, and still not yet done. Won't be right 'til I'm back on the island with that. And even then, I'm not sure. You're right about the break-in. I just hope it doesn't come back to haunt any of you.'

Jacob nodded. A more comfortable silence grew around them and they headed off to the cafeteria, to get some tea and to search the tables of customers for a lorry driver heading north.

THE CURSING STONE

part four

The Prince Returns

forty

Only his breathing interfered with the sea's conversation with the wind. The gulls too were quiet today, out hunting on the broad ocean. He turned, his eyes now sated by the blade of Skye's frosted crags, and trudged further along the beach. Trudged, because there was no other way to describe his daily searching along the foreshore. He had collected already some wood and plastic, all of which had long forgotten their original form, the shapes and colours erased by the workings of the irresistible sea. These pieces he had bundled together and tied with a length of sorry rope, so that they might be carried more easily back to the barn, to be sorted and stored wherever space permitted. Something might be of value to someone, and the wood would heat his water and his food, so that the remains of his father's insurance money might stretch a little further.

He had not expected to live so long. His calculations had been based on an accident, or worse, finishing him long ago. It was now impossible that the money would carry him to his pension. It was still two months before the man from Mallaig would visit, to weigh the shreds of plastic cluttering the barn and calculate the pittance he would offer for all these days of work. He wondered how he would have survived if he had had any trace of self-respect; if pride had kept him from clearing the beaches of detritus, clipping it by hand into slivers. He most probably would have starved by now. But fortunately his pride had been stolen from him with his father, as a boy. As a man, he had had none left to prevent him from sinking into the filth that the sea did not want.

A lone tern shrieked overhead, its cry carried on the wind high onto the cliffs above. The hidden mainland was surely still there, behind the purple rise of Rum, across the blue water, sparkling with the clear spring light. The brief snow of the previous week had cleared completely now and the wet air had given way to a more seasonal clarity. Had he gone then, after his father had died, to take up the offer of sanctuary with a cousin he had not met, with his wife and daughters in Kinlochleven, he would most probably have been happier. But it was not guaranteed. And he would have had to give up his father's place, his place, leave it undefended against the Buchannans, their avarice and entitlement. He would have had to give up the possibility of revenge.

The beach began to taper towards the little rocky headland at the point, and he stumbled on the large, flattened rocks that backed the bay above the tide line. He had crossed this bar of gnarled rock a thousand times or more and yet still he stepped gingerly on its slickness. The tern dropped into the sea just beyond the lacklustre surf. Duncannon paused, watching for it to break the surface, to see what bounty it carried; the fish flashed silver in the beak for a moment and then was gone; the tern tore itself from the water and rose again into the air, pulling against the insistent gravity. It wheeled once and set off back along the shoreline.

Alone again, Duncannon dropped heavily from the rock onto the beach. His knees complained in clicks and pops, but he walked on in spite of them. At the far end of this beach was a squat basalt stack that had been a fortress once, before the Christians and the Vikings came; after that, the Clanranalds had made it a gaol, which had passed on their leaving to the Buchanans. The stone remains of grim walls still clung to the crag, high above his barn. He had lived his whole life beneath the Buchanans' ancient prison and had not thought to escape.

Half way between the headland and the stack, he stopped. A large blue drum lay forlorn among the tufts and boulders at the cliff's foot. It was open at both ends, but nonetheless contained a great deal of plastic. It rested between two painfully familiar rocks. It was here that his father's head had split open. The barrel lay over the place where James Duncannon had stopped rolling, lifeless and bloodied.

It was a place he passed everyday but never now approached. Then, he had run to it, the hot blood of youth pushing him on, convinced that if he could reach him he could save him, could put right the crime. But his father had been dead before Duncannon had placed his hand on his chest. The bloody misshapen mass that had once been a handsome, noble face was smeared and distorted yet more by the tears that hung in the boy's eyes. But even through the distortion, the figure on the cliff edge above had remained as clear as before, when the wrestling and shouting had begun. The noise had startled him: his father had sent him out, so that he might receive a visitor, but Duncannon had assumed that it would be the woman, not the man; that the house would be closed up and silent. And yet instead, there had been his father, outside and arguing, up on the crag. And then he had been falling, and then he had been dead. Duncannon had been just a boy that day, but in the endless time that followed, weeping over his father's corpse, he had become a man.

He bent down by the barrel, one knee on the cold rock, and turned it in his hands, felt its weight, tried to calculate its value. His hands shaking, he took a length of rope and looped it through the empty drum, and tied it tight, like a chain through a pendant's clasp. And then he could avoid it no longer and he looked up to the crag above, expecting to see him staring down once more.

After the doctor had been, and the priest, Buchanan had visited the farm. He had not knocked, and had found the boy sobbing by the fire. He had been brief, wanting only to make sure that the Duncannon boy had understood him, to understand what had been clear from the stony face that had stared down at the beach, so long such that there could be no mistake: he did not care that the boy knew, only that he should be silent. And so he had been and so he was.

Behind him, the stutter of McCredie's boat coughed in the distance. Grateful for the intrusion, he rose to his feet once more, turning to watch the thin line of the *Tern's* wake cut the flat sea. Maybe this would be the day that the Buchanan boy would return with the cursing stone. If not today, then surely soon. Duncannon let the thought slip from him, as he had every day he had watched for McCredie since the boy had left.

When the boat had disappeared around the headland, he took up the loose end of the rope and slung it over his shoulder. The bright blue barrel rattled and jumped over the stones behind him, and he trudged on with his treasures towards the kettle by the hearth.

forty-one

The kitchen was empty. Only the garden door, swinging gently on its hinges in the morning breeze, betrayed the presence of others. Her mother would be out in the sunshine, cutting flowers for the table or hanging washing that would swell with fresh spring air. Tea warmed by the stove and she dashed red-brown gouts of it out of the pot into the cup that had been left for her. Taking her tea to the table, she waited, heedless of the need for the day to begin.

There were no sounds either, not even from her grandfather's room. No creaks or coughs, nor those frightening noises that had burst into the night, waking Mary and her parents, shaking the floors with their force and malice. She had let them go to him, fearful that it was the sound of death that raged in the darkness. He had looked so near to dying that evening. When she had arrived from the harbour she had been full of optimism and fortitude, enough to sustain the whole family; but at the sight of his paper skin and dull eyes, all her courage had fled. She hoped only that he was sleeping now, as near to peace as life would allow.

Her mother had told her what to expect, but with such little gravel in her voice. It was a story that had to be told as if it were true, so that her husband would be reassured in his anxiety and her daughter would come home to comfort him. But Mary had not believed it and now knew that her mother could not be blind to these simple facts: Fingal Buchanan would be dead before the end of the week. It would be a painful death.

'Your father's sleeping. It's a Sunday, after all, and he was with Fingal most of the night. I suppose you heard him well enough.'

She was silhouetted in the doorframe, and only the daffodils in the crook of her arm shone with their own colours. She was shorter and her shoulders were defeated by gravity, by hard work and worry. Yet her mother had managed a little joy for Mary, some shred of gladness, and her smile when it was revealed was effortless. The flowers were leant in the sink and, without question, Morag brought the pot and replenished Mary's cup. As always, she added too much milk and as always Mary did not object. Especially not today.

She was busy with the bread, her body swaying with the knife, her back to Mary, talking about the garden, about the characters of the island and their goings-on. Mary let her talk, let her escape the facts upstairs through other less desperate lives, through the colours of hyacinths. And then they were eating, mouths occupied with other things, safe from naming their fears for some moments more.

'I've been elected President of the Archaeological Society.'

Only crumbs remained and, to keep her mother from sweeping them into her hand and clearing plates, she had had to say something. Something pale, something from over there. She did not need to tell her that there had been no other candidates, that the

Society numbered only twelve people, and that its only function was to organise a series of poorly attended speaker meetings in the Student Union, which she now had the honour to oversee.

'I was thinking, once the cursing stone is back on the island, I might invite Mr Galbraith to address one of our meetings on it. Do you think he'd like that?'

Her mother's face twitched, flickering between tears and smiles, fear and pride. Her left hand weighted down her right so that it could not scratch at the table cloth, nor at her arm. At last, the twitches smoothed into a wide beam, shorn of her usual modesty.

'Look at you! It seems like only yesterday that Mr Galbraith was your teacher and now you're inviting him to Glasgow, to one of your own meetings. What's that thing they say in that film? The student becomes the master, is it?'

The laughter felt good. Years fell from her mother's face and the miles that separated their worlds dissolved. It had only been six months or so since Mary had left for the city, for her life, but already the bonds had weakened such that she knew she had had a choice over whether she should return to her family at this hour. She had not come through duty, but love.

'It's working out, then? Studying? The city? It's all you hoped?'

All she had hoped too. Her own happiness was bound closely to the success of her daughter's adventure with the mainland: she had willed it, fought for it, encouraged and supported her in taking this path. She had sent a part of herself with Mary to Glasgow, the part that could be spared, the part that was not needed on Hinba, would not be missed by the men, by the other islanders. She hung breathless on Mary's confirmation that all was as they had hoped, that her free spirit was at ease on those far horizons.

Only the boy. Craig. Only this troubled her. She had married young herself and knew what was lost in that. For Mary to have this chance and to surrender it all to a boy before she started would be too painful. And yet she did not want her daughter to be lonely, nor to be one of those girls, too liberal in her affections. She could say nothing of course, and could only trust in the good sense that she had fed her daughter as an infant.

'Do you think you'll come back, when it's finished? When you've got your degree, I mean.'

She willed Mary to say no, to laugh politely and shake her head, thoughtfully, without closing any doors, without condescension.

'I doubt it, mum. There is just so much to learn. I love it. Some of them, on my course, they spend their time carrying on. You never see them in the library. I don't understand it. I've got just three years to explore five-thousand of years of history. I don't want to waste the chance. Thank you, for… well, you know.'

She would not cry, even through happiness. If the tears started, Morag could not be sure that they would stop. She had wished him dead a thousand times, but now that the time was here, she could only think of the loss of the old fool from her life and imagine how vast was the pain that her husband laboured beneath.

'That's OK, sweetheart. I'm just pleased that it's what you wanted. I only ever wanted for you to be happy, to be what you wanted to be. You and Fergus. I think you're nearer to it than he is, if I'm honest.'

The ceiling creaked above them. Both women raised their eyes towards it, saying nothing. A door ticked its way open and footstep followed footstep before they ceased. The muffled sound of a human voice fell through wood and plaster and paper, its meaning and form lost in the dust. Mary looked towards her mother, whose own eyes remained fixed on the ceiling, intent and desperate. At last, no longer able simply to imagine her husband's reddened eyes, she pushed back her chair and, apologising, left the kitchen for the stairs.

forty-two

The singing lapped against the boat, fighting a butterfly battle with the sound of McCredie's motor. The little church sat lonely in a field between the village and the jetty, and the islanders' voices had rushed over the pasture and the brine to meet them as soon as they rounded the headland. It was as it had always been and yet seemed so dissonant now. The island itself no longer fitted snugly within him: on their approach, it's long, low slab had seemed sluggish on the horizon and the summit of Carn a' Ghaill was no longer exultant, but squat and insipid. He had expected to see Duncannon on the beach, even from so far out, but he had seen no-one.

At the first bump between boat and jetty, Fergus stepped from the deck and onto the solid concrete. While his legs settled into their new state, he paused for a moment, resting the brown holdall on the ground. McCredie and the young hand, a boy he vaguely recognised from Mallaig, began to unload boxes and drums and great spools of wire onto the harbour side. Their curses and laboured breathing provided a syncopated rhythm to the straining of *Abide With Me* that rose now from the church.

Swift to its close ebbs out life's little day. He knew the hymn well; it was a favourite of the Reverend Drummond. But he had never before felt its poignancy. Now, while his grandfather lay dying, it weighed heavily upon him. The decision made, he shouted a farewell to the labourers, grasped the handles of the holdall and set out for the village. Shona would have to wait, after all. He should probably wash and change first in any case. He had been in these same clothes for over 24 hours, had slept in them, lolling in the cab of the lorry that had brought him to Fort William. His mouth was repellent, even to him. Yet, as he passed the *Harbour Bell*, he prayed that she had gone to church with her parents, that she would not see him passing, forsaking her, as he hurried to his home. She would understand, of course, that he would need to see his grandfather as soon as possible, but to catch sight of him slipping passed without explanation would cause needless distress.

He was soon out of sight of the pub and slipping into the garden, where the high wall hid him from the whole island. He walked carefully over the flagstones, taking the time to remember the flowers that rose each spring, noting that his mother's secateurs still lay in the grass by the daffodil beds, neglected, forlorn. Otherwise, everything was as it should be. Pristine. Even after winter, the whitewashed walls of the house remained white, with no flakes to be seen. The windows gleamed back the late morning like quicksilver in prim frames. There were no weeds between the flagstones where he walked, nor in any of the flower beds; the runner beans ran up their canes from a flawless rectangle of peaty brown soil. Were they expecting him, he would have thought that they had spent days preparing the perfect scene for their reunion. But he had given no word about his return.

The back door was ajar and he had only to caress it with his free hand for it to fall open upon the kitchen. Mary did not look up for a moment, as if the presence of another did not surprise her. He cleared his throat, offered a greeting and a smile, and waited for his sister's thoughts to re-enter her body. Then there were smiles and embraces, and all of the curled and barbed things that both had held so tightly moments before fell away.

'Sorry, I was miles way. Must've been dreaming.'

She ushered him inside, took his bag and was jolted by its weight. Seated now, he watched her pour out tea for the two of them.

'That's odd, because I haven't dreamt at all, not for days. First time since I can remember. Nothing. Not since I got that.'

He nodded towards the bag by the back door. Mary stopped, the milk jug hovering still over a cup, and flicked her head between Fergus and the leather holdall. Her lips quivered and her nostrils flared slightly.

'You got it? And it's in there? It's that heavy? Of course it is. My god, I didn't even think, I was so happy to see you. Can I...'

She didn't wait and was on her knees before the question had trailed into nothingness. Clothes and books spilled from the leathery mouth and onto the floor, an unruly setting for this rarest of gems. Her freneticism collapsed into calm wonder. Cautiously, Mary brushed her fingertips across the smooth surface, tracing the ancient cut to the centre of the cross. With an effort she lifted the stone out of the bag and onto the table; she laid her cheek beside her cup and simply watched, waiting for something to transpire.

'How is he? I couldn't tell, not from what mum said. But dad, he wanted me to come home urgent. Whether I'd got the stone or not. So.'

The delight creased from Mary's face and she straightened in her chair. A hand still rested lightly on the stone, but otherwise her full attention was marshalled into answering her brother.

'It's not good. He looks terrible. And the sounds. When he coughs it sounds like his body is going to rip apart. The doctor is due over tomorrow again, so we should know more. But I don't think he'll last the week, Fergus.'

He'd known, of course. The knowing had borne down on him all week. But that did not slow the tears now. There were no convulsions, just quiet streaks that ran rapidly to his jaw and dropped disconsolate into his collar. Neither spoke until they had dried.

'I should go up and see him. Take him this. Maybe it will lift him. Give him hope.'

Mary did not join him on the stairs, but stayed in her seat, content to grant him this moment. She heard his heavy tread on the steps, the creaking of the house under the weight of the stone and its favoured son. Once she was sure that he had closed the bedroom door behind him, she pulled on her trainers and slipped from the kitchen and out into the day. The bells from the church began to peal as she pulled the garden gate onto its latch.

Fergus watched his grandfather's narrow chest stutter under the covers. His face was wan, lifeless, but his eyes flickered under papery lids. The stone became heavy in his arms and, as quietly as he could, he placed it on the wooden chair beside the bed, as if it were the visitor, not he. He waited. Through his socks and the threadbare rug, he could feel the twists and rises of the floor boards, could feel them squirm beneath his toes. All the years that they had lain here, and yet they still shifted, still sought that place of perfect repose.

The bed sheets whispered between themselves and slowly Fingal stirred from empty sleep. Fergus waited until his eyes were fully open and he had hauled himself a fraction up in bed, until he was fully in the world, before greeting his grandfather. The broad smile that he offered in return horrified Fergus, the gums were pulled back so far. Yet he offered his own calm happiness, careful not to reflect his grandfather's decline.

'I got it granddad. The stone. I brought it home. For you.'

Kneeling on the floor, between the bed and the chair, Fergus told Fingal about his journey south, about Maltravers and about the break-in. He talked about the new friends he had gained and the old friend he had lost at last; how big were the buildings, how constant the noise and the life of the city; the novelty of snow in April. While he described how they had found it on a table high above the city, he placed Fingal's hand on the stone: the fingers curled into its curve and brittle yellow nails skated on its skin. Fingal seemed to strengthen, to sit up further, to be more present. He asked questions, and nodded or shook his head at the answers he received. Slowly, the audience became a conversation, such as it ever had been, and the old savoured the vitality of the young, while the young drew deeply on the accumulations of age. Only when the ending of brief laughter by violent coughing reminded them both of the world as it had lately been and as it must be again, soon enough, did Fergus retreat into silence momentarily.

'Granddad, don't worry if you don't, but do you recognise this?'

Fingal closed up the handkerchief trembling in his hand and looked at the pendant turning slowly on a coarse chain. Squinting, he took the small gold block between the thumb and forefinger of his free hand, which trembled at the exertion. As he held it, he disappeared once more, not into sickness but into some other place or time, and only slowly did he return. A pale tongue ran along his emaciated lip, but it gave no moisture.

'Where did you find it, son?'

Fingal did not look at his grandson as he asked his question, but rather kept his eyes on the pendant. His face had lost again the vitality that Fergus's return had given him.

'Mr Duncannon. Before I left. He gave it to me. Said it rightly belonged to me. Gave it me for luck, he said. Granddad, do you know what it is? Is it something to do with grandma?'

'Duncannon. No, Fergus, I'm sorry; I can't think what it is. I've never seen it before. Bloody Duncannon. Why he has to make up stories like this, filling your head with nonsense. Always a trouble maker, that one.'

The voice contained a ferocity that seemed unlikely to have come from so frail a body. He had let the pendant hang loose now, but had still not looked at his grandson, instead turning his head to the window, to the sky and the world beyond. Fergus wrestled with what he should say next, certain that his grandfather was lying, but unsure whether he should defy him, after all these years, now, today, here on his death bed. The wheezing took the decision from him and he could instead soothe the old man while the coughing wracked his body.

When the convulsions had subsided, Fergus let his grandfather return to his rest. With the pendant in his pocket, he lifted the stone into his arms and headed to the door. Behind him Fingal mumbled something in his incipient slumber, but when he turned around, all was peaceful. He pulled the door to with his foot and started a careful descent of the staircase.

forty-three

A murmur of voices leaked beneath the kitchen door into the hallway. Men's voices too: he had left his grandfather in his bed and since he had heard his father upstairs, making deals with heaven behind the bedroom door, Fergus knew that there must be others in the house. He allowed the cursing stone to bow his spine a little as he exhaled wearily, reconciling himself to what lay beyond, then pushed against the door with his back, sliding it easily from its worn latch. As the wood gave way, he span slowly into the room. He stood for a moment in the threshold, the stone pulling at its cradle in his arms.

The voices fell silent at his appearance and everyone turned towards his framed form. His mother regarded him with barely contained joy, while the Reverend Drummond and Mary watched with pride. Mr Galbraith stared only at the stone, and Mr and Mrs MacLeod presented their best smiles, lifelessly. Even Duncannon was there, hiding by the back door, his eyes furtive, mobile, fluttering from the boy to the stone to his feet. Fergus looked from one face to the other, but Shona was nowhere to be found.

'Put that rock down, my love, and give your old mother a kiss.'

Morag patted the kitchen table with her palm and waited impatiently while her son placed the heavy stone onto the table top. Then, as soon as he was free, she pulled him to her. She allowed herself three jolting sobs before releasing him grudgingly to the handshakes and congratulations, which even Mr MacLeod was able to summon up. Galbraith and Drummond wanted to know everything about the journey and about the recovery of the stone, but their enquiries came so fast and were so uncontrolled that their words tied around each other, smothering every question before Fergus had a chance to feel his way towards an answer. Instead he merely looked from one to the other with each new enquiry, his mouth hanging a little ajar, his eyes drifting always to the door. It was in part because of this that, above the commotion and excitement, he found the calm of Duncannon's face so often. The hermit asked no questions, which was to be expected, but nor did he melt into the fervour of the moment. Quietly, he gazed at the stone on the kitchen table, contemplative, beatific.

'She's on her way, hen. She got up late this morning, so wasn't in church. She's making herself lovely for you, quick as she can.'

Mrs MacLeod had followed the boy's eyes to where her daughter should surely appear and she smiled broadly as the concern melted from Fergus's face. Happy that her putative son-in-law was still more interested in her daughter than the rock, she reached up to kiss his cheek, hands clasped to his broad shoulders. Fergus blushed.

The aimless inquisition continued. Eventually, Galbraith was able to form a solid question and asked it so solidly that even the Reverend paused so that it might be answered. He stood squarely in front of Fergus, his left arm and open hand trailing to where the stone sat behind him. For the first time, his eyes rested solely on the boy and were followed by the eyes of the others, who waited patiently for him to respond to this, the question at the nub of the matter.

'I didn't convince him, exactly. I tried, with both reason and righteousness. But Mr Maltravers isn't a man to deal fairly with someone like me. He did not want to give up the stone, not at all. But I had help. Some friends in London. They were able to help me find a way around his, uh, stubbornness...'

Fergus's voice thinned to nothingness against the incomprehension and discomfort of the faces before him. Galbraith sought to formulate a more precise question, a direct line to the truth about events in London, but his thoughts were scattered by Mrs Buchanan's interjection.

'Mr Duncannon! Might I ask you not to scratch my good kitchen table in that way?'

Morag had been the only one to notice Duncannon. While Fergus stumbled over the description of quite how, after all, the artefact had come to be in his possession, Duncannon had stepped purposefully to the table and had taken the cursing stone between his hands, had begun to turn it slowly, deliberately, passing its bulk from his right hand to his left. The scraping of the first turn had roused Morag's attention; the second she had seen; by the time her voice had risen to scold Duncannon, the third turn was complete.

Duncannon's hands dropped to his side and he took a short step back from the table. To everyone's surprise he uttered an apology, contrition curling into his shoulders. Only Fergus caught the fleeting glimpse of the smile that played about his friend's eyes. Chastised and satisfied, Duncannon slipped from the garden door into the bright outside even before Galbraith had reached the stone to ensure it remained undamaged. Mrs MacLeod joined Mrs Buchanan in her inspection of the dark varnish that covered the table itself.

It was into this silence that Shona appeared. She slipped in through the same garden door from which Duncannon had disappeared like a ghost only moments before. They must have passed in the garden, but Shona made no mention of the retreating Duncannon. Without regard for anyone else in the bright kitchen, she took three bold strides towards her fiancé and kissed him. It was not a restrained kiss, nor one delivered with shame or embarrassment. For some moments, she hung there from his unmoving shoulders, mouth pressed full onto his, until he pulled away, peeling his lips from hers. She regarded him with confusion across the few inches he had claimed between them, until the kitchen and the world, her parents and the Reverend, returned. Too late, she felt his arms about her, and they squeezed her to him, but it was as an offering, an apology. His weak smile underlined her dejection.

'Not here, not like this. With everyone looking on. Let's step into the garden, shall we? Get a little privacy?'

Fergus looked to his mother, as if to ask permission, before slipping his hand into Shona's and leading her from the house.

The sky was marked with some smears of white, but otherwise blazed blue. Above them, the wind made the day's only sounds, but behind the high garden wall the air was still and peaceful. The flowers grew unmolested, and only the very tops of the little apple tree swayed gently in the breeze that coaxed the first of the blossom from pink buds. Fergus led Shona to the swing seat by the north wall.

When it had arrived, six years before, Fingal had scorned his spendthrift daughter-in-law. She had persuaded her husband to order it from Fort William and, since the garden was accepted as her domain, Davey had not felt it necessary to mention the purchase to the old man. The boxes that appeared one morning had at first aroused no comment. Even when Davey had taken his tools into the garden, Fingal had assumed that the lengths of wood laid out on the lawn were the components of some useful structure, for the growing of runner beans or the protection of early vegetables.

As the shape became unmistakeable, however, he had flown into a rage, rebuking the waste and the self-indulgence, and berating his son for his cowardice in hiding the purchase from him. That summer, the swing seat had been barely used. At first, Morag would take some moments swinging in to the evening sunlight, when she thought Fingal was not watching; as she grew in confidence and in obstinacy, she made a point of sitting in the seat more frequently, and then at every opportunity.

Her daughter had been first to join her and they would sit with their tea, listening to the whisper of the sea rising from the harbour and to the creak of the seat as it swung gently under their weight. In subsequent years, Davey had also been seen in the seat, either talking with Morag or simply breathing in the still air, once his morning tasks had been completed, or with a glass of beer once the day's work was done, watching the kittiwakes glide over the village on their way back from the sea.

But this was the first time that Fergus had sat there. The welcome give of the wood, the easing of the springs against their weight brought a small smile, the premonition of laughter. He turned to Shona and kissed her cheek, her forehead, her nose; he let his lips brush against hers, once, twice, and then a third time.

'It is good to see you, Shona.'

'Is it? I thought, well, when you didn't want to kiss me before...'

Shona nodded towards the kitchen window. Something like fear or hurt flickered behind her frown. His absence had been filled with unexpected thoughts, of the possibility of aloneness, of rejection and abandonment; she had not allowed the possible reasons for his enduring loss to stray beyond the back of her mind, but they had lurked there, curled in cruel anticipation, waiting to burst from the darkness, ready to bite. The ambiguity of their reunion had loosed them from her grip; his protestations of bashfulness did little to quell them.

While Shona gripped his hand, Fergus recounted his adventures. She winced at the echo of the pain of his bruised ribs and, as he described the break-in at Lauderdale Tower, she hid her excitement beneath plastic disapproval. By the time he had finished describing the long drive north in the cabs of four separate lorries, he had omitted only Ruby from the details of the Stepney housemates. Shona did not press him, instead asking about the streets of Mayfair, the clothes of the women and the height of the buildings.

'Once we're married, maybe we should visit London together? I could meet your friends and you could show me the sights. I hear that one shop has a whole floor just of shoes.'

He had never lied to Shona before; he had never had cause to do so. Even now, he was not sure if he was lying. He had anticipated the question, the earnest enquiry or the half-joking suggestion, of being led astray by city women, but it had not arrived, not yet at least. Had it been asked, he had decided to tell the truth, but as little as was necessary and certainly not enough to confirm any suspicions, before taking offence at her lack of faith in him. But there were no questions, only her open face, tilted somewhat towards him.

Their kiss was interrupted by the click of the door. Davey Buchanan appeared, flanked by both Reverend Drummond and Mr Galbraith. He walked with them in the direction of the garden gate, and although his 'uh-huh's lacked the excitement of the two men's babble, they mimicked enthusiasm to a degree. Halfway along the path, Davey saw his son and paused, hanging on the right heel of his tattered garden slippers. Remembering himself, he excused himself and strode towards the swing seat. Fergus rose and extended his right arm to receive the expected hand shake, but instead and for the first time that he could remember, he disappeared into his father's embrace.

forty-four

Maybe if he had let them take him from the island. Had he let them put him in the hospital and have the doctors prod and poke him, like they'd said, let them put tubes in him and filled him with pills, maybe then he might have squeezed a few more years of life from the world. Maybe. But what would have been the point? Why risk everything, his dignity and the right to die where he had lived, on his island, when there was no reason.

Fingal had known it was hopeless, even before the full force of his cough had taken hold of his chest, had alarmed even his daughter-in-law by its persistence and force. Something inside him had told him that he would not see another summer through. So he had put his foot down. He had stayed. The doctors had had to come to him. They had brought the drugs to Hinba, pills to fight the invasion in his body, tablets to lessen the pain of the fight. He had stayed and he had waited, for Fergus to return.

And Fergus had now returned. He had won back the stone for the island. His position was secured and, with it, the Buchanan line. Fergus would marry the MacLeod girl and the island would belong wholly to the Buchanans. All would be as it should be.

As it should have been since the Buchanans had thrown out the Clanranalds. The boy would run things properly, the post office, the pub, the island. They were all one in any case, and Fergus would make a fine Laird for Hinba. And in turn his own sons and grandsons would carry on the name, the line. All would be well, and all would be as it should be.

Except Duncannon. He should have driven the little bastard off the island all those years ago, when he had the chance, when he could have made it seem like charity. What was best for the little orphan boy. But he'd not and that had been a mistake. Duncannon had kept his silence for thirty years, but was now set on causing trouble, with his games and riddles. Fingal could only admire the man that had held his will for revenge so long, to choose his moment so precisely. Duncannon had endured penury and isolation for his whole adult life, not through guilt but through guile. As unworthy of trust as his father. And yet, and yet. Fingal had to admire him: to orchestrate so stark a reminder as that crass token of betrayal, and in the blameless hands of his own grandson.

The night was turning to morning and once again he had not slept: the room was filling with the grey light of the dawn. A tearing cough ripped through his chest to split the stillness. Fingal raised his hand to wipe the spittle from around his mouth. He felt the thinning hair of his beard. It was no longer the rich lustrous beard of years gone by: time and illness had worn away some patches almost entirely. He did not need a mirror to know that it was now no longer white. It too had started to yellow, but it was still the testament of a good, long life. He did not need to live longer. It would have been grand to have seen the boy turn twenty one, and to see him wed. But these things were certain now, and witnessing their passing was simply gravy to the banquet of his reign. To know that he was back on the island, to have seen his strong youthfulness once more, was sufficient.

He loved Fergus not just for what he represented, but also for who he was. Since the boy had been a baby, Fingal had doted on him. He had lavished the devotion he had withheld from his own son onto his grandson. His final gift had been to send him out to win back the stone, to make him a king among the islanders. Whatever was to come, his life was now complete, save for the loose ends of a birthday party and a wedding breakfast. He was prepared to pass on, secure in the knowledge that Fergus would be ready to take his place. He had never had the time to feel things like this for his own son: Davey had been born at a time when there had not been enough time or money, or love. And of course his son had been too close to his wife. He even looked like her.

He tried to shift in his bed, to ease the pain in his chest. Instead, there was only another convulsion, a wet tearing of coughing, this time so fierce that he felt as if his sternum had cracked. The bed shook in echo, the vibrations remaining even after the eruption had subsided. Again he wiped the saliva from his mouth on the back of his hand and, in the dawn half-light, he caught sight of the black smudge on his knuckle. For a moment he was perplexed, before he recognised the darkness as blood. He ran his other, clean, hand over his chin and, sure enough, it too was traced with sticky blackness. His chest cracked once more, but with a violence that surprised him and, before he could make his wish, his life slipped through his skin; seventy two years turned to a vapour that could not be contained by his will, nor his body.

The blood flowed for a brief while, until it hardened, crusting his whiskers and drawing a line from his mouth, downwards, towards the bed that had cosseted him since he was an adolescent, down towards the floorboards that he had buffed to a dull sheen with ten thousand shambling steps; down further, into the kitchen where the boy was sitting, had been sitting since he had crept into the house in the dead of night, crept back from the darkened bar of the Harbour Bell, where he had left Shona and, despite his half-hearted protestations, his innocence too.

Fergus sat beneath his grandfather and thought about his prize. Everything that had been promised had been given. He had completed the task, and returned the cursing stone to Hinba. He was now the man of the house, of the island. He was the hero of his neighbours. He had his bride. And yet, during those silent minutes, staring out at the moon, the stars, the blackness of the edge of the world, he had been unable to staunch the flow of his satisfaction into the cold kitchen air. By the time his grandfather's cough broke the stillness, he knew that even at the very moment that all had been given, it had already been lost.

The old man's stiffening body lay undisturbed for two or three hours. By the time Morag brought in the tea, Fingal was stone cold, the colour of ash. She let out a small whimper but regained herself quickly. Placing the tea on the night stand, she moved cautiously to the bed. There was a smear of blood across the old man's beard, and other red flecks covered the bedsheet that was pulled under his chin; flecks also on the crisp white of the pillow case, on the thin pale skin under his eyes. His harsh grey eyes still stared out to the ceiling, as if to sea, and Morag almost doubted that he was indeed dead. The thought flitted through her mind that he was simply pretending, just to raise her hopes, to see if he could catch her out in a moment of relief. But it was quickly gone. The lifeless stare and the smell of the chilled air proclaimed the incontrovertibility of the situation. Morag gingerly slid the eyelids down to cover that stare for once and for all.

'Oh, you old fool! What have you done? Always wanting to be the centre of everything. You wait for Fergus to come home then you claim the limelight from him. Oh, you poor, old fool...'

She gave up her chiding and felt the tears rise. She stood by the bed, eyes closed, gently weeping, for a few minutes, her arms awkward at her sides. She wanted for someone to embrace, someone to comfort her, for someone to comfort. Opening her eyes, she stretched her face to regain her emotions. Things needed to be done. She would have to alert the house, fetch the vicar, make everything presentable for when the doctor arrived from Mallaig.

She decided that it would be best to wake her husband first, to give him the time he needed with his dead father, before Fergus woke and threatened the peace. Fergus. He would be heart-broken. At least he had made it back in time to say goodbye. Morag shook the creeping thoughts out of her head and paced, stealthy as a thief back onto the landing and into her bedroom, where Davey was already pulling himself from a light sleep in anticipation of his alarm.

forty-five

'He's not here, hen.'

The redness no longer ringed her eyes, but Morag Buchanan still bore the mark of her family's despondency. She tried her best to sympathise with the girl at the kitchen door, but Shona's troubles would pass soon enough, while hers would last well beyond the time when Fingal's coffin was covered over and the last of the island's mourners had left her living room that evening. At least then, she would be able to begin the job of rebuilding her husband.

Over the past days, since the doctor had come over to pronounce what by then was already known to every soul on Hinba, the remaining Buchanans had clutched each other close, receiving the neighbours and their condolences one after the other. Through three afternoons Shona had hung from her distant Fergus, breaking from him only briefly to help Morag with kettles and teas and sandwiches, until the dusk came around again and she had slipped unnoticed from the house.

It was barely half past eight now. Shona had waited by the gate until she had heard the sounds of morning clatter in the house behind the post office, and then some moments more, before she had knocked at the garden door. Morag had ushered her in, and explained that Fergus had left to walk the moors sometime after dawn, before the tea was made. The weight of the old man's body in the room above pushed down on them and Shona left as soon as was polite. She heard but did not heed Morag's advice to leave Fergus to his thoughts until he was ready to return and she scurried from the village, up the track towards the slopes above the harbour, where Fergus went to think things that needed to be thought.

The dry days had not yet sucked the winter's damp from the turf. The soft give of the ground slowed her progress as much as the toil of the hill; grass snared her ankles, tangling around her steps. But soon, Shona reached the broad crag under Cnoc Brostan. She paused to catch her breath among the loops of stone, the remnants of ancient houses, where Fergus had often come in the past, but there was no sign of him. A gust of wind shook through a clump of gorse and sent tiny birds scrambling into the sky; the wind chilled Shona and she pulled her cardigan to her throat.

Her shoes were sodden from the dew damp grass and the coldness in her feet rose up, until it crashed into a shiver between her shoulder blades. She wished she had brought a jacket; she wished that Fergus had been here. Perhaps she knew him less well than she had believed. Perhaps now that she had given herself to him, his passion had cooled. Perhaps guilt, of being with her while Fingal died, had pushed him away from her, onto the hills, out of sight, out of reach. Despondent, she began to descend from the other side of the crag, her long strides tearing through the still tenacious sedge.

Under Compass Hill, she reached the cliffs at the eastern end of the island. Across the sea, the sun sparkled from snow-flecked peaks on the blue horizon, but Shona turned south oblivious. She found the track that led down to the village, lost in her thoughts and looking only at her feet; she did not see Fergus until he was only a few strides distant. Seated at the brink, he was lost somewhere among the distant mountains, and she had to call his name to rouse him.

His face turned up towards her, the bright sunlight burnishing his hair. Fergus released a smile so sweetly wrapped in sadness that Shona had to gulp back her pity. She dropped to the ground beside him and embraced him, forehead pressed to temple, while the wet earth soaked into her knees.

'It's alright. I'm alright. Just watching the birds. The terns are busying themselves for nesting. New life returning.'

There was nothing for Shona to do but to hold on, keep her mouth close to his ear and murmur whatever reassurances she could. Later, in a few hours, Fergus would bury his grandfather under the grass beside the church where they would marry in a few months. By then summer would dress the moors in pinks and yellows and the evening's light would stretch far into the night; the breezes would be warm, like the breath of a loved one on your neck. Would the sadness that encased him be gone by then, she wondered?

'I don't dream anymore. That all stopped about a week ago. Since then, my sleep has been as black as pitch. At first I thought, great, I'm free of them. But now, especially now, I just feel, well, the best I can call it is, I feel their shadow.'

Shona pulled away slightly to study his face for a moment before returning to her rest, head on head. She ran her hand down the length of his arm and the fabric of his coat rustled, the sound merging with that of the wind in the gorse. He had dreamt as long as she could remember. She had never found his dreaming strange, had never asked to read his notebooks; she had listened to him dutifully when he recounted those parts of his dreams he had wanted to share, but had not pried further. That they were now gone saddened her more than she could have anticipated.

Neither spoke again for some time, until the distant stutter of a marine engine reached them, carried on the wind. Fergus shielded his eyes to make out its origin, out there in the rich ocean-blue, and Shona followed his gaze, grateful for the relief of mundane curiosity. It could not be McCredie; his boat had arrived early as always that morning, and he was on the island still, dressed in stiff black.

'Who do you think it is? Maybe someone coming for the funeral?'

'It's headed from Mallaig – there's no-one on the mainland who would come. Not that I know of, anyway. Granddad didn't have a lot of friends over there, and no family.'

Fergus squinted, as if to make out the faces of those on board the distant boat. The thin line of its wake left only a fleeting mark upon the sea before blurring into the blue and vanishing forever. Fergus slipped loose of Shona's embrace with a kiss and got to his feet. He pulled her up after him.

'We'll find out, I suppose. Anyhow, we should be getting back. It's almost time.'

Ahead of them, a tern rose from below the lip of the cliff and into the wind, hanging motionless for a moment before soaring into the sky. Its cry pierced the air and it wheeled off over the headland. They watched its progress until it disappeared beyond the slope that tumbled down from Compass Hill. Wordless, they headed down towards the village, its church and its people, both the living and the dead.

forty-six

Alasdair McLeish straightened his tunic as he stepped off the boat. The harsh concrete of the quayside swayed momentarily beneath him until the fluids behind his ears reached their equilibrium. Despite a lifetime of living on the edge of the swelling sea, he was still not accustomed to its unreliability even on a fine day like today.

A fine day marred by his duties. He never enjoyed official visits to the homes of his distant neighbours out on the islands. They were good people, by and large, and the intrusion of the law into their isolation was usually the result of ignorance or foolishness, rather than malice. He was all the more resistant to making such visits on behalf of the Strathclyde Constabulary. That this particular instruction had originated not from Glasgow, but from New Scotland Yard, saddened him almost as much as the instruction itself. To question, and probably arrest, a school friend was not why he joined the force. Alasdair had been two years above Fergus Buchanan at the High School but, as a boy, Fergus had lodged at his mother's house during the school week and they had had formed a respectful acquaintanceship, which was almost a friendship in the isolation of the Small Isles.

Alasdair had heard, of course, about Fergus's journey south. Quite why the Reverend hadn't called him or one of the other officers at the Mallaig station, he did not know. They could have investigated the theft and, were there sufficient grounds, retrieved the stolen artefact without fuss. There had been no need to send Fergus off on this misconceived quest – the law would be enforced. You had only to trust in the system, to co-operate, to be vigilant. Not a vigilante. There was no place for that and there was no excuse. Alasdair could not believe it, would not believe it, despite the evidence he had seen, emailed from London to Glasgow to Mallaig.

Closing the harbour gate behind him, he set off along the road towards the village. As he strode on along the thin tarmac, his eye was caught by the large group of people standing by the church. It was not a Sunday, and all appeared to be dressed in black clothes: a funeral then. By the iron gate, where the road passed closest to the church, he paused and removed his cap. His head lowered, he watched his fingers clench on the glossy brim for a moment and mumbled what he could remember of his prayers. He would find out who had passed when he reached the village, and pay his respects more formally later, when he made his way back to the harbour. Replacing his cap, he turned slowly on his heel, the leather crunching and squealing on its pivot, and he took one, two steps onwards. He paused. He looked again at the gathering in the grave yard and concluded that it must comprise the entire population of Hinba, and several more besides. There would be no-one in the village of whom to make enquiries. Better to wait until after the interment was complete and conduct his investigation then.

Alasdair leant against the cold grey stone of the gatepost and looked out across the harbour, his arms folded at his chest. White walled houses dotted the green slopes and, out on the bay, kittiwakes patrolled the wind-ruffled water. The tide was receding and the marshy banks that lurked beneath the surface had begun to reveal themselves; sheep that had missed the last low tide, forgetful in their grazing, would soon be able to leave the islets in the bay to find their way back to the shore. Alasdair wondered if the sheep experienced their isolation as concern or were simply content with the abundant grass at their feet.

Despite the beauty of the place, he had never envied the islanders, on Rum and Eigg as much as here. Alasdair considered the line of cliffs that stretched off in ragged procession for five miles along the southern limits of Hinba before they simply stopped: there was nothing but blue beyond them. On other days, they would become quickly lost in greyness, if you could see them at all, and Alasdair was too familiar with days such as those.

Behind him, the sound of feet champing on gravel washed past him on the wind and Alasdair twisted back towards the grave yard. The first of the mourners were making their way back, the rites completed. He straightened his tie and removed his cap once more, taking two steps into the road to face the gateway.

'Young Alasdair McLeish. Well, it's good of you to come over to pay your respects. A pity you missed the service, but you'll come to the Bell for the wake?'

The gate squealed on its rusted hinges before Mr MacLeod could prevent it from swinging a little towards his wife, who caught it in time and held it while the steady stream of islanders passed through. Alasdair nodded acknowledgement to each while he spoke.

'Actually, Mr MacLeod, I'm here on other business. I didn't know that there had been a death on the island until I arrived, I'm afraid.

Who, might I ask, was the deceased?'

The news that the old man had died was not a surprise – his illness and age were well known – but it was a blow nonetheless. Not least, it made his duties more delicate. The publican watched the boy's frown for a short while, unsure of its cause, while his mind raced around the possibilities as to the nature of the officer's business on the island. With hungry curiosity, MacLeod placed his hand on the constable's shoulder to guide him towards the warmth of the Bell.

'It is a sad day indeed. Death comes to us all of course, but Fingal Buchanan was well respected by many on the island. Even if he was loved by very few.'

In a few minutes, the head of the black snake winding back from the church reached the little timber jetty of the old harbour, and then the entrance to the Bell. MacLeod swung the door back and led the constable, his wife and the others into the lounge bar. The tables were pushed against one wall and were covered by an assortment of table-cloths and platters of sandwiches and sausage rolls and slices of meat pie. While Mrs MacLeod pulled the cling film from the plates, her husband took his place behind the bar. The first drink, a measure of whisky, he offered to the constable who, to his surprise, accepted. In three short sips he had drained the glass, while MacLeod looked on quizzically. Only the arrival of Mrs Robertson, her arm supported by Mr McCulloch, pulled him away and he turned reluctantly to fetch the sherry; when he had dealt with Mr McCredie's insistent thirst, Alasdair McLeish was nowhere to be seen. Soon, there was such a bramble of hands reaching for the bar, that he had no time to wonder where he might have gone.

Despite the throng, the bar hushed as the Buchanans arrived. Davey took each hand presented to him and shook it robustly but with appropriate solemnity. When Cameron MacLeod strode through the parting mourners with a double whisky proffered in his outstretched hand, Davey Buchanan accepted it with grace and put an arm around the publican and embraced him without reserve. Their glasses clanked, and Davey wondered how things might have been had he stood up to his father all those years before.

Time passed, mellowed by good whisky, and the mixed emotions for the deceased blurred into a hopeful nostalgia. The sandwiches were exhausted; the mourners left as the afternoon wore off until all that remained were the Buchanans and the McCleods, the Reverend and Mr Galbraith. Mrs Robertson, who had remained as long as her duty to her husband demanded, slipped out before Chrissie MacLeod could refill her glass.

'It is a sad day, of course,' Galbraith shifted in his chair, the wooden feet scraping painfully at the stone floor, *'but it is also a time for hopefulness, no? We have the nuptials of Shona and Fergus to come. And we have the triumph of that young man to celebrate – bringing home the bullaun stone. It might be considered inappropriate, this being his grandfather's wake, and if it is you have my most profound apologies, but I would nevertheless like to raise a toast to the labours of our Fergus and, of course, to his success.'*

The whisky slopped over the side of his glass as he reached up his arm abruptly. A moment passed before MacLeod joined the school teacher in raising his glass; Davey Buchanan did the same, and was followed by the others; Shona beamed in pride. Fergus dropped his eyes to his hands, which seemed unusually large, clumsy and pink.

'Thank you, John. If I may, I'd like to say some words myself about my son, and about my father too...'

Davey had hauled himself to his feet, but was interrupted by the shudder of the door in its frame and the subsequent appearance of Constable McLeish who stood uncertain at the threshold for some moments before intruding further. His steely face could not mask the uncertainty that quivered about his mouth, laced his eyes. He looked from each face to the next until he found Fergus. Despite his gaze, he addressed the Reverend.

He explained that he had taken a short walk up to the meadow behind the village, where the nearer of the island's ancient crosses was to be found, weathered and forlorn. There, at the foot of the monolith, he had found not a puddle in the bowl worn into the pediment, but a stone, round and smooth, a cross cut into it. He was curious to know, he continued, if the Reverend could explain how such a thing had come to be there, in that meadow, at the base of that cross. He was certain that it had not been there that last time he had visited Hinba.

Shreds of grass still clung to his black boots. Fergus watched a bead of dew crawl over the curve of leather and spread across the stitching at the sole and smiled: how had Alasdair McLeish known so precisely where to look? It had been at the insistence of Mr Galbraith that the cursing stone had been placed under the shattered cross above the village, pending its return to St Ernan's ruined monastery. The Reverend had been uncertain of the theological propriety of housing the artefact within the church and, while the islanders squabbled over the alternatives, Galbraith had simply acted, silencing the grumbles of Mr MacLeod with a look familiar to every pupil of the little island school. He would have wasted no time in letting the world know that the stone was back on Hinba, that his decade-long search had at last borne fruit.

'Now, Alasdair, surely you can see that this is not the time. Can we not finish mourning my father first? No-one is going anywhere: everyone will still be here in a day or two. As will that stone. We'll be happy to answer your questions then.'

Davey was the first to understand and had moved to stand between the constable and his son. Alasdair McLeish clasped his wrist behind his back and fixed his eyes to the run of bottles on the shelf behind the bar. He did not want to pursue the matter, but orders were just that. He had been instructed to return to Mallaig with the suspect in custody and he had little choice but to do so. Perhaps he had been wrong to seek to soften the blow by beginning with friendly questions, when he had sufficient evidence simply to arrest Fergus Buchanan. He had, it would seem, only managed to postpone the inevitable.

'It's OK, Alasdair. Officer. I'll not make you dance around this any longer. I'll come with you.'

Fergus had gently moved his father out of the way to stand before the constable. Despite his efforts, the young officer's face belied his dispassion and the two schoolmates smiled their understanding to each other.

'Fergus, what's going on?'

Shona's voice quavered. Fergus interrupted Alasdair before he could set out the full details of the case, to explain in his own words.

'It's like I said, Shona. Did you think that there'd be no reckoning? There's always a reckoning, even on Hinba.' Fergus turned to the others. 'You see, Dad, Mr Galbraith, to get the cursing stone back, I had to break into Maltravers' house. He wouldn't see reason. When

I heard how sick granddad was, I had to do something, and that was the only something I could do. So I broke in. In the circumstances, it was only a matter of time before the police came. I'm sorry. Mum, dad, really I am sorry. But I had to bring the stone back before granddad died. You see that don't you?'

Morag embraced her son, but Fergus slipped loose from his mother and went to the door to stand beside Alasdair McLeish. He gave a brief soft smile towards his sister.

'Mr Galbraith, if you wouldn't mind, I would be grateful for your assistance in carrying the stone to the harbour.' Galbraith looked about him in desperation, but no-one came to his aid, unconcerned by his anguish, his loss. That it should be him that should carry from the island that which he had sought for so long was such cruelty, but he was too afraid to refuse the constable's request.

Once the three men had left the Bell, MacLeod stood up, rising to something beyond his full height. He sought to maintain a sombre and serious demeanour, postponing his full enjoyment of the moment until after everyone had gone home, until his wife and daughter had gone to bed and he was alone, able to drink a toast to his victory. For now, he turned to Davey Buchanan.

'I think we both know that there will be no wedding now. I'll not let my Shona endure the shame of being married to a convict.'

'He's not yet convicted of anything, you sanctimonious bastard!'

Morag was grateful for some target for her rage. She looked imploringly to Shona, but the girl stayed silent as she wrestled with her own wretchedness, struggling to accommodate herself to her shattered world; she made no defence of Fergus. Morag turned and ran from the pub, after her son.

There was silence for a moment or two. The others looked at their feet, their pints, and shrank into their most unobtrusive shapes. Without a word, Davey Buchanan stood squarely in front of Cameron MacLeod, so that his eyes were level with his tormentor, but he said nothing. In the past five days, he had lost his father, his son, and now these MacLeods wanted to have what was left of his pride as well. He was Davey Buchanan. He was better than this. He picked up his pint and drained it in one long swallow; the empty glass he thumped onto the table.

'I'm away to my son. You'll not be gossiping while I'm gone.'

Davey Buchanan turned calmly to the door and left the silence behind him.

forty-seven

At the sound of the engine, Duncannon paused and tilted his attention towards the sea. Unable to be sure without seeing for himself, he left the spool of packing tape on the work bench and ambled from the barn. Sure enough, the police launch was rounding the headland on its return journey. It was a less lumbering vessel than McCredie's boat, and it cut a clean swathe through the waves as it motored swiftly away from Hinba. Despite the speed, Duncannon could clearly see two figures on the little deck: one a police officer, the other unmistakably Fergus Buchanan. Duncannon's frown passed soon enough. It didn't matter what the Buchanan boy had done, only that the Buchanans' mourning had been deepened further.

Whatever crime the boy had committed was as nothing to that of his grandfather, but it was reassuring all the same to see that the family's criminality was at last being punished. He allowed himself a small smile: being punished by the law, rather than by Duncannon. If only the old man had lived long enough to see this. A murmur of regret washed through him on the wind, but was soon gone. Fingal's passing was sweet enough, certain as he was that Fergus would have asked about the pendant, would have shown it to Fingal, asked how Duncannon could have come by his grandmother's love token, a token so clearly given to another man. That would have been poison enough, even without the turns of the cursing stone.

Thirty years. For thirty years, Duncannon had held his hatred close, waiting. Befriending Fergus, encouraging him to spend time at Duncannon's farm, in the place where his grandfather had made his threats, where Fingal had committed his crime; this had been the first blow. The discovery of the cursing stone had been an unexpected boon: his grandfather had swaddled him in the old stories, of the curse that had rid the island of the Clanranalds, of the magic worked by the Buchanans and MacLeods, of their brief truce in which they had hidden the stone so that neither could use it against the other, of insidious magic that could bring down both houses and the island itself if wielded with sufficient loathing. The rediscovery of the stone had provided the petrol, but Duncannon's revenge had been a slow fuse that had burned through all these years. Now at last it had burned to the nub; there was no more fire. His whole adult life had been spent under the shadow of the crime and the retribution and now he did not know how to live. Except to leave.

Tonight however, despite the expense, he would venture down to the village, to the Harbour Bell, to buy Cameron MacLeod a large whisky. He would stand at the bar with him and they would drink down the smoke together, and he would curse the ghost of Fingal Buchanan, not caring who might hear. And then he would announce the sale of the farm and the land and everything that he could not carry from the island. And he would be free of it all.

There was nothing further to keep him on Hinba. He had no more obligations, to the living or to the dead. He could start his life now,

now that his work was done. Now the cursing stone had done its work. He had two decades more before he could claim his pension; the insurance money was practically spent, but the sale of the farm would raise enough to keep him comfortable for a time. To stretch it further, he could take a job in the fish sheds at Mallaig; better yet, he could travel, live simply, on his wits. He was well practised in such a life. Or there was that cousin at Kinlochleven, of course. Duncannon laughed at the richness of the choices that his freedom gave him and his laugh spiralled up on the wind to carry far across the hills, to weave among the yellow gorse.

The engine's stutter no longer carried to shore and the launch itself was little more than a vanishing dot. Duncannon held up his arm in a gesture of farewell to the tiny boat before turning back towards the barn. Most of his good hand tools were already packed into boxes, along with the few other things of value. He had only to seal them tight and carry them to the house, and then he could start packing his things there. He would talk to McCredie in the morning about arranging passage to Mallaig, once he knew how much he would take and how much would be left behind.

forty-eight

The gulls' cries pierced the roar of the wind and rattle of the boat's motor. All other sound was lost, drowned. Fergus found the enveloping cacophony comforting, and he was grateful that it allowed for no intrusion upon his mute vigil. He was at liberty to watch the shores of Hinba recede, fading from green to purple to blue. And then it was gone, lost like some mythical land that he could no longer reach.

Behind him, Alasdair was in silent conversation with the pilot of the launch. He was grateful that he had left him undisturbed to watch the island vanish this last time. He would probably avoid a custodial sentence, the officer had said: a first offence and a guilty plea counted in his favour. Most likely, there would be community service and Fergus had felt a little hope that he might be able to serve his sentence in London, maybe in EC1 or even in E1 itself. But whatever the outcome of the trial, he knew that he would not return to Hinba, or at least only as an outsider, a visitor; a mourner at another funeral perhaps, or to bring flowers to his mother's sick bed. He wondered who would become post master after his father; he only knew that it would not be him. A MacLeod perhaps.

THE CURSING STONE

Maybe Cameron would finally have his victory, and maybe Shona would come to live in his childhood home after all.

Even bulky Rum was fading behind them now: they would soon be in Mallaig. He would be taken to the cells at the police station to await his transit to London. And the cursing stone would be taken from the launch and away from Hinba once more. Maltravers would have his treasure restored, to be lost and ignored among all the others. And the island would go on without it, as it had before. Nothing had changed yet everything was different.

'Sorry about the handcuffs, Fergus. Procedure. You understand?'

Fergus felt the hand of his friend and captor rest gently on his shoulder, a faint act of well-meant consolation. The launch was nudging its way into the bay. The smell of seaweed and fish coursed on the breeze pouring from the shore, colliding with memories and dreams. The light of the low sun burst onto the hillside that rose above the harbour, paving the land beyond Mallaig with a golden glow. Fergus closed his eyes, drew the salt tang into his lungs. He felt his feet rise from the deck, slowly at first and then with growing certainty. He could picture the startled face of Alasdair McLeish beneath him, feel the curiosity of the gulls as he rose among them, see the golden slopes fall away, the harbour and the boats, the railway station and the school, the sea. The sensation was effortless and familiar. It was not weightlessness; the lull of gravity still pulled at him. But the air beneath him felt solid enough and carried his weight without complaint, without danger of injury, without fear of falling.

acknowledgements

A number of people have played their part in turning a loose set of ideas into The Cursing Stone. Early on, Graeme Laughlan gave me valuable advice on ferry times and convivial pubs in both Lochaber and in Glasgow; later, Mairi Robertson Carrey rescued me from the Glasgow night and went on to provide inspiration, advice and insight; and insightful comments came also from Tom Bolton, Rachel Fisher and Mark Harvey. The errors that remain are mine, despite their good counsel.

Special thanks are due to the inimitable Matthew Smith at Urbane Publications for his support, enthusiasm and wisdom.

And to Katherine Heaton for, well, everything really.

Since escaping the East Midlands to find adventure in the big city, Adrian Harvey has combined a career in and around government with trying to see as much of the world as he can. He lives in North London, which he believes to be the finest corner of the world's greatest city. *The Cursing Stone* is his second novel.

ALSO BY ADRIAN HARVEY......

£8.99, ISBN 978-1909273092

Being Someone is a life story, a love story, a human story. James has fallen through life, plotting a course of least resistance.

Taking each day as it comes and waiting for that indefinable something to turn up, to give his story meaning. His journey lacks one vital element; a fellow traveller.

Then he meets Lainey. Confident. Beautiful. Captivating. And James rewrites himself to win her heart. Lainey gives James a reason to grow, paints a bright future, promises the happy ending he has sought so keenly.

But when we discover we can live the greatest story of all, are we able to share the pages with someone else? Being Someone is an emotive tale of love, of self-discovery and adventure; a story of the eternal search for happiness in another, without ultimately losing ourselves.

Available from the Urbane website, Amazon and all good bookshops.